TRAPPED WITHIN...

"Where's this light coming from?"

The soldier's surprise was unmistakable. "*Gott*," he said, "it was on when the earthquake stopped. I thought that it was some sort of emergency system . . . but it's the ship's panel, isn't it?"

"It appears to be so," agreed Jefferies, "which means that something on this ship is operating for the first time in a hundred thousand years. We may be caught in an alien spacecraft that's just about to crack open like an egg and finish its mission here on Earth."

THEY HAD TO ESCAPE!

**OTHER LEISURE BOOKS
BY STEVE VANCE:**

*THE ABYSS
THE HYDE EFFECT*

THE ASGARD RUN

STEVE VANCE

Book Margins, Inc.

A BMI Edition

Published by special arrangement with Dorchester Publishing Co., Inc.

If you purchased this book without a cover you should be aware that this book is stolen property. It was reported as "unsold and destroyed" to the publisher and neither the author nor the publisher has received any payment for this "stripped book."

Copyright © 1990 by Steve Vance

All rights reserved. No part of this book may be reproduced or transmitted in any form or by any electronic or mechanical means, including photocopying, recording or by any information storage and retrieval system, without the written permission of the Publisher, except where permitted by law.

Printed in the United States of America.

THE ASGARD RUN

Chapter One

When it came, there was no welcoming.
No trumpets, no parades.
There were none of the overtures that should have reached out to initiate the intellectual exchange between two species of totally disparate origins and development; and when it began its shallow, screaming, spiralling dive downward, there were no ovations or preparations to greet these visitors from far beyond the sky.

But there were upturned faces.

It was seen long before it was heard, long before the sounds that it dragged through the strange atmosphere echoed down to the earth. Awed humans standing in the noonday sun on what was to be Asia stared into the endless blue above them and followed the arc of the brilliant white flare as it passed. Like a tiny chunk of the formerly immutable sun, it blazed down the western horizon, across the forests that blanketed Europe and the unconquered waves of the Atlantic, over the New World that yet rested quietly before those who trod the landbridge that predated the Bering Strait could spread southward, and above the clean Pacific once again. It dazzled the inhabitants of Asia for a second time within one hour.

The glowing object from the stars completed three circuits of the globe before it began to slow. At that point its altitude had dropped from hundreds to tens of miles. Something was wrong within the controlling depths of the craft (for that was its true nature: a manufactured, functioning, and guided craft from beyond the Earth). Probes laced out invisibly from it and encountered the subjects they sought, but the collected data were ignored; preset instructions were broadcast on a tightly designed schedule, but the programmed reactions failed or were misfed; the vehicle and all of its vital cargo hesitated on the verge of destruction because of some unrecorded accident that had occurred during its long journey across space.

Finally, the craft responded to a repeated command. It was near a large range of mountains on that predominently uninhabited "new" continent, and its velocity had slowed to almost zero, so that it was hanging in the night sky like a second and larger full moon when the instruction successfully routed itself to the proper receptors. The huge, forested mounds were well-suited to its purposes, and it dropped to within a thousand feet of them before beginning the swift excavations necessary for its long-term plans.

THE ASGARD RUN

Far to the north, the only human beings in that hemisphere slept unaware of the ongoing function—the gallant wanderings of the Norsemen were still thousands of generations in the future—a function that rivalled the forces of nature in its scope and effect on the mountain range.

With almost unimaginable speed, the vessel worked, using its power cells to displace tons of rock and soil from within the mountains' heart, and its lonely duty was performed before the sun appeared behind it. It was a duty prescribed by minds belonging to other worlds and cultures, but designed specifically for the planets that constituted this particular category. None but the mute beasts of the forest witnessed the vast cavern that was so suddenly born deep in the mountains, and when the craft moved spectrally into this massive hollow, their clouded minds could no more comprehend the action or purpose than had the gaping men who had stood on the plains of Asia and watched its passage.

Once ensconced within the hollow, the dimensions of which were but an outline to its exterior shielding, the vehicle shifted the stresses that had supported the lips of the opening in order to create a landslide that completed the burial. Then the quiet vessel lost the white glow that had characterized it during flight and began secondary operations to invigorate its organic passengers; but these orders died in transmission, cut off by the same accident that had plagued the craft during its arrival and deceleration.

By sunrise all was quiet in the mountains. The vessel rested like a gigantic, unborn infant in its womb, protected by the depth of the earth itself. Within five years, the entry scar had healed; within ten, there was no visible evidence of its presence; and when men reached that far south, no one was even aware of the time when a blazing star had shaken loose from the heavens, circled the world, and prepared its own hiding place for a hibernation that would last for millennia.

"We Stop At Nothing."

That was the motto of his company, and Jack Hays did his dead level best to live up to that boast in every phase of his job. When the cross-country pneumatic subway system known commercially as "SubShot" had been announced eighteen months before (with primary routes given as New York City, Washington, D.C., and Atlanta to Seattle, Dallas, and LA) Hays had known with calm certainty that Northwest Halo Drilling would swing the Kansas City to Seattle contract because of the owners' political connections and the exemplary safety and performance records of the company itself in a decade of supervised mineral and oil drilling. And since he was one of the five best men who had ever handled the laser equipment, he felt reasonably sure that at least one section of the run would be under his supervision. He drew the Wyoming allotment.

Wyoming was the land of the world's largest mineral hot springs, Thermopolis, Yellowstone National Park and its geysers, the Buffalo Bill Museum, Wild West shows, dude ranches, Fort Laramie, and, of course, the Rocky Mountains. This was the nice, happy problem that the contract boys had dumped right on top of Jack Hays's head: to get that glorified blowgun tunnel from the sidestop of Cheyenne through the Laramie Mountains, under the various rivers, across more mountains at the Absaroka Range, and to another sidestop between the Grand National and Yellowstone National Parks before he could turn over the job to some other poor slob in Idaho. And, oh yes, he had to do all of this without varying the apparent inaugural level of the tunnel more than eleven point two inches in either direction, so that a commuter stepping into the tube at the Atlanta terminal could fold his newspaper and shuffle onto a Seattle sidewalk one hundred and sixty-five minutes later without undergoing any unpleasant bumps or dips.

But Hays was confident that if any equipment existed that was capable of moling cleanly through a solid mountain it belonged to the Northwest Halo Drilling Corporation. ("Halo" was derived from the corona-like vapor effect sometimes caused by the primary lasers employed in the rigs.) With the light-based claws excavating in the lead and an acrylic seal being instantly applied by the rear of the machine, the tunnel would snake across the wide state far faster than any burrowing animal after which it may have been modelled, and no one could play those drills the way old Jack could. So it was a challenge, all right, but not one that Hays would politely refuse to meet.

He met it and he drove that tunnel in a manner that might have inspired a folk song in the days of John Henry. In fact, he had the operation halfway across Wyoming, through the Laramies, under the Sweetwater, and was nearing the Togwotec Pass north of the Wind River Range when he found trouble.

Jack was on call as the Supervisor for all three of the eight-hour shifts that were pushing the tunnel, but he was actually on the scene of the drilling for sixteen out of every twenty-four hours, which all of his doctors repeatedly swore would kill him soon. Even so, like most of the world's driven men and women, he would have gone the full allotment if he had found some way of beating nature out of the sleep it required.

It was August 16th, a bright, clear morning, and they had just gotten the teeth of Halo's most reliable rig into the foot of a new mountain a full two days ahead of schedule. Hays was with the plotting crew in the mobile shack above ground and five miles behind the rig, but he was following its progress on the simulator unit when the trouble began.

"Holding speed and pressure," Hull Newbury, his righthand, said as Jack tried to swallow a cup of brown coffee that tasted more like battery acid. "Geological soundings are proving out. No surprises."

Hays was a big man with bushy gray hair, and any pleasure he may have taken at being ahead of schedule was totally hidden by his characteristically sour demeanor. "Any report of the backup spray unit for number seven, yet?" he demanded.

Newberry had worked with Hays for the better part of eight years, and he took no offense at the other's attitude. "Nothing. Pocatello says that we'd do better time ordering through McMillan and Fitch. They could have the whole exo-unit delivered by Saturday noon. You want me to call them?"

"Do it, and cancel the first order. Damn, look at that reading; that gal is going to gain us another ten hours or wreck the rig. Speed?"

Newberry consulted the big screen that covered the rear of the shack and replied, "Three-five per. She's a good mole, Jack."

"I know, I know." Hays crumpled an empty styrofoam cup and tossed it in the direction of a waste basket. "I'd still give anything if the hose hadn't caught Meister's kneecap." He grabbed up a handmike that connected him with the operating rig. "Come in, Mole One, this is Hays."

"Yeah, boss?" responded a woman's voice.

"You're riding it too hard; we're *ahead*, not behind, and you can lose stability at that rate. Ease up on the left—"

"How about letting me drive, Jack? I'm a big girl and the—*wow*! Holy Christ!"

In the shack, the simulator unit was going crazy. Hays thumbed in on her alarm. "Morrison! You're getting reflection! Shut down, shut down! You'll fry yourself!"

"It's off, but I've got fire!" she screamed.

"Hit the fire unit and shut off the sealer or you'll encase the whole damned rig!"

Newberry tore his eyes from the wildly fluctuating readings on the screen. "My lord, Jack, what did she hit? There's nothing down there! All the tests show—"

"Shut up and jump us to the nearest eyelet. I'm going down."

The pilot of the mobile shack swiftly complied, and the van-like vehicle soared the three miles across the wooded countryside to the foot of the mountain in which Mole One had been burrowing. The "eyelet" Hays had referred to was located at this point and was one of a series of tunnel-to-surface openings designed to allow access to the below-ground working area for people and equipment. The shack disgorged its passengers at the hole nearest the place where the Mole had run into trouble, and Hays and Newberry took a hastily gathered damage crew below to check out the situation.

The rig was stalled over two miles into the base of the mountain, so the men travelled through the tube via scootboards—single-passenger electric carts with rubber-tired wheels that moved well over the acrylic seal that the rig used to paint the tunnel walls behind it in order to guard against cave-ins. It was a brief, eerie ride, with their mounted lamps lighting the way.

When they reached the silent and dark rig, they found little real damage other than some laser fusing in the craft's forepart, caused when the energy had been reflected into its source. What shocked and amazed the group, however, was the shimmering silvery wall that blocked off the end of the tunnel and had stopped the advance of the Mole.

"What in the hell is it?" asked Jenny Morrison, the rigger, in amazement.

"Why didn't it show up in the geo soundings?" asked Newberry.

Hays ignored them and examined the barrier. It was at least as large across as the thirty-foot tunnel, because it stretched off into the surrounding rock at all points, and its surface was as smooth as ice and metallically cold. Instinctively, Hays knew that this thing, whatever it happened to be, was big, and they were grubbing around only a tiny patch of it.

"Newberry, get this rig out of here, take the bugeyes with you, send me a team of laser personel and an extra suit of coveralls and a gun," he ordered. "We're going to dig out around this bitch for a time."

They worked for an hour, and the segment of metal grew to eight times its original size without any evidence of ending. With the possibility of a cave-in increasing with each swipe of the lasers, Hays finally consented to calling in the government.

The federal investigators arrived within the day and quickly took over every part of the operation, in spite of Hays's strong objections. In fact, the mole rigger and his entire crew were expelled from the area, which had suddenly been tagged with a top-secret listing and was closed off to traffic of all forms by stonefaced military enforcements.

Any impenetrable substance that seemed to elude all forms of wave detection except direct sight was definitely interesting to the government and vital to national security.

It took another week of spot drilling into the mountain before investigators realized that what they had discovered was an object artificially constructed, at least eighty thousand years old, over twelve miles in total length, and more than two miles in thickness. This information was carefully guarded from the public, of course, as was the additional, unavoidable conclusion that the vessel was of non-terrestrial origin.

Only after three years of largely fruitless multinational cooperative investigation did the story break to the general public, and what a story it was.

Chapter Two

The car moved smoothly up the steep incline, riding on the air cushion that held it a foot above the highway. Its tightly closed windows separated the hot summer air outside from the circulating coolness of the interior where Aaron Doyle sat back hardly watching the road as the high-volume rage of music flooded over him and washed away yesterday's memories. He didn't want to think about anything.

But in spite of the stereo's efforts, her words returned to him like some acidic echo within the closed sphere of his mind:

"Aaron, I've applied for an adjunctive clause to our conjugal license."
"You put in for a rider without telling me? For crying out—"

"I want to begin a triad with Sheld."

"Glynna, you know how I feel about that kind of thing!"

"'That kind of thing?' Oh, grow up, Aaron, this is the twenty-first century! And I like Sheld! He's so kind and gentle."

"Then maybe you and he would be happy together, but leave me out of it! See how long you can live together on a damned poet's salary!"

And then the fight had begun. God, what a fight, filled with painful truth concerning his "obsessive materialism" and her inability to find whatever translucent ambition it was that fed the fires of her physical needs. It wasn't new ground—they had been through the same arguments many times before—but this was the first time that Glynna had gone so far as to make an official application for a change in their lifestyles, and she hadn't even warned him beforehand. He had answered with the only action open to him by taking the car and flying. But this time his usual cooling-off junket had grown with his anger to cover two full days and six states.

The realization suddenly struck him. He was in *Wyoming*, of all places. What had possessed him to come here all the way from Lancaster? Then he saw the sign above the gates at the top of the mountain.

"WELCOME TO SPACEWORLD," the huge letters said. "Home of the Buried Saucer."

Doyle had to chuckle then. His subconscious had been functioning at top level, even if nothing else had for the past forty-eight hours; since taking that minor in interstellar analysis three years earlier, he had burned with curiosity about the Spacecraft and planned to take the personal tour of it offered year round, but the suggestion had never met with Glynna's approval. Who wanted to go tramping around in some alien tomb when you could see the same display by simply dialing the television? she reasoned. Besides, with all their technology, the UN's best scientific minds still had been unable to make a scratch on the outside of the ship and had gotten inside a single compartment only because its door had been halfway open when they found it.

She was right about that, Doyle had to admit. Lasers, diamond drills, ultra-speed vibrational saws, and even low-yield atomic reactions had been used on the vast construction, but not even a heat splotch had appeared on the smooth, glistening hull. And the one open compartment had inspired volumes of intellectually badgering questions while answering no more than a handful.

That was where he and Glynna differed most basically: she could conceive of no reason even to consider leaving the creature comforts of her snug little world for the uncertainties of outer space, while Doyle would have given every cent that his lucrative seascape firm had earned for him just to have the opportunity to step from the limited stage of the Solar System into the unimaginable frontier of the Universe. Even to stand in an outer room of a vessel of alien construction sent tendrils of intoxicating awe through his brain.

For once something good had come out of one of their raging battles, he decided with a short laugh. He switched off the stereo. The ritual of leaving U.S. territory and entering the internationally held patch of ground known as SpaceWorld was well-recorded, but he switched on the dash television just to experience the full effect of this, his first trip into extraterrestrial reality.

A young woman's face appeared on the screen. "Good afternoon, sir," she said cordially, "and welcome to SpaceWorld, the home of the Buried Saucer."

"Thank you," he replied in a perfunctory tone. Even school kids knew by now that the craft was *not* saucer-shaped.

The young woman continued her opening lines, "As you may well know, SpaceWorld and the mountain that holds it have become, by an act of the 1996 Global Congress, an internationally held state within the confines of the U.S. state of Wyoming, much in the manner that the papal state of Vatican City exists within Rome, Italy.

"As you are therefore about to leave the United States for international territory, the law requires that I ask you and any other passengers in your vehicle to feed your citizen's license numbers into the dash computer terminal to facilitate a general check for outstanding violations. If you are not a citizen of the United States or have taken a Principle stand against the listing, please direct your vehicle into the line to your extreme right where you will be allowed to pass through personal inspection."

Doyle quickly punched MXTL997-83704 on the keys of his dash terminal. He briefly wondered if Glynna had reported his absence to the authorities. More likely she had turned in the jointly owned car as stolen, he concluded ironically.

"Thank you, sir," the woman said with a smile. "Are there any other passengers in your vehicle?"

Doyle recognized this as mere courtesy on her part, since she had the readout of monitoring machines that could detect a creature as small as a mouse within his car. "None," he said.

"Fine. Your vehicle has passed the primary inspections for the International Weapons Possession Act, so if you will please deposit twenty dollars at the entry gate, you may proceed."

"Thanks, and, hey!" he said, feeling his spirits lifted for the first time in months. "How do you feel about handsome, thirty-seven-year-old men who have just broken their conjugal contracts out of season?"

The face in the screen actually blushed a bit. "Sorry, sir, SpaceWorld rules do not permit fraternization between visitors and—"

"'. . . employees'. I've heard it before," Doyle said. "Well, what the heck, I gave it a shot."

"And a good one, too," she said. "Thank you, sir."

Pulling ahead to the brightly decorated gates, he flipped his window open and braved the wash of hot air long enough to drop a bill into the waiting currency slot. The mechanical gate instantly hummed open to allow him passage and Doyle let up on the brake and rolled into the large, almost three-quarters-filled parking lot that bordered the king-sized amusement park that had grown above the most important artifact ever to be discovered by the human race.

After parking and collecting his check, Doyle stood for a few moments and stretched the two-day kinks out of his body before beginning the walk to the nearest tram stand. He was tall, broad-shouldered, and trim, a physique attributable to his thirteen years as a professional deep sea diver and engineer before cadging enough securities to buy his own company; his hair was solid black uncompromised by any strands of brown or gray, and there was a certain spring to his walk, as if he were in a hurry to get to his destination wherever he went. Doyle's problem was that he didn't know where that destination would be found.

He waited at the stand for almost five minutes, wondering all the while how any location so high could be so hot, before a packed tram cruised up. It was filled with faces of a single mold: old or young, men, women, and children, all looked the same in their sheen of anticipatory excitement. Naturally, the more worldly of them attempted to cover their enthusiasm with appropriate amounts of jaded boredom, and the parents tried not to allow themselves to exhibit more exhilaration than their children, but the effect was visible on all of them. This was SpaceWorld.

And Doyle knew that he looked just like any of them.

"You know, I've written eight short stories, myself," the young girl said with perfect seriousness. "I suppose half of them could be called science fiction, though I may be weak as far as hard-science background goes."

"Really?" said Roger Griffin in a tone that he hoped was free of adult condescension. He was sixty-six years old and had spoken to countless convention audiences, but he could list the opportunities he'd had to speak with nine-year-old geniuses on one finger. "Have you submitted any of your work for publication?" he asked.

The little girl's air of competency faded. "I have had two pieces published in *Sparks*. That's a nationally distributed magazine written for and by children under the age of fourteen," she admitted.

"Yes, I've heard of it," Griffin said.

"But they don't have particularly high standards for fiction. They're happy just as long as you're a juvenile. And Mother submitted a story of mine called 'I'm Mary's Friend' to one of her favorite magazines, *McCall's*. It was accepted and printed last fall."

"That's certainly something to be proud of."

The girl sighed. "I suppose so, but it was run in conjunction with an article on exceptional children, so again I was published without any real regard to the merit of my work. I do plan to take a couple of journalism courses during my next school term, though."

"Anjanette," interrupted a tall woman sitting next to the girl, "I'm sure the gentleman is tiring of this conversation. We're almost to the park; why don't you pick out the rides that you want to try first?"

Griffin started to reply, but his wife, Maureen, beat him to the opening. "Please don't worry about tiring Roger, Mrs. Palmer. We've been married for thirty-four years, and I have yet to hear the old warhorse admit to being bored by talk dealing in any way with writing. My goodness, he attends as many as six of those science fiction conventions in a single year."

"Oh, I didn't realize that you were involved with writers, Mr. Griffin," the woman said.

Anjanette Palmer looked up at her mother and explained, "Roger Griffin is a living legend in the science fiction and fantasy genres. He has been one of the leading writers in the field for over forty years."

Griffin laughed aloud at the sober fashion in which the young girl had described him. Forty years ago, he had had constant problems selling enough of his work to buy doughnuts three times a day; thirty years ago, his stories had been summarily dismissed by the serious-minded critics as "imitative and exploitive;" twenty years ago, he'd scripted his first movie, which was an unqualified disaster; and now he was termed a "living legend" by not only this amazingly intelligent nine year old, but also by practically everyone he met at the many, many conventions. All you had to do in order to become a "living legend", it seemed, was outlive everyone else.

"Forgive me," the very proper Mrs. Palmer said, "might I have read any of your work?"

"Perhaps," he answered. "My most commercially successful novel was *The Guards at Gate Four*, published five years ago."

"Oh, Mother, I have at least a dozen of his books at home," Anjanette stated impatiently.

"You do?"

"Of course, they're the ones with the covers that you don't like me to look at."

Again Griffin threw back his head and laughed at life, so much of which was finally rewarding his youthful optimism. The words of babes, even babes with genius I.Q.'s, could deflate adult puffery just as swiftly as it could be so worthlessly cultivated. Waving aside the red-faced woman's attempts at apology, he looked at Anjanette. "Young lady," he said sternly, "as soon as you get home, I want you to send me your best, most polished efforts, and I assure you that they will receive fair and serious readings from the editors of the top magazines."

She smiled brightly at his evidently genuine interest. "You don't think I'm too young to be a real writer?"

Griffin paused for a moment before replying, "I knew from the time that I first learned to read that I wanted to write, and I began mailing my attempts when I was in high school, but I was twenty-six years old before I saw the first thing in print. Didn't even receive payment for that, either. Now, you're . . . ?"

"Nine."

"Nine, yes, and already you've published three stories and received checks for them."

"Which went directly into her education account at the bank," supplied Mrs. Palmer.

"Naturally. But Anjanette, remember, you can do whatever you want, if you'll keep the promises that you make to yourself."

"Hallelujah," whispered Maureen into his ear.

June had been a hot month from its beginning that year, and that part of Wyoming was especially distinguished with temperatures that ran from eight to fourteen degrees above average for the period. In spite of this run of heat, SpaceWorld had seen record crowds pass through its gates to leave behind massive amounts of good American capital to fill the coffer of the United Nations Special Committee for the Modernization of Socio-Economically Impeded Countries. With its large complement of advanced and thrilling rides—including a legitimate three-mile-high by seventeen-mile-broad, radio-controlled "space" missile—and its endless souvenir shops and restaurants, the park had zoomed in popularity to the position of one of the six top moneymaking entertainment centers in the world.

That was not to say that the mountain containing the buried spacecraft had been designed and managed solely as a profit-drawing tourist attraction. The international scientific community unanimously recognized the vehicle itself as the real treasure, if only they could crack its shell and decipher its clues. But in eight years of trying, science had been unable to cut, blast, melt, or wrinkle the impassive hulk.

What had been accomplished since the momentous discovery had come through slow and tedious digging. Excavating the entire vessel was out of the question due to its sheer size and its position beneath the mountain range, and any form of surface sounding was thwarted by the unique wave "invisibility" of the craft, so the only effective answer was to worm around the hull with modified versions of Jack Hays's Moles combined with verticle shafts sunk from above it.

THE ASGARD RUN

These operations gave the investigators the dimensions of the tremendous vehicle. Its shape was aptly termed "three-D double diamond", because it resembled a pair of Brobdingnagian hat boxes placed corner to corner and melded there into a thick, strong joint. In length, it was 64,781.5 feet, in height, 11,403.2, and because of various factors, not even a ballpark figure was offered as a guess to its weight. The only path into the structure was discovered at the bottom of the east-southeastern face a little more than a quarter of a mile from where Hays's drill team had happened upon it. This gap had been created when a double-chambered door had frozen at the beginning of its upward climb and remained in this half-clenched smile for eighty thousand years or more. Unfortunately, this door led to only one room, and that was a cathedral-like, but basically empty hall that was lined with blank screens and unresponsive mechanical controls. The only question that this enigmatic room definitely answered concerned the size of the creatures for whom the vessel had been designed. They were giants.

But how the people of Earth flocked to see that room. They came from all lands and backgrounds, sometimes travelling thousands of miles, just to stand for a few minutes inside a ship that had been forged on another planet and piloted across the empty light years of space to finally die beneath this quiet mountain. It was an irresistable attraction that was worth every mile of the trip and even the ultimate silence of the alien chamber.

* * *

The tram that was carrying Aaron Doyle, the Griffins, and Carol Palmer and her daughter Anjanette finally crossed the parking area and reached the outskirts of the park itself. They left the hovercraft with mounting excitement and blended into the festive crowd that already covered the grounds. Roger Griffin resembled nothing so much as an aged child on Christmas morning, and his shock of pure white hair (that had already begun a full retreat from his advancing forehead) and matching mustache combined to make him appear at least a decade older than his true age, though his movements and energy contradicted any suggestion of infirmity.

Maureen Griffin was taller than her husband and looked like a confident, successful businesswoman, but she had been at the center of most of the wildest parties that the various SF conventions could boast. She was always urging her husband to spend less time submerged in animated but restrictive discussions with fellow authors and to lead a more social life among the truly important people in his profession—those who bought the books.

Anjanette, who tagged closely behind her new friends, was small even for her age and had bright red hair and green eyes. She looked like a child actress, and, because of this, her mother dressed her in dresses and frills that accentuated the youthful look, which Anjanette hated. She was acutely aware of having an adult mind that resided in an immature body, and the mask of conceited knowledge that she wore by choice hid a volcanic struggle for identity. Anjanette Palmer knew her name, address, and I.Q. score, but she could never get a grasp on who the child behind the phenomenon truly wanted to be.

There were seventy-nine other people on the tram, among them Daniel Levya of Hermiston, Oregon, Patrice Rutherford of Winona, Minnesota, Con Jefferies, who had flown with his family from Ireland, and Kim Shawlee of Baltimore, but none of these new arrivals entertained worries greater than tomorrow's sunburns and tired feet. Just like the safe thrills offered by the shooting and dipping roller coasters that trundled screaming passengers above them, the people expected to be intellectually titillated by a visit to the dead saucer. But nothing threatening clouded the brilliant sun overhead, because all true disasters are unforeseen and sudden.

Lines. The American public is born to them, tagged as the next body on the conveyer belt, and all of their lives, no matter how individualistically oriented, they find themselves stalled at one time or another with a stranger ahead, another behind, and no end in sight.

The lines at SpaceWorld were the absolute worst Aaron Doyle could recall ever having been trapped in, and the most depressing part of it all was the fact that while each of the countless lines had a definite beginning at the turnstile to whatever ride they serviced, they were so obscenely long that they spilled out of the waiting shed and into the paved walkways to mingle like stimulated coral snakes thrown together in a pit. Doyle had to sift slowly through a number of other writhing columns of human beings just to make his way to the only point in the entire park that immediately interested him: the Buried Saucer tour, where, naturally, he would be forced to get in line.

Some of the comments that he endured while worming his large form toward his goal were less than cordial, but the large majority of the assembled people appeared to be willing to undergo heat and closeness just to hold on to the emotional charge that was radiating from everyone who stepped, laughing, from the rides.

After some ten minutes that would have done credit to the Lewis and Clark expedition, Doyle stumbled upon the mass of people patiently awaiting their turn to stand inside the indestructable space vehicle and wonder where it had begun. He wasn't at all surprised to find that the covered shed erected just outside the cavern-like entrance had long since surpassed its recommended limit of three hundred and expelled a long, coiling stream of human beings into the leech-like heat of the afternoon sun; so he took his place at the line's end with resignation rather than dejection.

For an hour and fifty minutes, Doyle was one of the best customers of the walking vendors who serviced the various lines; he drank three orange sodas and a cup of Gatorade and ate two chilled apples while inching toward the fan-blown shade of the shed. But he refused to pay good money for one of the vivid red derbies that were proving so popular with his fellow customers for shielding themselves from the burning sun overhead. Just ahead of him, a substantial block of people purchased the hats, including a young executive type, his very attractive wife, a short and portly white-haired man, and a small girl whose natural hair color almost matched the shade of the bowler. The girl's derby was paid for by the older man, in spite of the protestations of a woman who must have been her mother.

When the snail's crawl of the line finally brought Doyle into the protection of the shed, the difference was dramatic. Large ceiling fans whipped the warm air into steady motion, though they failed actually to cool it, and just the blocking of the sun cut the misery by half. The fan sounds and the redoubled closeness of the people in the zig-zagging line caused the noise level to shoot upward, but Doyle was still able to tune in an unusual conversation that was developing between the white-haired man and the archetype executive.

"I really find it hard to believe that the craft has been under this mountain for eighty thousand years," the executive said to the other man, who resembled backcover photos that Doyle had seen of author Roger Griffin. "In fact, I *don't* believe that it has been here that long."

The second man nodded. "It's hard for the average person to really grasp such a passage of time, but for me, anyway, it seems far more likely than the discovery of this incredibly tough metal that can't be scratched by our most powerful laser beams."

The younger man paused, as if carefully weighing his reply or attempting to decide whether he should reply at all. After a moment, he answered, "I don't think that this ship has been here over six thousand years and I can't accept the theory that it's from anywhere other than the Earth."

That made Doyle blink. He'd heard a zooful of wild conjectures concerning the ship, but this was one of the few "American Indians built it" declarations that he had turned up. And the man looked so conservatively levelheaded, too.

The Griffin lookalike picked up on the same train of thought. "Do you mean to suggest that the Mayans or the Apaches are responsible for the craft? Even if that's true, surely some legends of a civilization so advanced as to turn out work like that would have survived until modern times. And what happened to the rest of their products?"

The well-dressed man sighed, and his wife muttered, "Here we go again," mostly to herself.

"Well," the man began almost regretfully, "maybe this isn't the time to go into theological discussion, but I can't accept the age or origin suggested for this thing because I know that this planet hasn't existed for longer than five or, at most, six thousand years."

Doyle inadvertently laughed, but neither of the speakers seemed to notice. "I believe I understand. You're a member of a . . . fundamentalist religious sect, right?" asked the older man.

"I believe in the Bible, and I believe that every word is inspired. There are many claims made by science that aren't in accord with biblical teachings, and the age of the Earth is one of the primary points of disagreement."

Doyle stepped back slightly in anticipation, wondering if the old guy would meet this blatant challenge to the human intellect with equal conviction or try to calmly reason out the particulars of conflict. Actually, the man did neither.

"I realize that your points are sincere and in keeping with your outlook on life, so I won't debate the matter with you," the older man said. "Neither of us would convince the other of anything, and since wars have been fought over less, I don't want to chance starting one in this line. I'm too out of shape to handle myself properly."

"You can say that again," added a woman who must have been *his* wife.

Doyle slumped mentally. He still had his hackles at half-mast due to the fight with Glynna and had been set for a fur shower, but the older man's refusal to become involved with such a personal scrap left him feeling like a kid opening an empty birthday present.

So, with nothing better to occupy him during the eternal wait—he was sure that this line disappeared into the cavern, ran twice around the interior of the earth and then shot straight down to Hell, where Satan's first words would be, "All right, fools, line up!"—he decided to enter the conversation to keep it from dying a graceful death. But he needed a better entrance line than, "Excuse me, but you're full of cow dung." Maybe the old guy's faint resemblance to the writer would come in handy.

"Pardon me," Doyle said, tapping the man's shoulder. "I know that this is going to sound pretty stupid, but . . . well, I'm sure you're not, but are you Roger Griffin, the science fiction writer?"

The man turned and, with a broad smile, answered, "Yes, I am. Are you a follower of the category?"

Doyle swallowed his prepared apology and tried to cover his embarrassment with a nervous cough.

"I, uh, just wanted to say that I . . . enjoy your work and would like to have you autograph my copies of your novels. Uh, if I had them with me, I mean," he finished lamely.

"Well, thank you, son. I've always disregarded the opinions of that great repository of angry human failures known as critics, but the people who lay out their own money for my products have earned my respect and the right to voice their judgments. I'll tell you what, give my wife your name and address, and as soon as we get home, I'll mail you a signed, numbered, and dated copy of my latest novel. Maureen?"

She began searching through her purse for a notepad. "Again with the addresses. Your book will have to sell better than anything Harold Robbins ever wrote just to break even with the free copies you hand out."

Doyle began covering his mistakes. "Oh, no, don't bother. I bought the book two weeks ago in New York. Loved it. How about if we get together for dinner or something so that I can unload some of these one-way questions that have been collecting in my mental attic?"

"That would be just great," Griffin said. "There's nothing that can open to full view the enigmas of the macrocosm like a little roast duck and Chianti."

"That's almost poetic," grinned Doyle.

"Poetic nothing, it's the title of his next short story," commented Maureen.

Doyle saw that the preacher with whom he had scheduled his bout was losing interest and turning away from Griffin and himself. "Uh, excuse me, Reverend," he said, around the Griffins and the mother-daughter combination.

The man looked back. "I would rather that you didn't call me that."

"Sorry, then, Father?"

He shook his head and smiled, but it was a very serious smile. "No, the word of God authorizes no such titles for common men, whether they are evangelists or working men." His little joke was designed to ease any building tension, and it worked in most cases.

"What should I call you, then?" asked Doyle, as he warmed to the task.

"Why not Jim? My name's James Aymdahle."

"Aaron Doyle, Jim. It's a pleasure to meet you."

"Why thanks. Did you know the name of Moses' brother was Aaron? Not many people remember things such as that these days. What was it you wanted to ask?"

Doyle considered the attack he was preparing to direct against this basically friendly man and wondered if he should follow through. Some nagging little demon had lodged itself in the posterior of his brain since the fight with Glynna and was frenziedly urging him to lash out at anybody handy. It was an even-odd situation that, had the preacher taken the ancient astronaut point of argument, he would have leaped to defend the Scriptual stand. So he committed himself.

"I think you're wrong about the age of the world, where the saucer is from, and just about everything else you said in your conversation with Mr. Griffin."

Aymdahle stared wordlessly at him, as did the others, all momentarily stunned by this verbal equivalent to a splash of ice water in the face. But the preacher had been in this position before, and he recovered quickly. "Might I be correct in understanding that you are an atheist, Mr. Doyle?"

"Perhaps an agnostic, Jim. An agnostic with an open mind, but one who can't understand why an apparently intelligent adult would dismiss sound, clear scientific evidence and accept the dicta of a collection of unproven tribal legends."

"The Bible is *not* a legend," Aymdahle responded with more passion than he had intended. "It has been proven to be the authentic record of the Divinely directed men and women of the Lord here on Earth."

"Proven? In what way?"

"Gentlemen," interrupted Griffin, "let's not allow ourselves to get carried away by our personal biases. The heat, the crowd—"

"Please, Mr. Griffin, let me finish," said Aymdahle. "The Scripture has been proven to be authentic by minute examination of the original scrolls—"

"What original scrolls?" Doyle asked. "Any theological researcher will admit that the most ancient of biblical writings in our possession are copies of copies, at least three times removed from the originals, whatever they may have been. Naturally, those copies are so filled with mistakes, changes, personal opinion on the part of the transcriber, and old-fashioned lying that even our closest copy is—"

"I won't be a part of this blasphemy!"

"Will both of you *shut up*?" Griffin's sudden shout was loud enough to startle both of the men and even overrode the continual hum of the conversation of people bunched in line close to them; it drew a gallery of baleful stares from people who were irritated at having this atmosphere of joyful abandon contaminated by conflicting emotions.

Griffin ignored their silent reproofs and continued with his stunned audience. "There is an old and crusty cliché that, nevertheless, holds true for almost any subject: there's a time and place for everything. This is quite definitely neither for a high-volume debate about religion. *I* am not here for arguments, *you* aren't, the other people in this line aren't; so if you have to slug it out right now, I suggest that you step from the line, work your way into the open, and start punching. I intend to enjoy my first visit aboard an alien spacecraft."

The applause started with one pair of hands belonging to a young woman five people up-line, but it grew among the footsore, excited group of people like a cresting river abruptly released. It moved so thoroughly to every corner of the shed and beyond that soon ninety percent of the crowd was applauding without knowing why. Griffin bowed his head and sighed with a small smile.

Even the solemn Aymdahle grinned. "Mr. Griffin, I know that there is no place or time inappropriate to the spreading of God's word, but on this occasion I'll drop the subject so that your trip won't be spoiled."

His wife hugged his arm and whispered, "Thanks, hon."

You've been a Class One Idiot, Aarie old boy, Doyle thought to himself. You needed somebody to swing at and to hell with anyone who got in the way, right? "Sorry, Roger," he said aloud. "Sometimes my clutch slips and I can't get my brain into gear."

Griffin forgave them, and the crowd returned to its normal, buzzing preparation for the excitement to come. Only then did the small, red-haired girl ahead of the writer speak up, "Mr. Griffin, were you lying just then? Is this really your first visit to SpaceWorld?"

"Anjanette!" her mother snapped.

Griffin shushed her concern. "Yes, my dear, I was telling the truth. For all of my working, following, and lecturing about things such as this before anyone knew it was true, I've never fitted a visit into my schedule."

Roger didn't add that he had been unbearably eager to come the first day that the find had been made public, but a stupid sense of pride had forced him to wait until invited by one of a number of film and tape crews that were snatching up writers of far less talent and standing; when this invitation had failed to arrive, his own assaulted ego had refused to allow him to make the trip to the place that he and Maureen had named "Asgard," the home of the gods.

"Yep, this is my maiden voyage," he repeated, "but I fully intend to make up for every second that I've missed."

There were two views one could take of SpaceWorld mountain, as Donald Buckley had discovered in two years of working there. One was that the Saucer was a purely natural phenomenon, gestated by the Earth the way an oyster forms a pearl, and Donald preferred to subscribe to this farfetched, but comforting theory as he stood, hour by hour in the cool, dark recesses of the mountain. The second and more popular concept was that the entire area was filled with spirits, shades, phantoms, the ghosts of two different worlds mingling with each other as pre-Columbian Indians sang and chanted in their afterlife while surrounded by the towering, faceless specters of the former pilots of the crashed saucer.

And it was quite easy to fall under the spell of supernatural visitation when moving through the carefully orchestrated channel designed by the overlords of SpaceWorld. In spite of the mass appeal of the thrill rides, the Buried Saucer was still the most popular attraction in the park, so the approach to it was well-designed.

Following a long, charbroiling wait under the blazing sun (and it was always hot on this damned mountain, except during the light, early evening showers), the tantilized visitor became a member of one of five tour groups of no more than thirty-five people each led by attractive young girls in SF costumes; then the group proceeded single file through an almost midnight-black passageway to the string of descending escalators that dropped them a good fifth of the way toward the base of the mountain in equally dim lighting, while fluorophoto screens to either side of the stairwell recreated the possible ancient arrival of the spaceship, its accidental burial in the collapse of some tremendous natural cave, and its discovery by the SubShot team eight years earlier. Added to this display were the glowing images of various artists' conceptions of how the aliens once appeared physically, as calculated by the little evidence obtained from the single open room.

After stepping from the last escalator, the group was shown to one of the three huge glass elevators —one piloted by Donald Buckley—that carried them the rest of the way down the slot to the ship's bottom, all the while providing them with in-the-field geology lessons as they watched the layers of color-treated strata pass beyond the transparent sheathing of acrylic that encased the entire elevator shaft. The cute tour guides delivered a spiel of deliciously extrapolated scientific theory throughout the descent until the eager visitors were allowed finally to crawl through the yard-high opening in the doorway and walk in fascination through the deserted and enigmatic alien chamber before being directed to a second set of elevators that carried them up to the exit.

It was all very impressive and made a terrific story to spin for the folks back home, but Buckley had tired of it rather soon after having been recruited as an elevator jockey from his starting job as an outdoor trashcollector and pooperscooper. Yet he stayed on for three reasons: (1) the pay and prestige were irresistable (even though he had been born in Jeffery City, Wyoming, and had never been out of the continental U.S. in all of his nineteen years, he was job-rated as I-5, a member of the International workforce, because he was employed by the UN on UN territory); (2) it was a lot more comfortable within the coolness of the mountain than outside; and (3) Susan Leipnitz.

Susan was the best-looking of all the tour guides in the entire park, and she led her groups during his duty shift, so every day, for the too short five minutes of the drop to the saucer level, he got to stand at her side at the elevator doors and smell her honey-blonde hair and fantasize about what would occur someday when the two of them were trapped in the otherwise empty elevator during a power failure. Susan wouldn't contract or even date him because, she explained, she "liked him . . . like a brother."

There was something to be said for the wholesome, big-ears-and-freckles Huck Finn look, but just as soon as he collected enough dough, Donald Buckley was going to have a little cosmetic surgery and come back to work as a second Tom Cruise.

"Bottom floor, ladies and gentlemen," he said professionally when the elevator doors shooshed open. "All out, please watch your step on the acrylic finish, it can be slick for some shoes, and please stay with your guide. Enjoy yourselves."

"Thank you, Donny," said Susan, leading her group off of the elevator. "This way, please."

Donald Buckley held the doors apart for a few seconds and watched Susan's ambrosial form undulate away from him once more. Then, sighing and nodding to himself, he turned away and hit the "UP" button.

Someday.

No one was disappointed by the trip into the heart of the mountain. The atmosphere had been exotically suggestive, and the fluorophoto presentations as they rode down had been, in many instances, awesome. Patrice Rutherford clutched her fiance's large hand with both of hers when the artists' visualizations of the Saucer's builders flashed inches from her eyes—partially because she knew he enjoyed her show of feminine dependence and partially due to the icy suspicion that something like that could well be waiting for her *down there*, in the locked recesses of the monolithic craft.

Roger Griffin was ecstatic. For years he had viewed the tri-dem tapes and listened with respect to first-hand accounts told by acquaintances, but now he was here, descending to the very threshold of interstellar travel. Oh god, the human race had to decipher the secrets held by this mint of knowledge, even if it meant destroying some of the vessel with hydrogen energy, because it had traversed the receding stairways and so much awaited the bold minds out there.

Griffin's excitement grew by the moment until it completely overshadowed and washed away his deeply felt "psychic" warnings against the trip. Nothing could happen to him in the presence of so much pure enlightenment.

The tours were purposely spaced so that each had about a five minute lead time on the one following, but this still meant that, at any given moment, three of the five were browsing through the church-like atmosphere of the alien room, in addition to the various scientists who came from all over the globe to spend weeks combing through the meager revelations provided by the vessel. When Susan Leipnitz's tour group crawled through the low opening, a total of one hundred and twenty people were inside the chamber: three tour guides, ninety-one tour members, six UN force soldiers there to guard against vandalism or souveniring, fifteen scientists, and five weary maintenance workers cleaning up litter left by previous visitors.

"I used to think I might be teleported aboard a UFO, but I never thought that I'd have to crawl into one," said Roger Griffin, as he dragged himself beneath the double-chambered, eleven-foot wide entrance on hands and knees.

"What's the matter, Grandpa? Has age taken the forceful spring from your muscles?" asked Maureen from his side.

He snorted. "At my last physical, the doctor said that my insides were still as fresh as a thirty-year-old's and that I'm good for at least seventy-five more years."

"It's the outside that bothers me. If you'd consent to a little surgical restructuring, at least I wouldn't look as if I'd married my first grade teacher." Maureen said this in a tone that was only half-joking.

"Never!" replied Griffin, still buoyant. "It's taken me sixty-six years to acquire these wrinkles and this balding dome, so don't try to force me into a return of puberty. Besides, this image makes me more attractive to women."

"It's a strange curse to be married to a man without vanity," his wife muttered.

"You know, eight years ago, I thought we were alone in the Universe," Doyle observed.

"We are," said James Aymdahle.

While the adults were slowly making their way into the interior, the few children in the group exalted in their sudden superiority by racing ahead of their parents and ignoring admonitions to be careful of their heads. Anjanette Palmer was small for nine years old, though still too tall to race beneath the door in an upright gait, but she solved the difficulty by proceeding in a modified, squatting duck-walk that quickly carried her ahead of her slower elders.

"Who said it's rotten to be a child?" she laughed, mocking her own attitude and problems.

" 'Not I', said the Walrus," puffed Griffin.

Susan Leipnitz finished the course well ahead of the others, dusted the knees of her pantsuit out of habit (the acrylic floor was cleaned at least once an hour), and reined in the excited children until their parents could take charge of them.

"Welcome, ladies and gentlemen," she said, "to the only artificial craft on this planet that was not constructed by human beings." Then she stepped back and allowed the natural wonder of the moment to evolve without interference.

Cries, whistles, and gasps followed. The sheer size of the room—it was three hundred yards long by a hundred wide by fifty in height—robbed the newcomers of speech for long moments, and thereafter the elaborate furnishings that had been installed by the UN teams took the average tourist's attention firmly and held it while the tour orbited slowly throughout the room on large, wheeled platforms. The numerous additons to the relatively empty room consisted of mounted artists' displays, recorded lectures by international experts in the field of extraterrestrial theory, and recreations of the best guesses concerning the craft's origin. These helped to disguise the basic lack of artifacts.

Everyone came to their feet to stare more fully at the scene, except for Griffin. He remained on his knees, transfixed by the sight that had been so integral a part of his imagination but now existed as

THE ASGARD RUN

the undeniable truth, and all that he seemed able to say was a whispered, "It's real, finally, it's real." Tears welled in his eyes and threatened to spill down his cheeks.

In spite of the dozens of people in the room with him, it was his moment alone.

Maureen understood her husband's reaction and stood quietly at his side so that it might play itself out within his soul. The only person who turned back from the astounding moment was Anjanette, and she immediately ran to Griffin's side.

"Mr. Griffin!" she cried. "What's wrong? Did you hurt your legs?"

He wrapped one arm about her shoulders, rubbed his eyes with the heel of his hand, and smiled. "No, my dear, I'm simply an old man who can't control his own emotions. You see, for most of my life, I've been unable to actually *see* my own work; oh, I can read the print and hold the books, but an architect can watch as life grows inside his buildings, a doctor can watch his patients recover, but I . . . I've worked only in other people's minds, and I couldn't be certain that *they* saw what *I* saw. This is like the moon landing for me. But I don't suppose that you understand—"

"Yes I do," the girl stated simply.

He looked at her. "You do, don't you? Here, help an aging fool to his feet and we'll get on with this tour."

The group stepped onto a waiting platform and some people took advantage of the mounted seats as the tour began moving down the right wall. Susan Leipnitz expertly helmed the discussion, explaining the various theories applicable to the craft (von Daniken's ancient astronauts, Gaddis's holes in time, the ideas of Gillfillan, Umbasso, and countless others), reviewing the known qualities of the vessel, and listing UN objectives in the coming five years, all without lapsing into the arid drone of the constant lecturer. She guided them past the single huge chair in the rear of the chamber, which suggested that the creators of the vehicle stood upright on at least two feet and towered to heights of ten feet or better (the pivot-based chair was located before a cluster of wall-screens and dials, and its seat reached to Doyle's waist). And Susan kept them hooked on her descriptions of what might lie behind the three impenetrable doors that lined the far end of the room.

Approximately halfway through the tour, before either of the other teams of visitors had completed the circuit, Carol Palmer began to feel faint. She realized that the medicine that she had counted on to hold her travel sickness at bay was wearing off. It was psychological, of course, she had known *that* long enough, and her medicine was a mental crutch, but psychological sickness did the same acrobatic maneuvers to her stomach as the real thing.

After tactfully breaking in on Susan's travelogue and discovering that she could leave the tour early by way of the elevators at the exit side of the door, Carol took her daughter's hand to begin the three-hundred-yard walk, but Anjanette resisted the action.

"*Mother*," she whispered, "I want to stay for the rest of it."

"Mummy is sick, Anjanette. Now, come on!"

THE ASGARD RUN

The Griffins had overheard and turned to them. "Mrs. Palmer, we'll watch after her for the rest of the tour, if you'd like," Maureen said.

"I couldn't ask you to—"

"Of course you could," interrupted Roger. "She can probably tell us more about this derelict than the guides can. Why not go ahead and wait for us by the upstairs exit?"

"Well," Carol said, her stomach registering severe complaints about remaining under all of those tons of mountain. "If you're certain that she won't trouble you."

"Run along," Maureen said, smiling.

"All right. Mummy will be right outside the elevator in the park, Anjanette, so don't be frightened."

"I won't," the girl assured her. "You'd better go; you look green."

After pecking her child on the cheek, Carol Palmer walked quickly across the long hall and slid beneath the constantly open door. Susan continued her narrative. "While most authoritative opinion places the age of this vessel at eighty thousand years due to research done on the geological strata and cosmic count, many experts are now placing its origin, at least in this mountain, as far back as two hundred thousand years in the past."

"Wow," said George Flanders. "I'm going to get a shot of that control center in the wall." Raising his holographic camera, he stepped from the rolling platform and went to one knee for the best angle. As he snapped the picture, a strange sensation, like a scrambling imp with tiny claws, danced up his right leg and into his hip. "What the hell?" he muttered, glancing at the white floor. "What was that?" The feeling darted up his leg again. "Hey, honey, do you have electricity or something running through this ship?"

Susan interrupted her speech to reply, "No, sir. The only energy coming into this craft is in insulated cables and provides power for the mounted lights and the displays."

"Humph," he grunted, stepping back to the platform.

"You feel that?"

Paula Tyre took her eyes from the world's largest ferris wheel. "That vibration?" she asked.

"Yeah," said the young man next to her, as he swept up a wad of paper. "What was it?"

"Who knows? Sonic booms, SubShot exploding, earthquake, the ghosts tap-dancing in the spaceship." She shrugged and turned back to the ride.

"Earthquake," the boy said. And he walked away.

Chapter Three

The brain stirred.
More than half liquid, it had settled without a struggle into peaceful oblivion tens of thousands of years before and remained in that state without complaint for all that time, insulated from the shocks of the world outside by layers of deadening soil. But now circumstances had changed: there were the minor stimuli provided by the intelligent inhabitants of the planet—the caustic solutions, the concussions, the trickle of energy running into Sub-Deck One—in addition to a massive, angry, building shift that radiated through the mountains and the land around it like a powerful heat.

The situation was close to developing into a total state conducive to cognizance.

The brain that had not fulfilled its programming

for the thousands of years that it had rested in the mountain stirred and tried to awaken.

Paula Tyre had made a series of suggestions to account for the strange ground vibrations to some boy whose name she couldn't recall, and at that time her interest in the matter had been minimal and her explanations facetious. After all, the missile ride caused the paving to jump enough to notice when it was launched, if you stood close enough to it. But after the boy had gone and she had dismissed the momentary interruption, a sense of uneasiness had remained, reenforced when another hesitant tremble ran beneath her soles.

It felt as if she were standing on a wooden porch and someone had slapped at a spot directly below her feet with a wide board.

How many times would the missile ride take off inside a minute? How many explosions would rip the SubShot fifteen miles away? Come on, Paula, you work around *heavy equipment*, this is the world's largest ferris wheel at your side . . .

She looked up at the exuberant, shining faces of the children, all of those little children.

"Wyant!" she called.

A passing man in the red-and-white-striped uniform of the SpaceWorld grounds unit stopped and answered, "Yeah, Paulawalla? What d'you want?"

"Take my place for ten, will you?" she asked with a sudden urgency. "I have to see Kelton."

"Sure I will, but why do you need to see him?"

"It's important, Wyant. Just take over for me, okay?"

He did so, and Paula quickly pushed through the unsuspecting crowd to the nearest parktram, where she hitched a ride with an outgoing garbage load. Jumping off at the supervisory center, she dodged by the rain of questions launched at her by fellow employees and knocked loudly on the office door of Franklin Kelton, the day supervisor.

"Enter," answered his aristocratic voice.

"Frank, I'm Paula Tyre. I work the rides on southside," she stated as the door closed behind her.

"Of course, Paula, I remember you," Kelton said through his plastic smile. Kelton made a point of memorizing the names and faces of everyone who worked "beneath" him, but actually he had terrible retention. "Have a seat."

"I really don't have time, Frank. I just came in to see if you have the seismic readings from those tremors we've been having?"

"Tremors?" he repeated. His right eyebrow rose a condescending half-inch, and he pulled a small strip of tape from the readout slot at the right side of his desk. "I haven't felt anything."

"You were in here," she began.

"And these readings from Pahaska aren't in the least alarming. You probably felt some of the construction work that is going on down range for the—"

"Franklin!" she said, genuinely surprised at his nonchalant attitude. "I would recognize construction work, wouldn't I? Those are tremors, just like you get before an earthquake, and this area had one ten years ago!"

"Mild," he countered. "And centered more than

a hundred miles away. Nothing that would concern us if it happened again. Look." He pushed a button on the arm of his chair and a wall panel slid back to reveal a lever resembling one used to control house current. "If a quake of any magnitude hit, all I'd have to do is flip that and every ride in the place would zip into a holding zone and all of you loyal workers would begin evacuating the customers to safety areas."

"I know that, and I want you to pull it now! If you wait for the main shake to begin, you'll kill half of those people out there!"

"Oh, Tyre, give me credit for some intelligence, will you?" he said in disgust. "The seismic center will put out a warning if anything should—"

"Damn your warnings!" Paula shouted.

"I'm not shutting down the park, girl!" he shouted just as loudly. "Do you realize the reports that would involve, the reride checks, the ordinances?"

From somewhere deep below the building in which they stood, something moved, and the low, hollow cry of the earth drifted up to their ears. To Paula, it was an accusation, to Kelton, a possible point of concern. He looked at the continuing readout and smiled.

"See?" he said. "Nothing to worry about at all, no warning."

"You're unbelievable!" Marching around his desk, she reached for the lever. "I'll take full responsibility if its a false alarm."

"Hey! What are you doing?" he demanded. Before she could throw the switch, he had grasped her shoulders and shoved her roughly away from the

THE ASGARD RUN

panel. "Don't you touch my equipment, do you hear, you little bitch?" He was much the larger of the two.

A different sort of fear washed over Paula, but her sense of purpose won out. Grasping a handful of neatly outtyped and stacked reports from the top of his desk, she threw them directly into his face, creating a momentary blizzard. That was all the time she needed to dart back to the important lever and flip it into an operative position.

"Look at what you've done!" screamed Kelton. "Get out of here, get out of my office!"

"Gladly," she said. "You sanctimonious idiot."

The rides slowed, stopped, and pulled off-track or revolution into a preplanned area for quick, effective evacuation. On the belt of each Space-World employee, a tiny crimson light flashed and a calm voice said, "Operation Three is now effective. Repeat, Operation Three is now effective."

For the first time in the history of the park, a full evacuation was on, but each worker went about the task swiftly and coolly, ignoring the confused and often irate reactions of the upset customers.

There were three point four minutes left until the first major shock.

The roller coaster died on the second from last uphill grade and began to roll backward at a fast, but not excessive speed. Some of the screams that greeted this action were more genuine than those inspired by the regulation course, though most of the riders hadn't become aware of the deviation.

Buster Jurgens recognized the variance in the

STEVE VANCE

run—he'd ridden the coaster twice that afternoon—and he was more angered than surprised when the car slowed to a stop in the valley between two slopes and then rolled onto an auxiliary span located at the foot of the forward hill. Buster didn't like the interruption a damned bit.

"What the hell's this?" he demanded as a couple of uniformed park employees began to direct the passengers off the track and onto a stairway that wound to the ground some forty feet below. More attendants waited there.

"Speed it up, sir, down the stairs, thank you, sir!" answered a wide-eyed skinny boy with a bad complexion, pushing Buster firmly on the shoulder.

"The stupid ride ain't over!" Jurgens stopped at the stairs and held up the rest of the long line.

"Please, sir, we must keep everyone moving!" the kid said with something close to panic.

"Do I get a refund? Answer me that, do I get one?"

The second employee, a short, bulky, husky-looking guy, stopped his work at the rear of the car and shouldered a path to where Buster stood, immovable, like the Spartan at the bridge. When this other boy spoke, there was no trace of the normal, polite customer-service deference in his voice, "Geo, what's the damned holdup?"

The tall boy replied, "This man won't leave unless we give him a refund of some kind."

"I paid enough to get into this place," Buster explained angrily, "and nobody shortchanges Buster Jurgens."

The stocky boy looked at the blinking light on his belt and listened to the placidly insistent voice

48

from the clip behind his right ear. It was all part of his training, and he knew what to do. "Sir, I assure you that you will be in the first carload of customers following this drill."

"That's not good enough, boyo, you can't push me around."

The park attendant realized that the other coaster riders were getting nervous, and it was his job to get all of these civilians down into the shelters before things began to bounce. Shaking his head as if somewhat disgusted with the situation, the boy half-turned to the left and, with a snake-like speed foreign to his size, his right fist lashed out and grabbed the front of Jurgens' shirt. He dragged the startled man to him with ease and forced his upper body over the metal railing until it seemed that only the boy's one-handed grip on the back of his neck kept the man from tumbling to an abrupt end on the paving below.

"Get 'em down, Geo!" the boy shouted. "Mr. Buster Jurgens is taking the express elevator!"

Geo reacted quickly, and the passengers resumed the fast, orderly flow to the ground, none bothering to stop and aid Jurgens, who was screaming hysterically.

"Help me, get me up!" he cried. "I didn't mean nothing by it!"

The boy took no pleasure in the fear he was inspiring in Jurgens—it was his job—and as soon as the majority of the other civilians were safely down, he jerked the trembling man into an upright position. "Had enough, loudmouth?" he whispered harshly.

"Yeah, yeah—"

"Listen!" He shook Jurgens. "You're going down those steps and do exactly as you're told, understand?"

"Sure, kid, I understand!"

The boy shoved the man toward the descending line and followed, sighing deeply. Only doing my job, he reaffirmed to himself, only my job. Then he observed ironically, Which I probably just lost.

A minute and ten seconds remained until disaster.

"Still overwhelmed?" whispered Doyle beneath the steady burr of the guide's speech.

Griffin's face had lost little if any of its excited luster. "Only when I think," he answered.

Carol Palmer had left perhaps five minutes before, and one of the three tour groups was just approaching the door to follow her path to the surface of the mountain.

The brain of the long-dormant craft was within degrees of consciousness.

Anjanette was speaking when the moment came —she had interrupted Susan's flow of words to ask a question concerning the size of the theorized shipbuilders—and in spite of the fact that that single instant in her young life was forever imprinted in her mind in dazzling detail, she could never recall the exact words of that unanswered question.

The quake arrived.

For everyone on the motorized platforms, there was a flash instant of certainty that the machine had exploded; but then they were thrown to the smooth metal floor along with the rest of the people in the craft and the terrifying dancing continued. Roger Griffin hit the floor on his back, driving his alarmed cry from his lungs along with the rest of his breath. Anjanette instinctively curled herself into a tight ball and slid across the metal as if it were ice. James Aymdahle clutched futilely at the air, caught his wife's shoulders, and twisted his body below hers as they hit the floor. The lighting system, run in from the outside, began to flicker, racing the world through a series of alternating midnights and dawns, and the tall displays and reconstructions built within the vessel by the park's designers joined in the hysteria of the moment by swaying ponderously above the struggling people.

The warning system set in motion by Paula Tyre was highly effective despite the fact that it had never before been employed. Well over half of the passengers on the various rides had been evacuated to safety, and most of the terrified civilians on the ground were rushing to the reinforced shelters while the ground shuddered beneath them.

The roller coaster seemed to become elastic and stretched at incredible angles before it collapsed into an arching mass of rubble. The overhead skylift began to rain to the earth amid wails of terror. The world's largest ferris wheel could not be cleared fast enough to prevent loss of life, either, and seventeen unlucky people were trapped near its top when the huge steel columns that held it locked into static paralysis screamed and began to twist. The massive structure broke free and dropped the short distance to the ground with a terrible explosion; it stood balanced briefly like some gargantuan wheel before making a half-roll and toppling slowly to one side.

Franklin Kelton stood inside an office that shook as if on rough seas and stared through a window at SpaceWorld while it collapsed upon itself. He realized that he should be screaming, crying, raging against the forces that were destroying him, but he found it hard to dredge any honest feeling out of the iceberg of his soul.

That Tyre kid had saved his ass; he couldn't be held responsible for an act of God, but if he had been successful in denying the emergency signal to her, the UN courts would have fried him alive (if he managed to survive, of course.) But because of her actions, they might come out of the mess with minimal deaths, perhaps as few as fifty or sixty.

The little bitch.

Donald Buckley was waiting at the top of his elevator shaft when the alarm came in. He had felt the small tremors that had been flitting through the mountain, but he had paid little attention to them until he heard that spinechilling "moan" from somewhere down there. Then the light on his belt had gone off and the voice had begun announcing the implementation of Operation Three levelly but firmly, so Buckley didn't wait to find out if it was a drill or the real thing.

His instructions in the case of Operation Three were clear: if he had no passengers in his elevator (which he hadn't) he was to shift himself into high drive and evacuate through the emergency exit stairs at the right ascending elevators, which he intended to do. Elevator shafts weren't the safest

THE ASGARD RUN

places to wait out emergencies, whatever they turned out to be.

The level on which Buckley was running for his life was located five hundred feet below Space-World park and was designed so that visitors to the Buried Saucer could move from the illustrious escalators to the quicker elevators for the rest of the trip down. The emergency stairway led straight out of the side of the mountain and had been devised to allow the elevator jockies and their passengers to get out of danger as quickly as possible, and Buckley and his fellow operators dashed past the ascending cars as they headed for the way out. These elevators zipped to a stop just before the first shock rolled through the floor with a deafening roar that seemed to come from the very center of the earth.

Donald felt like a bowling pin. He bounced from his feet and reeled against a couple of other boys before he had enough room to fall. Once on the cold acrylic floor, his jerking body tripped all three of the operators who were spilling out of the newly arrived cars. Tangled in struggling arms and legs, Buckley had a doubly tough chore in squirming from under them and climbing to his feet. It was like trying to stand in shoes soled with ball bearings.

"Come on, let's get out of here before the tunnel collapses!" he shouted at the rest. "Come on!"

Like slapstick comedians, the boys lurched forward to the stairs, where they found the going easier due to the handrails they clung to as they climbed. Donald was forty steps toward daylight before he realized what he was doing.

Grabbing the shoulder of the boy ahead of him, he yelled, "Where are the people who were in the saucer?" He was just barely heard above the noise.

The other pointed down and away.

Buckley caught his arm. "You *left* them down there?"

"This is an *earthquake*!" exploded the boy.

"There are over a hundred people in that thing! We've got to get them out!"

The boy shook himself free, responding, "I ain't crazy enough to go back down that hole!"

"Freddy, Ian!" Buckley shouted after the fleeing group. "We've got to help them! Somebody!" No one responded. "All right, you damned cowards!" He turned back into the mountain, his courage like a cold fist in his throat.

One of the running boys did notice his actions and called back, "Don't be a fool, Don!" But he didn't pause.

The strip lights began to flare and dim before Donald could reach the nearest elevator. When they went out all together, he was suddenly lost in a reborn version of black Chaos, with a floor that jumped under his feet and walls that slammed at him blindly from either side. Even the flashing light on his belt and the too composed voice near his ear deserted him. Twice he misstepped and caught a faceful of floor, but he didn't turn back to the stairs because he knew that the elevator shafts had auxiliary power sources independent of the lighting system.

By the time he found the open door and stumbled in, his face was wet with his own blood and his head was whirling. His hand groped for and found the power button. Light hammered at his eyes so roughly that he had to shield them with a forearm while he punched the car into downward motion.

When the elevator began to shriek, Donald wasn't sure if it was a new sound or just another note of the cacophony that surrounded him; when the walls of the shaft slowed and then stopped in their upward flow, he knew it was over. None of the operational buttons responded to his futile poundings, so Donald Buckley sat limply on the floor.

The walls were visibly closing on the car. Next the lights would go out.

The brain of the ship awoke in a state of inefficiency. Its sensors were flooded with wildly fluctuating data that was in severe conflict with the in-flight collation of the planet's natural ecological system, but, of course, the brain had no way of realizing that it had been aroused during an earthquake.

Responding to incomplete and jumbled information and with a portion of its systems yet malfunctioning, the craft prepared for a hovering maneuver designed to lift it out of the potentially disruptive ground tremors. Lateral control had failed in the implementation of the order, so only half of the vessel responded to the emergency action. The displacement cells cleared an area sixty-eight percent of the way to the surface, but only along the southern face of the craft, and when it lifted, only half of the ship raised itself.

After several seconds of holding at a plus seventy

-degree angle, full control was re-established and all lifting power was restored in the operating portion of the machine.

Aaron Doyle thought the disaster was over. He had been tossed to the floor along with everyone else when the earthquake hit. (It had been an earthquake, of course; what else could have shaken a truly massive structure like the spacecraft, although he had entertained for one mad instant a flash vision of the thing actually *lifting* . . .) The lights were gone, so he lay in the dark, panting and feeling order settle slowly back upon the world. He anticipated another shock. The only sounds came from terrified children crying for their parents.

It's going to be a long, dark climb back upstairs, Doyle thought to himself. And then the entire planet tilted.

Doyle's scream mixed with the others as he found himself sliding with increasing speed head down on the hillside that the vessel's deck had become. He thrashed out with both hands just as James Aymdahle had done so frantically before, and he clawed at anything to stop his fall, though his hands found only black air. The cries filled his mind and added to his own terror so that he could formulate no thoughts beyond animal instinct. His speed increased, his feet were where his head should have been—

He was going to slam into the wall of the craft headfirst.

The path to salvation came to Donald Buckley like a proclamation from the Divinity. Instead of sitting resignedly on the floor of his glass coffin and waiting for the converging walls of the shaft to smash him like some insignificant bug, he could pull down the lightweight metal ladder, shove open the hatch, and monkey up the elevator cables to the next level, at least.

In the stygian darkness, it was difficult to catch the ladder while hopping like a rabbit, but he had worked so long in the elevators and had seen the equipment lining the ceilings so many days on end that its position had been buried in his consciousness beneath layers of familiarity. The grinding scream of the trapped car spurred him on, and finally his left hand wrapped around one of the rungs and jerked the structure down as he fell. The bottom of the ladder whipped across his temple so that his skull rang like a church bell and he dropped to his knees, a hundred and sixty pounds of cold meat.

The situation produced a continuous stream of adrenalin into his system and prevented him from surrendering to a numbing warmth inside his head. He used the ladder to climb up again and managed to drop one foot above the other until he banged his throbbing head against the roof, sending even more charges of pain through his body.

His hand found the lever release. Twisting it with a frantic strength, Buckley waited for the spring action to throw the trap panel up and back, just as it had in the two practice sessions he had run through, and then he would be outside and up those cables . . .

But the panel remained closed and solid, another bar in this death row cell.

"Open up, damn you!" he shouted, slamming his fist into the roof. Hysteria narcotized the pain. But the panel remained closed. "Oh my God, open!"

The pressures that were working to crush the elevator car were also holding the trap panel shut.

Donald slumped against the ladder, thinking that he was beyond caring anymore. He had tried so hard, just to die alone in this hole . . . I'm sorry Susan, I would have gotten you out if I could have, but you're down there in that unbreakable saucer while I'm about to be crushed between sunlight and Hell . . .

Then the spacecraft did its half-flip and the phenomenal pressures that were surrounding the frozen elevator multiplied immensely.

Donald Buckley suddenly screamed and spewed blood from his throat and ruptured ears. The elevator car resisted for a moment, and then it crumpled at its base like a used paper cup. The air in the sealed compartment rushed upward and blew the top away with a force that shot everything within it toward the surface like shells from a gun.

Buckley really thought that he was dead and only half-perceived the sensation of flying among the flotsam of the elevator. A length of severed cable writhed sinuously before his dazed face, and shards of treated glass embedded themselves in his legs and back, though none cut deeply enough to kill him. Had there been any light in this shaft, he would have seen the upwash of debris as well as the blurred uniformity of the walls that were diving so incredibly swiftly toward the planet's center.

His left forearm brushed against one of those walls, and even with the smoothness of the acrylics that coated it, a searing iron pressed into his exposed flesh; this sharp new pain laced through the insulating haze, forcing Donald to realize who and where he was and how few seconds he had left before the flow reversed and sent him hurtling back into the pit.

He reached out, away from the direction that had burned his arm, and, just as the massive forces began to equalize in a prelude to his death, both of his arms folded around a mass of wrist-thick cables and his legs clutched at them hungrily. After a moment of ponderous weight which painfully tugged him back toward the gaping mouth, he found the strength to fight.

Donald Buckley began to climb.

When the floor had become almost vertical, Doyle performed an acrobatic backflip and found himself bouncing down into the darkness like a human basketball, skimming along the smooth surface rather than slapping against it. He tucked to avoid the dangers of flailing limbs and prayed—though to no particular deity—that his skull wouldn't shatter like crystal when he hit the northern wall, which had now become the floor.

Susan Leipnitz had been as totally surprised by the quake as any of the civilians who were now falling about her in crying terror. She and the other park employees inside the ship possessed the same emergency equipment that had alerted the surface personnel to the imminent danger, but the sophisticated devices were completely useless inside the vessel, which was an almost perfect barrier to any type of wave transmission. This had been considered by the park management, but all alternate suggestions (such as placing a cable-fed auxiliary system inside the ship) were turned down as too potentially alarming. The responsibility of warning those in the saucer was delegated to the elevator operators, whose alarms could be reached by the primary signals.

As she tumbled like a wad of paper in a storm, Susan thought with startling clarity that the boys in the elevators must have been too far up-shaft to relay the alert before the shocks began.

Roger Griffin could not understand it. In the midst of his fear, his mind tried to comprehend how the floor to the spacecraft had broken free—hard to accept even considering the tremendous stresses of an earthquake—and dropped like a hinged trap door from beneath them. Then some cyclopean creature from the caverns below reached up and swatted his sliding form to a dead halt that robbed Griffin of all traces of consciousness.

Finally the last shrieking body tumbled into the struggling and broken mass of its fellows and the long dark fall was ended. The ship hovered there for an endless, knife-edged moment during which a kind of silence formed; the quake had ended and taken away the noise of roaring monsters, the terrified people were either unconscious or filling lungs drained by their fear and impact, and the functioning space vehicle created no sound or vibration in spite of the enormous thrust that had been generated just to raise it into that nearly perpendicular posture.

Without any warning, the ship fell back into the hutch it had occupied for thousands of years, and a strong new chorus of agonized cries answered the movement. Even though it crashed into its former resting place with a force heightened by its countless tons of weight, the noise that should have accompanied the fall was largely absent, and only the terror and pain were real as the one hundred and twenty people fell from the wall onto the relevelled floor.

The darkness encased their anguish within a hot, tight prison.

Chapter Four

He was in bed again, with Glynna, and he was demanding to know what she wanted, what more he could do to fulfill the voracious beast within her. In return, she wanted to find out where *he* was mentally, emotionally, psychically.... Why was it that, though she could always touch him, there was always a void where his *essence* (Glynna used that word a lot) should have been? What was it that had captured his yearnings so thoroughly that nothing she could say or do was able to really touch that which was Aaron Doyle?

Maybe that was what had driven him so far away from her: he could not answer her because he didn't know what it was that created the ache deep within his soul.

Doyle rolled away from Glynna to staunch the rising argument, but when his outflung arm swept across his chest and over the edge of the bed, it dropped roughly against something hard and cold and not the deep carpet that usually scrubbed his knuckles. The pain that shot up to his shoulder saved him the long moments of confusion that peppered so many of the others who had lost consciousness in the upheaval. He knew instantly that he was lying on the floor of an alien machine beneath hundreds of thousands of tons of quake-jolted earth.

It was nearly quiet. Groans that sounded like the mumbled voices of unsettled sleepers escaped through dry lips and fluttered to the far corners of the vast room. Then a child began to cry.

Doyle himself released a long sigh that verged on a groan and painfully worked open his eyelids. To his continued and harrassed surprise, the darkness that he had expected to find in the chamber was not complete; a diffused, short-range type of glow was emanating from a wide spot on the wall along which the people had been dumped so carelessly by the vessel's handstand, and though its greenish radiance provided a stark contrast to the general darkness, it was still so faint that shock-slackened, uncomprehending faces were distinguishable only within a dozen feet of the source of light.

Doyle decided to chance sitting up, since it would be easier to get out of the craft by walking to the rescuing elevators (once they arrived) than waiting around to be evacuated by stretcher along with the *really* injured people. Actually, he didn't have any way of knowing if he were one of the *really* injured people himself unless he sat up and made a thorough inspection, so that was another reason to make the effort.

Slowly, very carefully, as if he were afraid to tear away some film of numbness that might be insulating him from the torture of a fracture or rupture, Doyle eased himself into a sitting position. No sudden, gashing pains accompanied his actions, and, in fact, the only quickly evident pains were from the hand he had slapped so innocently onto the indestructable floor and from a thumb-sized lump on the back of his head.

By that time, the room was echoing with the cries of the seriously injured. A large portion of the young children he had seen inside the ship had apparently survived, to judge by their united voices.

Survived. God, that was a hard-edged word to apply to the situation. Doyle wondered if many people had been killed in the brief disaster and hoped, without much conviction, that no one had died.

Some of the conscious were now beginning to call specific names and questions over the wails of the rest, and Doyle felt that he should be doing so, as well, while he stood clumsily and leaned against the wall for support. But he had no wife or child in the conglomeration, and the only person he knew was Roger Griffin, who was more of an acquaintance through his work than actual association.

If it would give him some sort of fix in the madness, why not? "Griffin! Roger Griffin!" he added a shout to the numerous others. "Can you hear me, Griffin?"

Surprisingly, an answer came from the swirl of

voices, from somewhere close to Doyle's present location. "Yes, here! Who's calling me?" The writer's voice was dazed and confused.

"It's Aaron Doyle. I'm okay. Just stay there, and I'll come to you."

Doyle took a light, tentative step, found no one beneath his foot, and tried another. He had moved about three yards before he stumbled into someone still lying on the cold floor. He had trod heavily on the slim upper arm of a young woman, but she hadn't moaned, twitched, or even drawn a breath. He was no longer involved in an exciting, victimless adventure; death was as real below a mountain as he recalled it below the ocean waves.

Doyle took just a moment to realign himself and then continued to move toward Griffin. Less than a minute passed before he was close enough to pick out the distinctive cottony hair and mustache from among the faintly seen ghosts surrounding him.

Aaron stooped to where the older man sat, apparently uninjured, and said loudly enough to be heard, "It's Aaron Doyle, Griffin. Can I help you stand?"

Griffin was still shaken by the events of the past few minutes, and this condition was evident in his voice, "What? Oh, yes, I think I'm all right. At least, I haven't found any broken bones, yet. Have you seen Maureen?"

"Your wife? To be honest, I haven't seen much of anything since I woke up.

"I need to find her. We always called this vessel Asgard, you know, the Norse legend, home of the gods, but now . . . Aaron, what happened to us?"

Wasn't it clear? Doyle wondered. He had just

assumed that everyone had picked up on the cause of the catastrophe as quickly as he, but that had always been another of his big problems with Glynna, his assumptions. "Well, it's only a guess, but I'd say that we've recently experienced an earthquake of major proportions. The way the floor—"

"Yes, yes, I know that much," Griffin interrupted. "But what caused the floor to drop the way it did and then return to level? Did we fall into a gigantic cave or something?"

Doyle shrugged. "Who knows? We'll have to ask the park people when they get an elevator down here to us. If the elevators are still working, that is."

"Do you think they are?"

"Now that I think about it, probably not. A tremor of that magnitude could have easily collapsed the shafts. But don't get panicky; with all the laser equipment that places like this have, they'll have an emergency well sunk to us in a matter of hours."

"I hope that it's not too long to help these people. Lord, it sounds like a battlefield in here."

"Mostly fear," Doyle commented unconvincingly. "Nearly everybody here is used to a nice, safe, *solid* world underfoot, and this is the first real danger they've ever been thrown into. Literally."

"Ah, but it's easy for us to talk, isn't it? *We're* not hurt." Griffin extended his right hand toward the silhouette that was Doyle. "Help me up, if you don't mind. I have to find Maureen. She was too nervous to ride the roller coaster with me, so you can imagine what *this* has done to her."

"Sure."

After lifting the man to his feet, Doyle stood where he was, amid the gradually subsiding voices of pain, and tried to decide what to do next. He knew that sitting down again would only return that uncomfortable feeling of incompetence, but standing in the darkness without any plan made him feel about as useful as a dead roach. The weight of decision was taken from his brow when another tall shape moved into the light from the wall and began calling for quiet.

"Ladies and gentlemen, please calm yourselves," the man said, with a slight Swedish accent. "I am Sergeant Boras of the United Nations Management Team, and I assure you that the situation is now past the critical stage." He swiftly repeated the speech in Spanish and French before reverting to English. "I realize that many of you have received injuries in the preceeding events, but we must remain calm until qualified help can arrive."

"What in the hell happened to us?" shouted a loud, uninjured voice.

"Sir, that is an unanswerable question at the moment, but it seems probable that the destruction was caused by an earthquake, which, though rare, is not unknown in this area."

"Well, how are you going to get us out of here?"

"You can be certain that rescue teams are even now working their way down the elevator shafts to assist us," the Sergeant replied. "In the event that these shafts have been . . . crushed by the movement of the soil, emergency drilling teams will be able to reach us within two hours."

A perceptive but frightened woman spoke up. "If the tremor has sealed us in here, what about our oxygen supply?"

This abrupt return to immediate danger created a swell of concerned and angry questions that seemed only a step removed from hysteria, but Boras answered quickly to quell the tide. "I must *insist* that you remain calm!" he said forcefully. "There is no danger of suffocation! Even with the number of people we have here, a room of this size contains enough oxygen to supply us for days, far longer than the time that will be required for our rescue." The time estimation was only a guess by the soldier, but he did know that he had to keep everyone quiet and that there certainly was enough air to allow them to breathe until help arrived.

While Doyle listened for explanations from the soldier, Griffin wandered through the murkiness in search of his wife. They had been standing together at the moment of the quake, and it seemed logical to believe that she would have fallen close by him in the disaster, but as he moved to examine face after face, some still unconscious, some staring incredulously back at him, he realized that she could have been dropped practically anywhere along that side of the room.

He repeated her name constantly as he searched. Some people, such as George Flanders, a big, heavyset man, responded with angry replies as he passed, but the only familiar face that he came across was that of Anjanette Palmer, who sat huddled against the wall, crying softly.

"Anjanette?" Griffin asked as he dropped carefully to one knee. "Here, my child, are you hurt?"

She tried to control her sobs and trembled with the effort. "I—my knee hurts, but it's only bruised. I'm okay."

"That's good, but we have to be brave now, dear, all of us. We'll be all right if we keep our heads about us, you know, like Kipling said—"

She suddenly threw her arms about his neck and buried her face in his shoulder. "My mother's dead!" she cried.

The words hit Griffin as hard as the blow that had knocked him unconscious. Taking her by the arms, he pulled her away and asked, "Anjanette, how can you even say that? We don't know what sort of damage was done on the surface!"

"But she was in the elevator, and they said it had collapsed! You heard them!" she said, almost screaming through her sobs. "I *love* her, no matter what she did or how she treated me!"

"Of course you do! Anjanette, Anjanette!" He shook her easily. "Your mother left us ten or twelve minutes before the quake began, and that's plenty of time for her to have reached the surface. Right now, she's probably up there crying her eyes out over *you*."

The girl's shivering stopped. "Do you really think so?"

"I'd stake my reputation on it, if I had one," he said, trying to lift her spirits with a joke. He drew a white handkerchief from his shirt pocket and handed it to her. "Dry your face. I need some help to find my wife, and everyone else is preoccupied with their own problems, so you're my last hope."

"I'm sorry I acted like a baby," Anjanette said.

Griffin smiled and patted her shoulder.

Con Jefferies was a young, broad-shouldered man with a wide face that resembled a map of Ireland, which he had left only a week before on this vacation. Clonakilty, which was in the extreme southern part of Cork, was his lifelong home, and this was his first trip across the Atlantic. What a reception he'd gotten.

Jefferies had been dribbled about by the tremors as roughly as any of them, and he had skidded into the wall with enough force to set off fireworks inside his head, but as soon as he was able to shake the loose parts back into place, his first thoughts concerned his parents, sister, brother-in-law, and four-year-old twin nephews.

It took a good two minutes before he could be certain that they had all stayed topside, more interested in the thrills of cars leaping and diving along winding tracks than with the mysteries of the Universe. Besides, most of them were afflicted with galloping claustrophobia. A flush of relief flooded through him when he established this fact, and he forced himself to blot out any dark suppositions as he envisioned the possible devastation up in the park.

With no plan to follow, Jefferies seated himself on the floor directly beneath the glowing control panel set into the wall and listened to the cries of the casualties and the calming words of the Swedish sergeant. He spoke only when Boras had exhausted his supply of consoling phrases.

"Excuse me, Lieutenant," Jefferies said, "but I've got a question that may be important under the circumstances."

Boras swivelled around to look at Jefferies. "I will be glad to do what I can to help you, sir. My men and I are trained in first aid, so if your problem is physical I may be able to offer some assistance."

Jefferies laughed. "I'm fine, General, ready to tackle a Wyoming grizzly, in fact. My question could probably be classed as a scientific one." In the faint green illumination, he could see the obvious confusion that coated the Sergeant's face, so he cut through the malarky and spoke bluntly, "Where's this light coming from?"

The soldier's surprise was unmistakable. "*Gott*," he said, "it was on when the earthquake stopped . . . I though that it was some sort of emergency system . . . but it's the ship's panel, isn't it?"

"It appears to be so," agreed Jefferies, "which means that something on this ship is operating for the first time in a hundred-thousand years."

Boras had been a part of more historic episodes in the last hour than he had even considered possible, and this reawakening of the vessel's circuits was beyond the parameters of reality that he had set up for himself as an effective soldier. This development was going to fall into the laps of those more suited to its handling. "Corporal!" he shouted.

"Sergeant!" snapped another shadow.

"What was our complement of scientific personnel at the time of the disaster?"

"Fifteen representatives, Sergeant," answered the corporal without hesitation.

"Find a working hand torch and any of the men

who are still mobile. I want as many of the scientists as possible investigating this development immediately."

The weak relief from the darkness that the greenish light had provided was cut to almost nothing as nine of the fifteen visiting scientists bunched together between the giant chair and the glowing panels and blocked nearly all the output.

"After hundreds of generations, it still works," said one scientist. "My God, what kind of intelligence built this ship?"

"Do you think the quake jarred it into operation?" asked another, an Englishman with a seriously fractured left arm.

"It had to be, didn't it?" answered an Asian man. "Not even coincidence can be stretched to explain its sudden reawakening during the tremor without some sort of vibrational effect as the cause."

"But surely there've been earthquakes of equal or greater magnitude in this area since its landing," an American woman stated. "Why didn't one of those shake it to life?"

"Speculation such as that simply wastes time, Thirkell," snapped the Asian. "Perhaps the presence of other stimuli, such as human tampering, was required. Perhaps the ship *did* switch itself—"

Jefferies realized that it was up to the common mind to grasp and point out the most important part of the matter, so he whistled shrilly for the unanimous attention of the group. The scientists had seen him squatting in the glow beneath the oddly shaped dials and screens of the control panel, but they had unanimously ignored him as just another frightened and uncomprehending park visitor; his whistle knifed through their wide-ranging discussions and forced them to take full notice of his presence.

"Now that I have your attention," Jefferies said, "I'd very much like to point out one vital factor in this situation which seems to have eluded you."

"What? Who are you?" demanded a bearded man.

"A voice crying in the wilderness of overeducation," he said. "My point is: if these lights are working in this room, that should lead us to suspect that the rest of the ship is also percolating. We may be caught in an alien spacecraft that's just about to crack open like an egg and finish its mission here on Earth."

"Christ," whispered a woman, "he's right."

As if Jefferies' words had rung a bell, the noise level in the immediate area shot up several decibels. The possibilities inherent in his suggestion were overwhelming from the viewpoints of technology, anthropology, psychology, personal survival, and almost any other category of human consideration. Before the earthquake, examination of the vessel and the questions it raised had been exciting but impersonal. Now the examiners had to take into account that not only were they witnessing the possible return to performance of the craft, but that they were, at least temporarily, unable to escape being in the midst of its rebirth.

"What might be waiting to greet us beyond those long-sealed doors?" asked Jefferies, unable to resist pressing the point a little deeper.

Boras, the UN sergeant, had heard most of this speculation, and he noted a widespread rise in the conversation level among the ninety-plus already frightened park visitors and employees, who had picked up on the change in attitude and tone of the scientists' speech, if not their exact words. He didn't know very much about the growing life within the circuits and memory banks of the ship, but he did know that a panic on top of the recent quake could only result in more injuries to the people in his charge. He walked quickly to the group of scientists.

"Good people," he whispered formally but firmly, "I must ask that you keep your conversation down. You're upsetting the rest of those present. Especially you, sir."

Jefferies briefly considered this and wondered how much further this wounded, moaning, and crying mass of unfortunates could be upset by a little realistic supposition. "We're not exactly guests at a resort hotel, Mr. Sergeant, we're a group of injured, frightened, and trapped souls who may be about to become a part of an ancient alien resurrection. I don't believe you have the right to withhold the facts just because they're disagreeable. Some of these people may want to pray."

To his credit, Boras maintained his composure quite well. "Neither do we have the right to spread groundless rumors that may initiate a general panic. Our most favorable choice of action would be to wait calmly where we are for rescue workers from the surface to reach us."

"Sure, and if people like you had your way, the public would never have been told about World War One." Jefferies laboriously pulled himself to his feet. He hadn't conceded anything to the soldier.

"While we're speaking of it, Mr. Sergeant, how do you know that anyone is coming for us? Everybody down here was protected from the quake by an indestructable shell, and it still fractured arms and legs and skulls like glass. So what guarantee do you have that there's anybody left alive topside?"

Boras had no immediate reply. If everyone had been killed above ground, there was no way of predicting how long it would take outside relief groups to check the craft for survivors.

The small group among whom the discussion had begun was rapidly swelling as nearby listeners moved closer to pick up all that they were able, and this growth only added to the tension that was building inside Boras. Among those who were drawn closer to the animated conversation were Aaron Doyle, Susan Leipnitz, James Aymdahle, and another UN soldier, though all remained a discreet distance back, near the titanic chair.

"Okay, Sergeant," Con Jefferies went on, "let's for argument's sake agree that a rescue squad is on its way down to us and will arrive in, oh, how long? Two, three hours? They could still find a morgue when they get here."

The soldier's voice was modulated ice. "Sir, I don't know what you're speaking of, and I'm convinced that neither do you."

"What I mean, Colonel, is that this *operating* spacecraft may be adjusting itself for the comfort of its owners. What if these creatures are most relaxed at three degrees Celsius, or at sixty?" At least a part of Jefferies' goading of Boras was in response to fear and a feeling of having been failed by those people who were employed to protect him, but even in his irrational anger, he knew that the points that he was making were valid. "And what are the chances that the aliens thrive in an atmosphere identical to our own? How about a lungful of methane, Lieutenant?"

"Folks," said an American scientist, "this layman is doing our thinking for us."

"Nevertheless, I must insist that you halt this conversation," Boras continued in a tone that was louder than he had intended. "This is not the time to debate questions that are so frightening to the rest of the people in this situation."

"Damn, Lieutenant, have you been listening? Look at that!" Jefferies speared his right forefinger at the nearest of the shining panels where a collection of small, black outlines were swiftly turning, reshaping, and inverting themselves somewhat like cartoon projections. "Those squiggles are numbers, this is a clock of some sort, and there is one hell of a good chance that they are counting down toward some preprogrammed event! Don't tell me that this isn't the time to bring up questions that damned well affect us all!"

"That's more than enough, sir," Boras said simply.

"Perhaps he's right, Sergeant," began one scientist. "It may be better if everyone does realize the possibilities—"

"I am in charge, sir, and I say that we will remain calm and not confront problems that don't exist," Boras reaffirmed.

Jefferies snorted derisively and stepped away from the confrontation in symbolic defiance. "You need to stop looking at the circumstances through your blowhole, Sergeant."

That parting vulgarity was one comment too many for the second soldier in the group. He was a corporal named Krupp, and though he had no special respect for Boras as a superior, he did honor the rank that the man held. Suddenly Krupp shoved Jefferies around by the shoulder to face Boras once more.

"The Sergeant isn't finished, mister!" he said.

Con Jefferies instinctively clenched his fists as he stumbled back, off-balance, but even before the cold and cunning portion of his mind could whisper a warning about the idiocy of tangling with an armed man, his back hit the alien control board. Instantly, a series of short snapping sounds came from the board.

Overhead, the ceiling became a sheet of white light.

Cries rose like a choral refrain from the mass of people on the floor. Mixed in each voice was surprise at the unexpected light, short-lived terror of its source, and the sharp discomfort that the strong illumination produced in all those fully dilated pupils. There was no recognizable light-producing fixture overhead, but the entire metallic roof shone with a cool, steady, and colorless glow that—once the observer's eyes adjusted to it—was actually welcome.

"Well, I'll be cut," laughed Jefferies.

Not everything was better in the light, however. Fractures and open wounds seemed to generate more pain once clearly seen, and the frantic hope that had been held for the still forms in the cover of darkness was cruelly dissipated by the glare of reality. Death is hard to view.

The once hospital-clean chamber was littered with the remains of the large metal and plastic displays and recreations that the park had used to decorate the room, and there was more than enough weight in all that rubble to have killed anyone accidentally caught in its fall. Everyone stood or sat dazedly where the sudden light had pinned them.

"Look at the door," Jefferies said with devastating coolness.

All eyes turned together to the far end of the long room. The door was tightly closed.

"I knew it was the ship!" Jefferies heard the British scientist repeating over the hubbub of the crowd. "And the turn—during the earthquake, the ship didn't *fall*, it turned on its side! I *knew* it!"

But most of the comments concerning the thick and invulnerable door, now closed, were shaded with a dawning horror. The door hadn't moved up or down in thousands of years. George Flanders had taken reassurance in Boras' words about the rescue team, but this sudden development fanned the fears he had yet held, and his near-hysterical demands of the soldier were only a small part of the growing tide.

"How are they going to cut through that?" he asked. "I watch the shows, I know that nothing our technology has come up with can scratch the hull of this thing! Even if they dig down to us, how're they going to get us out of this coffin?"

Flanders was a big man with a bigger voice, and

when he fired these words at the Sergeant, he thrust his face forward so that it was only inches from the other man. Little sprays of spittle stung Boras.

"Please, sir, just stay calm! Everyone! You must remain calm!" he shouted. "We know now that this control panel is active because it switched on the lights, so there is certainly another button for controlling the outer door!"

"I wouldn't advise tampering with the panel any further," said a scientist.

Boras whirled on him. "I order you to shut up, mister! You and your fellows and the Irishman! If I hear another word from any of you, my man will deal with you!"

"God bless the UN," Jefferies said.

A group of people who had been near the southeast wall prior to the earthquake swarmed over the sealed door looking for any crack in its set or any device that might raise it. They found none. It was their contention that the door had closed during the tremor, since they couldn't conceive of anything so massive moving with a silence that wouldn't have alerted them.

While they made their futile search, however, a sound did come to Patrice Rutherford. She had been thoroughly shaken up during the disaster, though not really hurt, and now she stood next to her seated fiancé, who remained motionless with his face in his hands, wishing that he were out of this trap. He wasn't crying, but he answered her concerned questions only in monosyllables and didn't seem to want to move at all, not even to stand. It was as if he feared that moving would bring down the rest of the mountain upon him.

What Patrice heard in spite of the rising and falling roar of the others was the cry of a child coming from somewhere in the smashed remains of what had been a huge, animated billboard displaying the most current activities and projects of the United Nations' Scientific Fund. Somewhere beneath all that plastic and wire, she realized, a child was calling out to be released.

"Gerry!" she said as the realization hit her. "Help me! There's somebody under this!" She began to pull ineffectively at the large pieces of the machine. "Help me, Gerry!"

"Leave me alone," he muttered in a low voice.

"What? My God, that's a *kid* under there!"

"It doesn't matter."

Patrice started to reply, but the dead response of the young man at her feet overwhelmed her with a revulsion that was directed at herself as much as Gerry. Turning from him, she raised her voice to the entire room. "Someone please help me here! There's a child underneath this rubble!"

The reaction was immediate. At least ten men and women rushed to help, but their frenzied aid was as dangerous to the trapped child as Gerry's refusal. This was something that Doyle knew, a situation that he could control, and he moved to the scene with a feeling of purpose that had been absent since before the split with Glynna.

"Hold it!" he bellowed. "Get back, get away from there before you crush the poor kid!" The would-be rescuers were stopped dead by the power of his voice, and when he repeated himself, they stepped carefully back from the rubble. "Okay, I need five men—you, you, you, and you two. Together now, we'll move the bigger sections first."

With Doyle's back bearing as much weight as any two of the other men, the remains of the display, which had fallen into a slanting mass against the north wall, were shifted from a single large pile into a number of small ones, and the tiny voice became clearer and more urgent by the instant. Finally, a slab of plastic the size of a dining table was lowered away from the wall and the child was revealed, a boy no more than two years old clutching the still form of his mother tightly around the neck. Only Doyle moved forward; none of the other men had had any intimate association with death.

Doyle placed his right hand on the woman's face and neck. The coldness of her flesh told him all he needed to know. Gently he took the little boy in his arms and carried him away from the ruins to where a woman sat tearfully.

Meanwhile, Roger Griffin had paused in his search for his wife to witness Doyle's mission; he, too, had felt the violent extremes of emotion created by the saving of the little boy and the discovery of his mother's death. Then Griffin returned to the problem that was foremost in his mind.

It wasn't like Maureen to be missing this way for so long—it had been twenty minutes since the quake—and though the overhead light helped him immensely, he still hadn't found her or had any response to his calls. He had help in his quest: Anjanette Palmer was at his side, squeezing his hand with a grip that was almost painful.

But for all Roger's earnest effort, it was one of the five men who had helped Doyle reach the child who found Maureen Griffin. He had been combing through the wreckage to assure himself that no other children were trapped when he made the discovery that froze him for a moment. Composing himself, he said loudly enough for Doyle to hear, "Jesus! There's another body over here. It's a woman."

Doyle moved quickly toward him, but Griffin, who had been closer to the spot, reached the spot first.

"The little girl shouldn't look at this, mister," the discoverer said in a hoarse voice. "It's not . . . an easy thing to look at."

Roger Griffin looked down.

His cry was instinctive, a reaction handed down to him from a time before languages when anguish could be expressed only in sounds. His mind was still numb, though he could feel his heart pounding like a sprinter's as it forced his blood to flow through his suddenly weak body. His scream of denial muted to a low moan when he could no longer refuse to accept what his eyes saw. He dropped to his knees next to her.

"Oh hell," Doyle muttered to himself as Griffin began to shake. This had been a *dream* of Roger Griffin, to tour the saucer and inspire his inner self with the reality of other intelligent life in the universe. But this . . . this was a nightmare.

"Oh, Maureen, my life, my life," Griffin was moaning over and over.

I have to do something, thought Doyle, and I haven't got the words or the guts to do a halfway decent job of consoling the man. Why did the damned thing have to fall on *her*?

"Roger," he said, feeling himself in the spotlight

of this emotional scene and hating it. He placed one hand on the older man's shoulder. "Roger, you've got to . . . to leave her here. There's nothing you can do now, and this will just tear you apart."

Griffin turned his head and looked up at Doyle with an expression of total disbelief in his eyes. "I can't *leave* her."

"You've got to, Roger. She's dead. Please. She gave you thirty-five years, a lifetime that can never be taken from you. She wouldn't want this last . . . time spent together to ruin all that love." Doyle took a deep breath and waited for Griffin's response, which he hoped would be a tearful but logical break with his dead wife.

Griffin spoke, "You shut your goddamned mouth!"

"Roger, I—"

"Shut up! It was thirty-four years, and that can't begin to fill the need I have for this woman! I *know* she's dead, Aaron! God, I'm not an idiot! But I still need her!"

"But, Roger, it's the only—"

"Get away from me!"

Doyle opened his mouth to continue, but a woman at his side touched his arm and shook her head; so he fell silent as Griffin returned to his anguish.

Away from Griffin and Doyle, George Flanders was doing his best to open an escape passage to the outside. He'd seen how Con Jefferies had accidentally turned on the ceiling illumination, and he knew that the indecipherable control panel was in working order. So, he reasoned, if it had closed the stupid hatch, it could just as quickly open it. He was trying to put this theory to the test by doing some experimentation of his own, but four of the scientists were trying to stop him from any further tinkering with all the logical arguments they could muster. None of the two men or two women came close to matching Flanders in size or weight.

"Don't you want to get out of this mess?" he demanded in frustration.

"Of course we do," answered the British scientist.

"Then why in the name of Christ don't you let me try out a few of those pressure panels on the wall?"

"Because we don't know which one to push!"

"Aw, man, we'll just push them all," George said.

"Certainly, and we may well poison ourselves, burn the flesh from our bones, or—or *launch* ourselves into interstellar space! This is not a toy, Mr. Flanders, this is a functioning extraterrestrial vessel in which we are trapped. To fiddle blindly with the controls would be the height of stupidity."

"And waiting here to starve to death is smart, I guess?" Flanders said with a heavy dose of sarcasm. "You brainy types are so nearsighted that it's pathetic. This ship can't take off because we're still under a whole damned mountain!"

"Which is probably no more a barrier to this vessel than a cloud!" shouted one of the women. "The ship tilted nearly ninety degrees during the earthquake, and you know that there's no room for such a maneuver in the cavern that holds it!"

Flanders glared at them for a long moment and then pushed by the group, saying, "I don't care what you say, I'm going to get us out of this can!"

Con Jefferies seemed to come out of nowhere. He had been quite a way down the length of the room when the argument began, but before the heavy man could plant one thick finger on any part of the panel, Jefferies stepped through the scientists and clamped an arm on his shoulders. It was a friendly, but meaningful action.

"Ah, Mr. Flanders, maybe it wouldn't be the best idea to tackle this panel without a touch of pre-planning," he said with his most ingratiating Irish brogue.

George shrugged, as if to rid himself of the new arrival. "I'm tired of waiting while these mouths try to decide what hole to whistle down. I saw how you handled that thick sergeant; good work."

"Thanks. But don't touch that panel, Georgeo. I'm on your side, but we're going to go about this after sound consideration."

Flanders realized that he had no accomplice in the young man, so he fixed a scowl on his face and lifted Jefferies' arm from his shoulder. "Who are you to decide, Clancy?" he asked. At least three inches separated them in height.

Jefferies grinned. "Just another victim, friend, but one who is distantly related to a great Irish prizefighter named Peter Maher, who, in the 1890's, fought heavyweight champion-to-be Bob Fitzsimmons several times. They tell me I strongly take after Great-uncle Peter."

Flanders' angry resolve evaporated; he was wont to talk and act tough, but none of his relatives or acquaintances could ever recall having seen George engaged in a physical battle with an antagonist who had not been intimidated by his size. Sure, this

Jefferies kid was a lot smaller than he, but under the circumstances, why promote a fight? "Fitzsimmons, huh? I've heard of him. Won three titles, didn't he?"

"That's right," said Con.

"Well, maybe you've got something. If we take the time to study this control board, there's a chance we can locate the button that controls the door without hitting too many wrong numbers and, who knows, maybe blowing ourselves up."

"That's smart thinking," agreed Jefferies, still casually friendly. "And then again, we can always go out the back door."

"Back door?"

"Sure." He pointed to the trio of hingeless, garage-style doors that lined the rear of the room and, more specifically, to the lightly fluorescent spots on the right side of each at about the height of the average head. "I'll wager that those glowing dots will open the doors following some simple motion performed over them, or maybe at a touch, and they'll allow us to go deeper into the ship, where we can search for another way out."

"Oh no!" said the English scientist quickly. "We can't afford to open those. What if the alien atmosphere has been restored on the other side?"

"What if a quick death beats starvation in here?" responded Flanders.

Jefferies simply folded his arms and grinned.

The brain noted the presence of the indigenous animals in its malfunctioning Forward SubDeck One compartment, but no active interest was taken in them, since it had been designed originally to accommodate representatives of species flung across the galaxy. Its life support systems had scanned the beings, taken into file their physiological requirements and atmospheric needs, and was supplying these in the absence of any direct instructions from a member of the primary programmers. The ship easily could have sprayed them with a corrosive gas had it considered them to be classified in the order of vermin, but it didn't, and the control of the vessel was not operating at peak capacity, in any case. The accident that had befallen the ship had done extensive damage to the system that ran it.

The vessel picked up its programming at the point of interruption, which had been reincited by the natural geological tremor, and reevaluated it, doing a rather poor job in the process. Years of fastidiously planned operations were lost or ignored by the brain as it took up a "loose thread" far beyond the appropriate starting point.

The preliminary signal flashed to all compartments in the massive body.

The first soundings from the emergency equipment set atop the SpaceWorld mountain were jumbled and inconclusive, but after three more soundings clearly showed the huge growth of the cavern in which the craft rested and the lack of corresponding shifted soil, they had to be taken as proof that the long dormant vessel had been self-activated at some time since the tremor. Additional soundings confirmed this by showing that the eternally open hatchway into the ship had been closed.

It was also known that as many as one hundred

and twenty human beings were trapped inside the ship, and something had to be done to reach them. In spite of the fact that every man and women working on the rescue team was sure that all attempts were doomed to failure, four laser drilling machines were put into operation in one desperate effort to free the group from their gigantic prison.

Paula Tyre was crying without realizing it. She knew that she had saved a thousand or more lives by sending out the disaster code before the quake hit, but so many people still had not made it to safety. The official guess was in excess of fifty, not including those trapped in the spacecraft.

One of those unfortunates to whom she could give a face and name was the man she had asked to take her place at the ferris wheel, Lionel Wyant. It wasn't guilt that made her tears flow—he had had plenty of time to get out of the danger zone and into shelter—but the way he had chosen to confront the disaster. He had stayed with the slowly emptying ferris wheel until the height of the quake, when it had broken from its stanchions and crushed him, and that made Paula cry in spite of the fact that she herself had narrowly escaped the same fate while working almost at his side on the same ride. Fortune had smiled on her when the wheel fell the way it had; Wyant had received no such favor.

Another acquaintance of hers was dead as well, and in equally heroic circumstances. Donald Buckley had taken an elevator into the very teeth of the roaring monster in an effort to reach the people in the saucer, but the shaft had collapsed and crushed his car like a punctured balloon.

Paula herself was on the open elevator level within the mountain, though by all rights she should have been in the nearest town resting, receiving medical treatment, and playing heroine of the day to the media. But she felt more useful here, monitoring the progress of the drill teams; she was too hyped to rest, not injured enough for medical attention, and too private to deal with loudmouth reporters and blinding lights.

Let Kelton bask in the glow of publicity; it was his element and he would take all the credit for the effective early warning anyway.

"I guess that's the slot that the Buckley kid got crushed in," said one of the four near-giants the drilling company had dispatched to assist the teams that were cutting their way toward the closed spacecraft. Paula, who wasn't tall by any standards, felt like a midget among them, and the men merely tolerated her presence as they hunched over their portable monitoring machines.

"I suppose it has to be," grunted another. "It's the only shaft without an elevator car in it."

"Stupid asshole," concluded the first.

Paula could feel her body temperature rising, but she kept reminding herself that she was only an observer here and that this park was no longer her territory.

"How far are they now?"

"Inside a kilometer, though I don't know what in hell they're supposed to do when they get there. Use a can opener?"

Paula wandered away from the group and toward the elevator shafts, with the ghosts of the newly dead already rising to torment her. Who was she kidding? She felt full responsibility for Wyant and everybody else who hadn't survived. Why she always accepted the guilt for any situation—even one as unpredictable as an earthquake—was a fit topic for psychological study, but that was the way she was constructed and the way she knew her conscience would respond to the disaster. Perhaps it wouldn't have been so bad if she had forced the issue a little earlier, not wasted precious seconds arguing with that idiot Kelton, and given Donny more time to get down to the people below. Instead, that brave young man was no more than a red stain in the metal corpse of his elevator car.

She stared into the inky blackness of the empty shaft.

The center cable moved. The five heavy strands that had held the large car should have been hanging free after being sheared of the weight at their ends, and four of them were dangling there like cords of giants' hair, but the one in the middle, the one that had carried power and communications to the glass car, was taut and weaving slowly in an east/west line.

"Hey, can somebody come here for a minute?" she called.

One of the men lifted his face from the monitoring equipment. "What's wrong, babe?"

"There's something in this shaft!"

He laughed. "Yeah, a lot of demolished elevator."

"No, it's moving! Bring a flashlight!"

Cursing, but with good-humored condescension, the man drew a flashlight from his workjacket and thumbed it on, generating a cone of brilliance that knifed through the oppressive gloom. It fell on Paula, and she waved it toward the shaft.

"Over there," she said.

"There's nothing there, girl, it's just the atmosphere of this hole getting to you on top of the tragedy—"

"Don't talk to me that way!" she snapped. "Just shut up and hold the light steady!"

"Listen, Miss," the man stated coldly, "we can have you removed from this area, you know, for your own good."

Paula had already begun her reply when the specter suddenly appeared at the bottom of the lighted circle in the elevator shaft and cut off all conversation, leaving the woman and the four men staring without comprehension at the image before them. At first, it seemed to be a sparkling crimson snake that was slithering up the central cable, but then it was joined by a matching partner and Paula recognized a pair of blood-soaked hands and forearms.

"Donny!" she screamed, and the man holding the flashlight almost dropped it. "Donny!"

His head, as it came into the field of light, resembled that of a war victim, awash in blood, mouth open gasping for breath and drooling dust-black saliva, eyes painfully wide in the bright light from the flash. "The Two Thousand Yard Stare," Paula had heard it called when found in soldiers who had seen too much combat.

"I'll be damned," whispered the man with the light. Then, louder, "Riley! Get me something to catch that line and drag this kid out of the shaft!"

Paula Tyre watched the salvation of Donald

Buckley, who had drifted as close to death and returned as anyone she had ever known, and a smile moved unconsciously across her lips. The guilt was still there like a wreath of stone around her neck, and it was a defect that probably would linger with her forever, but as the bleeding and still dazed form of her friend was lowered gently to the cold floor, part of the burden disappeared. Thank you, Donny.

"This *is* a clock," said the British scientist, whose name was Stallybrass. Peter G. Stallybrass.

The other assembled men and women looked to the active, double-fist-sized, recessed and glass plated panel with the writhing black cord below what looked like nineteen-twentieths of a dark circle or a large chocolate pie with a small slice removed. They had seen the moving images as soon as Jefferies had pointed out the functioning status of the board, but with no real frame of interpretation, most had ignored the enigma. Stallybrass hadn't.

"Are you prepared to expound upon that?" asked another.

"Of course. I've been watching this device for the last, oh, fifteen minutes, and I noticed that the mutating line, here," he pointed to the twisting line at the bottom of the dial, "began as a rather long, flattened figure eight shape upon which various changes were rapidly evolving. As the minutes passed, the wriggling continued as fast as ever, though the overall size of the component began to lessen. Minutely, yes, but appreciably over a period of time. Just a moment ago, the line was no longer than . . . than an American nickel, and then it vanished entirely for an instant and the first wedge was removed from the large black circle. See, here, you can count the finely divided sections that are left in it."

"Um, nineteen, which means that it was made up of twenty segments," an American woman said after a brief count. "How long would you say that it took for the line to 'run down'?"

"I'd estimate twenty minutes."

"So the entire orb represents something like . . . six hours and forty minutes."

Standing to one side, Con Jefferies marvelled at the woman's calculating abilities. He had always had trouble remembering his age.

One of the American scientists spoke up with a tone of impatience that was in part caused by the growing anxiety he was undergoing, "All right, Peter, even if we accept that the chronological days of this race are split into periods of roughly six-and-a-half hours, this is still an unusual way of logging time—surely not as efficient as an on-going chronometer, whether digital or calibrated."

Stallybrass nodded slowly. "You're right, Kenneth. But, really, what I meant to say is that this is a clock of a sort, though not necessarily a chronometer of regular standards."

"Then what purpose does it serve?"

"It's a countdown clock," Jefferies supplied. The others stared at him as he assumed a nonchalant pose against the wall, and he revelled in the mosaic of confusion and dawning comprehension that was offered by their faces. It wasn't often that a woefully undereducated layman such as he could continually confound the ultraintelligent by picking out the obvious with the help of a little common sense.

"A countdown—" began Stallybrass.

Jefferies interrupted, "Suppose you're aboard an earthship on a mission to some unexplored planet and the scheduled time for the mission has just about expired. You'd have to do a lot of battening down in preparation for a long trip home, run system checks, stow away gathered samples, and like that, right? So what would be a better way of keeping the large crew aware of the time to liftoff than by displaying a shrinking pie? After the last slice is eaten by the clock, you lift."

"Ridiculous!" barked Kenneth Braam, who was exhibiting his growing tension.

"That would mean that we have just over six hours until this vessel launches itself," said the woman.

"And we're trapped here," added Stallybrass.

"Quite a prospect, isn't it?" Con asked.

Elizabeth Rules, the guide who had led the next-to-last tour into the craft, had been a silent participant in the conversation almost since the moment Jefferies had asked the pivotal question concerning the lights. She was a tall, slender girl with dark brown hair and a normally self-confident manner that had been savagely stripped from her by the mindless act of nature.

Elizabeth had heard Flanders' plans to experiment with the control panel by random selection, as well as the united argument against such action. But in view of Jefferies' apparently reasonable explanation of the strange dial as an indication that the craft was preparing for a return flight to wherever it had originated, Flanders' idea was quickly becoming the only realistic one that had been offered. That door had to be opened, no matter what chances were taken.

"Excuse me for interrupting, but don't you think it's time that we began to do something about this situation?" she asked.

Jefferies was surprised that anyone else had chosen to breach the intellectual barrier that had formed around the scientists. "All suggestions welcome," he said.

"Start pushing the buttons! Good God! They turned on the lights, and the temperature's unchanged! It won't flood us with air that will scorch our lungs! We have to get out of here, and that's the way!"

"I still think we should proceed cautiously," stated another of the men.

"The lady has a point," Jefferies said. "It's just six hours or so until whatever happens happens, so why not give it a shot?"

"All right, but let me do it!" said Braam. He stepped up to the control panel and raised his forefinger above one of the series of olive-colored squares that lined one side of the panels. "At least this way it won't be some hysterical neophyte at the controls."

"It'll be a trained scientific mind," Jefferies muttered.

Steeling himself for an instant, the man looked briefly at the boxes and then jabbed viciously at the nearest. All of the trapped people who realized what was occurring, including Doyle, Aymdahle, Patrice Rutherford, and little Anjanette Palmer, clenched their teeth and waited for whatever was to come.

It was nothing dramatic, at first. The climate control of the vessel was almost total, and though the atmospheric pressure and content was basically determined by the central brain, the conditions could be slightly modified from chamber to chamber. The switch that Braam's touch triggered merely increased the circulation of air from an unnoticeable drift to a somewhat stinging—and noisy-wind. It whistled by their ears, snatched at their hair, ruffled their clothing, and lifted the smaller bits of debris and dust into a swirling dance across the long room. Braam touched the square again in an effort to counteract the result, but nothing happened.

"Oh yeah, that's a whole damned sight better!" Flanders shouted over the howling. His allegiance to individual escape measures shifted from moment to moment.

"I'll keep trying!" Braam called to the others. He punched another square and the light dimmed to half-brilliance.

"Okay, you do that, you keep trying! I'm going to get the hell out of here!" cried Flanders.

No one paid attention as he broke from the group and ran toward the big doors at the rear of the room.

The brain of the vessel noted the unusual actions taking place in its Forward SubDeck chamber. The control console was being operated in an erratic manner and instigating atmospheric conditions that had not been observed to be helpful to the living processes of the lifeforms enclosed within it, though yet no conditions had been instrumented that were immediately threatening to their survival.

The brain was programmed and it was following this; it also contained emergency directives, though these had not been instituted as yet. This situation fell somewhere between normal progression and crisis. The awakening of a primary programmer for exigency instructions would be a long, slow process which might not be warranted by the circumstances. The autonomy of the brain's capacity allowed for determination within certain limits, and since the programming was going well otherwise, the appropriate steps appeared to be along this line.

Forces designed to quell the disturbance flowed into the various circuits.

The attack on the control panel was turning into a farce, as far as Aaron Doyle was concerned. The wind still roared and slapped at him, the lights were muted in one half of the room and painfully bright in the other, and Braam's frantic tick-tack-toe on the panel was only complicating matters. Doyle looked among the growing number of people who were watching the operation, found the guide Susan Leipnitz, and worked his way to her. Taking her arm, he pulled her away from the group.

"Do you know the size and shape of this ship?" he called to her.

Susan was a study in contrasts. An attractive young woman of eighteen, she had suffered extensive bruises about her face during the long slide. Her left eye and cheek were purple masses, and dried blood lay in a slash across her upper lip.

"Yes," she answered loudly. "It's double diamond shaped, almost sixty-five thousand feet long, more than—"

"Good, but spare me the details! Is there *anything* anywhere else that has been found that could be another door out of this thing? I mean back in the body of the ship?"

She was having trouble keeping her long blonde hair out of her face due to the high wind. "There's never been another opening found!" she replied.

"I *know* that!"

"Well, there are the spurs at the other side!"

"Spurs?"

"Yes, they were found during the first survey. Here, help me!"

She ran to one of the several piles of rubble left by the fallen displays and quickly found a plastic board that looked to be about two feet wide by five long. Doyle dragged it from beneath several others and turned it over.

"This is a scale reproduction of the outline of the craft, but there's not much detail; we don't know much!" she shouted.

Doyle stared at the plain graph of the vessel.

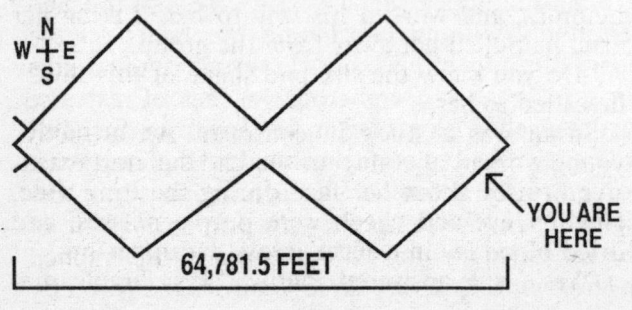

"Where are the spurs?"

"There, on the western side, those tiny lines!"

"*Those* are spurs?"

"They're some sort of projections that extend away from the body of the ship for almost two hundred yards, nearly out the side of the mountain," she said. "But they're sealed and don't seem to have doors of any kind! Some people think they're emergency exits, but most scientists believe that they're merely part of the design!"

Ornaments on an otherwise blank vessel? Doyle thought suspiciously. "They could be tunnels meant to provide a way to the outside!" he said. "This compartment is sealed, maybe for launching, but if we get to those outlets, maybe we can blow the covers off of them, like escape hatches!"

"But they're twelve miles away, and we'd have to go *through the body of the ship*!"

"I know," he replied, too low for her to hear. "It will be a last-ditch plan, if the scientists can't open the outer door!"

At that moment, the brain of the ship froze the chamber's control panel.

Braam thumped the last button he had touched repeatedly without effect, and the lights on the board abruptly blinked off. He turned to the others for some help in deciphering this lack of response just as a yellowish gas began to spew from the point where the wall met the ceiling at the northeast corner of the room. It was a narcotic vapor designed to induce temporary sleep in animal life of the general physiological makeup of those trapped in the room. To assist the operation, the formerly white ceiling began to oscillate through a series of radiant gold and blue hues to soothe and mesmerize the frightened creatures, while the overall light level of the compartment slowly dimmed.

Doyle saw the lights and gas and screamed, "Oh my God!" before pushing Susan toward the rear exits and shouting for Anjanette and Griffin. Jefferies took a single look at the advancing tide of fumes and began to lope toward the interior doors. But, most importantly, George Flanders realized instantly what was happening and slapped his hand hard against the glowing spot next to the door closest to him, the center door, and prayed aloud that it would open.

The room had not been sealed within itself—free access to the main body of the craft remained throughout the voyage—and the brain had overestimated the effectiveness of its synthesized gas, so the door slid obediently upward to reveal a tremendous hallway that seemed to go on forever.

Flanders forgot his panic before the white vastness that stretched before him.

The gas was dispensed into the whistling winds high above the floor, allowing the people nearest the outside door to step away from it and watch its frenzied but slow descent. This fascination combined with the carefully modulated colorplay to hold the men and women in a state of suspension until the fumes had reached them. Only when the gas overcame the first few individuals, did the others shook themselves free of the paralyzing influence of the light and turn to run.

They came like the first wave through a burst dam, at least forty people of all ages hurling their screams before them. Doyle stopped his search for Griffin to watch helplessly as a chilling sight unfolded a hundred yards away: a flood of shrieking victims running madly through the rubble and bodies to escape the billowing menace that chased them, people dropping regularly, like suits of clothing filled with mud, as the gas attached itself to their heads and drew all energy from them. Before they had covered half the distance to where Doyle stood, stupefied, the last staggering form reeled drunkenly against the north wall and collapsed. By then, it was nearly dark in the chamber.

"Mr. Doyle!" cried a high-pitched voice at his side. "Let's go, please!"

He looked down. Anjanette Palmer had found him.

"The door's open!" she yelled, pointing.

Doyle looked over his shoulder to see the icy whiteness of the hall and George Flanders stationed next to it. "You go ahead! Run to where that man is, see him? I've got to find Mr. Griffin! Scat!"

"He's over here, by his wife! The child dashed ahead of him into the growing maelstrom. When Doyle tracked her down, she was already at Griffin's side and tugging frantically at his arm. The writer was still stooped beside his wife's body. "Please, please, Mr. Griffin, you *have* to come with us before the gas gets you!" Anjanette cried.

Griffin remained as quiet as a statue.

Doyle slapped him heavily across the back, as if to break the trance. "Roger, let's go, old boy! The door's open! We can get out of here!"

"Leave me," the man answered dully.

"Roger, they're filling this room with knockout

gas! Flanders has a way out, but they won't let the door remain open much longer, so get off of your knees and come on!"

"I'm staying here with Maureen!" Griffin responded with feeling.

"Goddamn it, she's *dead*!"

The older man spun about as he came to his feet and clutched the front of Doyle's shirt in both fists.

"We're all dead, you stupid fool!" Griffin shouted. "That's not knockout gas, it's poison! Bug poison! They're spraying us like insects to sterilize the vessel! Run if you want to, and let them crush you in some other room. I'm staying here."

"Don't you give up on me, you bastard! You're going to stay here with a corpse while the rest of us escape, is that it? This is the *spaceship*, and even if we die, we'll still get to see their secrets first!" Doyle was shaking with fear and the necessity of getting this visionary man out of the closing jaws of the trap.

"Mr. Griffin, you've got to help me find my mother because I need you, please come with us!" begged Anjanette. "You promised to take care of me!" The words were calculated for their effect by her adult mind, but the emotion was deeply real.

Griffin seemed to understand the moment for the first time. He looked at the approaching gas cloud, then to the glistening promise of the open hallway, and finally to the quiet form of his wife. He went slowly to his knees and tenderly kissed Maureen's cold lips. "I have to go now, darling," he whispered. "Aaron's right, this is my dream. Asgard . . . the home of the gods . . . but at what cost . . . oh Jesus. . . . And there's the child. We promised her mother, so I have to get her out. Please forgive me. Goodbye, my only love."

Then he stood and walked toward the door with a steady, purposeful stride as if oblivious to the advancing tide of gas.

Near the door, Boras stood like Cerberus and watched the madness of the fleeing people as they fought with one another to reach safety, however tentative it might prove to be. Moments earlier, Flanders had relaxed his grip on the opening device to dart through the door, but as soon as his hand had fallen away, the door had slowly begun its long descent. Knowing that it was all his responsibility, Boras had taken up his position and held the way open by the pressure of the rear of his shoulder so that the fast and the lucky who escaped the gas would have some place to run.

"Sergeant, what are we to do?" asked Corporal Krupp. He had just run out of the mass of terrified confusion.

"Where are the others?" Boras asked.

"Dusek's dead, in the quake, Hralkalko broke his back, Treacher and Rahmahid are heading this way!"

"Good. You three go out with the rest of the people and get them through this ship to the spurs at the far end. There's a chance that you can escape there before this thing blasts off."

"Is it going to?"

"I think so. Get out there and direct traffic."

"What about you?"

Boras flipped the clear plastic shield at the top of

his helmet over his face. It was connected to a small oxygen tank on his back. "The gas can't affect me through this."

"No, Sergeant, you can't stay—"

"I'm doing my job, Corporal, just as you shall do yours. These people are mine, and I am going to confront whatever it is that will come for them. Now, move!"

Krupp looked at him for a moment, as if just realizing this aspect of duty, and then he nodded. "I'll man the next door, Sergeant."

"Krupp!"

"Two doors, sir, twice the opportunity for these people to escape. I'll send one man through with each group. Besides, the spurs are probably nothing but deadends."

Boras sighed and then laughed. "All right, Corporal. Assume your post."

Patrice Rutherford looked for Gerry until the cloud was almost on top of her, but she didn't catch so much as a glimpse of the young man who had changed so much during the brief reign of the earthquake. He probably wouldn't have come with her, anyway.

In the insanity of the darkening room, she hadn't yet seen the open doors at the other end, but she did see the wild flow of the other victims of the saucer and trusted enough to join them. Once in the current, she couldn't have refused to run if she'd wanted to.

The fog overcame dozens of hapless men and women and seemed to slide faster once it had reached floor level. Of the forty-seven people who had been more than halfway to the eastern side of the chamber when the gas was released, only one, a fleet, middle-aged insurance salesman named Daniel Levya, made it through the door and into the hall.

Con Jefferies was one of the last to escape the spreading fumes, even though he had started his run to the opening as soon as anyone. Jefferies liked to consider himself a First Person individual, that is, outside of his immediate family and his sister's kids, he looked out for Con Jefferies first and foremost. But this was a harmless private lie, as he had already proven during the ordeal.

He had been halfway to the door before the woman directly before him stumbled and fell. Normally, he wouldn't have stopped—she was healthy-looking, and the fall had not been caused by anything *he* had done—but this was different. He saw the small boy the woman had been carrying spill from her arms and run, crying hysterically, back into the lemon-colored storm that was swelling behind him.

"Get him!" the woman screamed.

Jefferies had been forced to break his stride at her fall, and now he hesitated. The kid was disappearing, almost gone, and that damned gas was boiling forward nearly as fast as he could run. Let the little brat go, his intellect ordered. You do that and you'll never again be able to call yourself a man, his emotions prophesied accurately.

"Move on into the hall!" he shouted at the woman. Then he leaped about and charged for the thick vapors.

In seconds, he was engulfed by the gas, though he had sucked in a chestful of clean oxygen that would have to provide for his pounding heart. The only instant effect of the fumes was a sharp stinging in his eyes. He quickly began stumbling over unconscious bodies that he could barely make out through the gloom and haze of tears.

The kid couldn't have gone too deeply into the fog, he knew, but it still took long seconds of casting around almost on all fours before his hand fell across the small arm of a very young child. He swept the boy into his arms, with his eyes searching for the way out; a faint trace of light to his left was his only hope.

Jefferies emerged from the cloud with an exaltation that was quickly transformed into an ice-cold fear as he saw the gate to salvation closing before him. Both of the open doors were gliding downward in spite of the pounding that their control dials were taking from the soldiers.

"Come on!" shouted one soldier. "I can't stop it!"

Jefferies was already in full sprint. "Go ahead, I can make it!" he called back. But the other man remained at the side of the door.

It was so clearly a race that there was no need for thought on Jefferies' part. The only decision that faced him was which of the two doors to go through. He quickly chose the one located in the middle of the three, simply because it was closer. Like the beak of some gargantuan turtle, the white wall slid downward, and his tortured lungs were called upon to squeeze even more energy into his numb legs.

Eight feet. Head high. Five feet. Four.

With the child in his arms, he had only one

chance to make it. Forgive me, spinal column, he thought giddily, and then he kicked both feet from beneath himself, spun like a falling cat, and hit the smooth floor on his back, sliding like a tobogganer with the limp boy riding on his chest.

As he passed beneath the door, the last thing he saw in the gas-filled chamber that had claimed at least seventy of his fellows was the face of the soldier, filled with fear, anger, joy, and determination. The toes of both his feet clipped the bottom of the descending metal curtain as he sailed into the hall, and then the door closed impenetrably behind him.

Chapter Five

There was, in the beginning of all things, a light pure and without hue, and in this achromatic white radiance was contained the essential elements of everything that would evolve and grow before the ultimate death and rebirth of the Universe. This was only one of the many explanations pertaining to the origin of the physical cosmos, but for nineteen people who had just escaped a prison filled with gas and terror, the tale embraced reality, for it seemed to them that they were totally surrounded by that same brilliant, colorless light.

Aaron Doyle had been stationed outside the descending door, urging those still within the clouding room to escape, but when Jefferies and the kid slipped just underneath the barrier, he slumped against one smooth wall, looked at those who were clustered behind him, and was struck dumb by the vision he beheld. A vast, endless cavern of ice.

The walls were snow white, bowed concavely away from the center, the floor was the same lustrous color, making it difficult to recognize where its level smoothness ran into the curve of the walls, and the ceiling glowed with a muted, yet permeating light that could no more be assigned to any one source of emanation than the clean air they were breathing. This uniformity of color and illumination was united with the almost unimaginable length of the unbending corridor to create an image of perpetuity, with no visible point of ending.

"Christ, it's *twelve miles long*," Doyle whispered in awed memory.

The stupefaction that the big man felt was not unique to him, and the entire group of frightened, confused people ceased their cries and gasps as if on silent command to stare into the depths of the passage that lay before them.

Peter G. Stallybrass, of Birmingham, England, was a sixty-seven year old, slightly built biologist who had been on his first visit to the spacecraft, after extensive reading on the subject during the preceeding five years. His main purpose had been to study the chair and the exposed panel indicators in an effort to prepare a guess as to what type of beings, if any, had piloted it into Earth's atmosphere, but when the quake shocked the tremendous vessel into automatic life, that purpose had been dissolved by the terror he had experienced. Since that instant, his normally unquenchable curiosity had been struggling to reassert itself over an extremely vigorous rival for his attention: his left forearm had sustained a fractured ulna during the ship's aborted liftoff, and even though now tightly wrapped in cloth strips, it throbbed with agonizing regularity in harmony with the beating of his heart.

While fleeing from the advancing gas, he had momentarily been able to sublimate the pain with general urgency, but now, "safe" in the corridor behind the closed door, the sharp ache returned and forced him to try to form a sling from his already tattered shirt. Setting his face against the pain, he guided his injured limb into a position across his stomach and looked up.

"Good Heavens!" he gasped.

All his physical discomfort vanished as his eyes flowed over the virginal sheen of the white walls and floor. But the brilliance was not so startling to him as the echoing size of the corridor. It was, perhaps, twenty-five feet from the floor to the top of the curving ceiling and thirty across at the widest point—though these dimensions weren't very impressive to a man who had stood in buildings large enough to allow for condensation and indoor rainfall.

But the third dimension outstripped any measurement that could be boasted by modern human construction. The tunnel ran like an arrow into the distance, like a pathway to the sun.

"That's sure going to be one long way to walk," stated George Flanders. His normally derisive tone was noticeably softened by the awe of the moment.

"Where? Where are we going?" Elizabeth Rules demanded with more than a trace of hysteria. She pointed to the door that had just closed tightly behind them. "That's where the exit is! They'll dig us out there!"

Susan Leipnitz stood and spoke for the first time since she had slipped and fallen after sprinting through the doorway. "Think for a minute, Liz; the door was closed and the air was full of poison gas, so how in the world will we get through all of that even if we try to go back that way?"

"Well, I don't want to go there!" she shouted, pointing down the hall. "Susan, don't you realize where we are? This is the saucer, further inside than anybody has ever been before! There's no way of telling what's waiting in here, and I don't want to find out!"

"Hey, you know, she's probably right," Flanders said. "The rescue squad will be coming for us at the outer door, not in this part of the ship, so how will they be able to find us? I mean, it might not be a bad idea to go back in there. The gas should be gone by now and we can wait for them to come get us, instead of wandering around inside this tank." His voice echoed down the still corridor.

Aaron waited. His instincts were to take his natural position as leader of this shaken, injured, and almost panicky group, just as he had when organizing the men who dug out the little boy (who was now asleep or dead in the arms of a man on the floor beside him). But he paused in deference to the husky, medium-height uniformed soldier standing deeper in the hall and nervously handling the wickedly beautiful Converse rifle. Doyle figured that this UN employee had been trained to take command in such a situation and wouldn't appreciate the intervention of a civilian; this was hardly a time to become involved in a power struggle.

The other seventeen people in the immense, quiet hallway continued to stand about in a cluster, checking themselves for injury and gazing at the endless stretch yawning before them. Some muttered darkly about the comments made by Flanders and Rules.

Doyle looked sternly at the soldier, who realized that he was being scrutinized, but there was no calming voice to lead them out of the web that seemed to be looping itself tighter around them by the instant. The level of edgy conversation grew in the absence of any reassurances.

"Why don't we just wait here for a couple of hours and give the crew time to dig down to us?" suggested James Aymdahle, who had beaten the vapor into the corridor along with his young wife Kay. "We can listen at this panel until we hear them breaking through on the other side."

"Good idea," Flanders agreed quickly.

Doyle didn't like this idea, and he swiftly moved around the people separating him from the UN man. "Soldier, you need to step in and take charge of this before it gets out of hand," he stated in a low tone. "You know that we can't go back in there."

The dark-haired man smiled and answered in a detectable Cockney accent, "Never been the leader type, sir. This job got me off the streets back home, but I can tell you that I didn't ask for these corporal's stripes at all."

"You're not going to do *anything*?" Doyle asked.

"Well, it's really a votin' situation now, isn't it? Group rule, you can say. We can vote on whether to stay here or try to force our way back inside. Anything evil-lookin' appears on the scene and I can put in a stopper with this," he held up the rifle, "but other than that I intend to follow the paths of smarter minds."

"Damn, you don't even know what's going on here," Aaron said. Okay, he had tried to let the matter gravitate to official outlets, and his reward had been spongy vacillation from a man with a gun. So the steering wheel had been handed back to him. In a way that was not so deeply buried in his subconscious, he was glad that the position had been refused by the English corporal.

"Ladies and gentlemen!" he said loudly, and the deep words rolled upward against the perfect metal surroundings before spiralling into eternity in the white distance behind his back. The interruption had the desired effect before fading, and all the haunted faces of his companions turned to look at him. "Please give me a moment to make a few very important points about where we are and what we need to do about it," he continued.

"Yeah, well, be quick about it," answered George Flanders from the safe anonymity of a crowd.

Doyle ignored him. "I hardly need to tell you that we are in the main body of the spacecraft, the first humans to move this deeply into it. In addition, we are effectively sealed inside until we are able to find our way out. There is no possibility that anyone from the outside can force their way through the hull, which is something that we have to accept."

"We could have done it from in there, at that control board!" Elizabeth Rules said with fear-heightened vehemence.

"The panel was frozen by some action of the ship or its pilots before the gas was released," Stallybrass told her. "Give the man the time he asked for."

"Thank you, doctor," Aaron responded. "Right, the controls that we were using went dead due to an interference from somewhere else in the ship, meaning that we have been detected in here, and the gas was sprayed on us either to kill or incapacitate."

"Excuse me," Con Jefferies spoke up. "I think it was only knockout fumes of some kind because this little guy caught a chestful of it and he's unconscious but breathing steady." He cocked his head at the small, towheaded form that lay across his left shoulder.

Doyle grinned almost savagely. "Good, terrific, that means the people who were trapped in the other room are still alive. But even if the gas has been removed from the air in there, we can't go back that way, because we've already made our choice. You, the man next to the touch panel to the doorway."

"James Aymdahle," the man supplied with more than a little sarcasm.

It wasn't wasted on Doyle. "Okay, James, hit the panel."

The fundamentalist preacher nodded and pressed the radiant circular spot. Nothing happened.

"Again," Aaron directed.

Aymdahle slapped the panel a second time with enough energy to force a short, urgent grunt from his lungs. The door remained closed.

"*Hit* it, man; make an effort!"

Aymdahle closed his right hand into a fist and swung it like a hammer against the yellowish glow, but there was no more result than had accompanied his previous attempts. "It won't open," he observed needlessly, and a sort of communal sigh emerged from the anxious group.

"Perhaps it was never meant to operate by direct pressure, rather in response to some signal—even a mental one—given out by the aliens who designed it," offered Kenneth Braam.

"Damn it, it opened that way on the other side, didn't it?" Doyle demanded. "What happened is that the panel was overridden from another control system within the ship! We weren't supposed to escape from the gassing, but we did, and now we aren't able to return to the room even if we want to, which we shouldn't!"

"Oh, I see," said Elizabeth Rules, who, along with Flanders and Braam, was unwilling to accept as truth *anything* put forth by *anyone*. "That means you 'saved' us from being put to sleep out there, but now we're trapped on this side of the door where rescue people won't be able to reach us."

Early, old-fashioned social training prevented Doyle from answering the young woman with the tone he had used with Braam, and he paused a moment to allow the other tour guide to answer her. He got no help this time, however.

"We're wasting time," he said. "Yes, the people inside the first room are probably alive, yes, we're locked out of there, and yes, there certainly is a rescue operation of some sort underway, but we can't rely on them to reach us, and we sure as hell can't stay here arguing among ourselves! There is a definite chance that this ship is preparing to lift off for whatever star system it originated in!"

Shocked and frightened cries burst from the group immediately. They were stunned to think that this craft, which had rested in this spot for maybe a hundred thousand years, could rise from beneath the mountain and return to the endless depths of space with them sealed aboard like laboratory mice.

"That's crazy, that's bullshit!" Flanders shouted in near panic.

"Shut up, mister!" Doyle snapped. "Doctor, you understand this, so explain it to them!"

Stallybrass coughed slightly and produced a weak smile on finding the questioning eyes focused upon him. He realized the necessity of swift action and launched into a brief explanation.

"While examing the control panel, which appeared to have been shaken into operation by the earthquake, I and several of my colleagues came across a calibration device which we took to be a 'countdown' clock, as someone put it, set to some action or point in time. It didn't impress us as being involved in on-going chronology, such as a regular timepiece, a watch or clock; it was more like an indicator of short duration programmed to inform the vessel's operators of a coming occurence in the ship's mission.

"We, and Mr. Doyle, are fairly well convinced that the event in question will be the launching of this craft."

"Though it doesn't *have* to be," Braam quickly pointed out.

Stallybrass seemed to have absorbed some of Doyle's sense of emergency and command as he resumed by practically shouting over other comments and questions, "You're correct, of course, the 'clock' could be set to display the time remaining until any number of alternate happenings occurs, but it would be in our best interests to treat this situation as if we *knew* that we had only a certain amount of time remaining before liftoff. Speculation may be personally satisfying, but in the end it only wastes precious minutes."

Anjanette Palmer had made her way into the corridor long before the door closed, apparently forever, and she had remained calm while watching the awful drama that had taken place among those who were desperately trying to outrace the yellow gas. She had been comforted only by the one person she knew to any extent, Roger Griffin.

In the midst of all of this emotional debate over the next move to be made by the few survivors of the gas attack, she had been content to play the child's role, but with Stallybrass and Doyle assuring all who would listen that they were about to be carried away not only from this place in the mountains but even from the *world*, an entirely new chord of terror was plucked within her soul. Only moments before, she had cried at the thought of being separated from a parent whom she thought to be dead, and now she was confronted with separation from everything she had ever known and loved.

"Mr. Griffin, I don't want to be carried into space!" she said to the white-haired man. Her voice rose in pitch with each word. "You've got to stop them! I don't want to go into outer space!"

Griffin was, she knew, an intelligent but ultimately powerless old man, yet she directed her fears and pleas for salvation to him because he was an adult and she, at this instant, was more helplessly young than she had ever been in her life.

He patted her hand and looked down, but Anjanette couldn't see anything rational in his glazed eyes, only numb bewilderment created by the incredible path his life had suddenly taken. "Into space," Roger said in a wondering tone. "Not just to Mars or the moon systems, but to the *stars* . . ."

"You have to do something!" she said.

"I don't know, I just don't know . . ."

About them, the confusion continued to swell. "If you're right, my God, there's nothing for us to do but sit here and wait for it to happen," gasped Kim Shawlee, a middle-aged widow from Baltimore.

Doyle replied quickly to avert the rising swell of panic, "No, that's not our only option! We've got—we've got . . . how long, someone?"

Gloria Thirkell glanced at her wristwatch. "We know from the broken watches that the tremor hit at four-thirteen, local time; it's now four-forty-three, and the segments take approximately twenty minutes to elapse, give or take a few seconds, so a good guess as to the remaining time would be six hours and ten minutes, if our extrapolations are correct."

A relieved sigh escaped the listening people. They had expected to be told that grace would expire within minutes, and pushing this form of Judgment back more than six hours made it easier to deal with.

"Six hours, that's not much time," Doyle said, sending their hopes crashing. He shook his head as if to chase all personal doubts and raised his voice to resume his address, "We are *not* stuck in here! Exploration of the exterior of the ship has uncovered a pair of protuberances at the far western end, almost directly opposite our present location, and they don't seem to be in anyway connected with what we can identify as the propulsion system; that is, excavation confirms that they're not exhaust tubes." He was improvising here, carefully shaping his lies; he had first heard of the "spurs" that same hour and knew no more about them than what Susan Leipnitz had told him. He looked to her, and she made no indication that he was wrong.

He continued, "We believe that they are emergency exits, designed to be used when evacuation of the craft is necessary and therefore they may be independently powered, which would make them functional even if the main portion of the ship is without operating energy."

"As it is now," said Flanders. His need to grasp at hope, however faint, was beginning to outweigh his natural querulousness. "You're saying that we may be able to open one of those tubes and escape through it?"

Doyle congradulated himself. He had to get them sold on the plan—the only plan he could come up with—and it seemed that he had succeeded in winning over the biggest obstacle. "Not if we sit here on our butts and whine. We have to move now, while we have some time, and we have to go that way!" He pointed his right hand into the glimmering snowfield that lay ahead of them.

"Don't you know what that is?" screamed Elizabeth. "It's the *spaceship*, damn it! We don't know *what* is down there!"

Braam joined her, "Infection is almost a certainty! The lighting system is functioning, so we have to believe that other, more hazardous devices are also in operation and may be activated by our passage! The atmosphere—"

"Is quite comfortable, Kenneth," interrupted Stallybrass. "At least fifty percent oxygen, I'd say, with no evident noxious gasses in its composition, and the temperature seems to be around twenty degrees Celsius. Of course, it's entirely possible that the conditions may be radically different in some other portions of the craft, but, realistically, that would have to be some section separate from this corridor. I'm willing to chance that this is the prevailing atmosphere and temperature all the way to the end."

Though fear was the primary motivation for Braam's resistance to the plan, he was torn between the urge to remain by this door and the impulse to join in this mad flight through a potential hell of impossible technology. He also realized that the main impetus for the probably futile journey was the unquenchable thirst lodged within the brain of Peter Stallybrass, a thirst that dampened the natural regard for his own safety or the safety of those with him.

Braam's mind longed for the knowledge that could be seized from the interior of this fabulous trove, but his gut wouldn't allow him to forget how much he feared death. It seemed to hover in every direction that he turned.

I'm not going to lose them, Doyle swore to himself. There may be no way out of this and we may be dead before the night comes, but, by God, I'm not going to die here on my ass or my knees!

He was ready to verbalize these feelings when something that none of them had anticipated struck without warning. An aftershock, not much weaker than the original tremor, rolled through the mountain and the surrounding area and threw every one of the startled people from their feet onto the smooth floor as visions of renewed destruction flooded through their minds.

The ship's brain was also unprepared for this sudden development, as unprepared as the men and women within its metallic body. In its state of low efficiency, it had recorded the capture and immobilization of the tresspassing specimens of the local fauna in the room located on SubDeck One. The escape of a small number of them into the main body of the ship had gone completely undetected. The atmospheric supplies to each section these renegades proceeded to invade were controlled by a craft-wide system that was so fully automatic that it was practically separate from the primary brain functioning unless specifically tied into it by particular design. In order to deal with these unusual circumstances, the brain had begun the process of revitalizing one of its primary programmers when the second large shock lanced through the surrounding earth.

The brain—injured, disoriented, without the direction of its biological creators, and functioning imperfectly—was severely impaired by this further violence and lapsed into a low degree of operation that was only slightly more cognizant than the state it had been trapped within during the preceeding eighty thousand years. Interrelated ship's systems continued their programmed duties, but they were now without the capacity of true thought, which left the band of conscious humans unmolested by capture attempts, yet at the mercy of their own ignorance.

And the countdown continued inexorably.

"I'm leaving!" The powerful voice shouted above the dying rumble of the angry Earth and the shrill cries of fear produced by his companions. "You can stay here if you want to!"

Aaron Doyle had never met Paula Tyre, and he never would, but he shared this attitude with her: the inescapable feeling of responsibility for all of those about him. He could lead and he had led, so if he failed to do so in a desperate time, guilt would become his constant preoccupation.

He had one advantage over the young woman, however, in that if his help was offered and rejected, his badgering conscience was placated. As he ran down the still-shuddering corridor, he was well aware that those who followed would be his to guide to safety, but the ones who chose to remain by the door would drift from his mind as if they had never actually been a part of his life.

"Wait! Wait!" screamed George Flanders. He scrambled to his feet with less grace than a panicked steer, and his action more than Doyle's words set the rest into motion with a herd instinct that affected them all.

They ran, crying out their fear and loss of control, and little Anjanette Palmer, who had every reasonable right to lapse into complete hysteria while the "stable" adults about her reacted that way, kept her head well enough to avoid being trampled in the stampede of giants; but she still found herself quickly being left behind by their much longer strides. The gap separating her from the group lengthened and became a growing gulf that threatened to extend into invisibility in the white distance.

"Mr. Griffin!" she cried thinly above the thunder of the disaster and the wailing of those who were abandoning her. "Help me, Mr. Griffin!"

The writer had locked himself deeply within the insulation of insensitivity, where Maureen still lived, and he had heeded the warnings of a perception that he couldn't believe in, so his body was responding only at a rudimentary level, as an animal following its peers. But those few, child-voiced words cut through the defensive layers to grip the man who remained there within the retreat. Almost against his will, Griffin stopped running and fell heavily to his knees, using the pain to further clean himself of the pity that had been drowning him.

The others left him there, and the little girl continued to fly along the floor toward him, until he turned at the last instant to catch her in his outstretched arms and clutch her to his chest. With her arrival, his tears broke; they flowed from him for all of the innocents who had died in the quake, all of the unfortunates who had been trapped by the gas in the room, and he cried for Maureen, the wonderful wife he had left behind in the debris.

"They're leaving us, Mr. Griffin," Anjanette said.

He didn't answer, but, still weeping, he lifted her and stood. Then he drove his sixty-six-year-old body into a run that was swift enough to catch and join the men and women who were fleeing one uncertainty for another.

They ran without speaking for nearly ten minutes, far longer than most would have believed that they could have forced their softened and civilized bodies to perform, and Doyle was always in the lead with his long strides. He could have gone on for an hour at that pace, but when those behind started to waver and gasp—the tremor had long since died—he held up his right hand like a wagonmaster of old to bring the flight to a halt. No one remained standing, even Doyle slid to the floor; and the red faces stared at one another without the power of speech because of the rapid panting that was required simply to feed their tissues and slow their hearts.

The corridor actually settled into near-silence once the group had controlled their breathing, but this didn't last for very long. The sound that broke the stillness wasn't words.

In addition to everything else that he possessed, Con Jefferies was blessed with an uninhibited sense of the absurd, which made it impossible for him to view the scene of which he was a part without succumbing to his equally freespirited laughter. It echoed through the vastness like audible madness.

At first, Jefferies' amusement drew irritated glances from the others, but he wasn't intimidated. The feeling spread among them like a virus. Within moments, their combined mirth filled the immediate area as completely as had their screams before it.

"You can't *outrun* an earthquake!" Susan Leipnitz managed to say between gasps.

"We must've looked like an army in full retreat!" added George Flanders.

Aaron had dealt with people and crises enough times to understand that this laughter was more closely related to hysteria than happiness, but he made no attempt to stop it because it drew them all into a stronger feeling of community and created a vent for their powerful fears that was more useful than crying or screaming. His wristwatch had been smashed in the initial shock so he leaned over to Gloria Thirkell and asked the time.

"Four-fifty-five," she answered. "That's forty-two minutes since the earthquake—the first one at four-thirteen, I mean—and gives us just under six hours until whatever is scheduled happens."

"Thanks." He glanced back in the direction they had taken. The huge door, as white as the rest of the surroundings, was lost to view at this distance, and the overall effect of the one-color hallway was that of an all-encompassing cloud high in a noonday sky. It created a soft, but ever-present sensation of dizziness, as if the floor weren't real and solid.

Aaron Doyle, Angel at Large, he thought and laughed to himself with the memory of only recently arguing with a fervent believer about the existence of a God.

Recently, yes, but already events occuring before the quake were taking on a "back then" quality.

Doyle was good with distances, and even without a sharp point of reference to work with, he felt confident in estimating that the panic-inspired sprint the group had just completed had covered a little better than one mile into the craft, which wasn't bad for the mostly non-athletic assembly. He guessed that they had eleven miles to go until they reached the spurs at the far end of the craft, and that apparently left them in a quite viable position, with six hours of time at a pace of around five miles per hour.

But Doyle wasn't as satisfied with the calculations as he might have been. He realized that he couldn't expect these men and women to keep up that high rate of speed, even if the aftershocks of the quake rumbled continuously until they were safely through, and there was good reason to believe that some would tire out at even a brisk walk with plenty of rest periods such as this one.

With cold honesty, Doyle calculated the chances of all who met his gaze and decided that, in addition to himself, those who appeared to have the best odds of making it to the other side—even if the path through the entire ship were as straight and empty as it had been so far—were the Irish fellow (who looked capable of making it with or without the burden of the child), the young Aymdahles (providing, of course, their God didn't divinely inform them that they were not to follow a trail blazed by an agnostic), the two guides, the English UN soldier (as long as he didn't have to make any important decisions on his own), possibly the two

American scientists Braam and Thirkell (though both showed signs of injury and oncoming exhaustion), and just maybe the heavy-set guy, Flanders, who was obviously out of shape but too much of a loudmouthed coward to give in to physical tiredness and be left behind.

Ten possibles out of nineteen was not a good ratio, he realized, but there was only so much that even a strong leader could do for other people.

And, he swore fiercely to himself, he would not allow any neurotic feelings of responsibility to trap him here, in the ship, with some exhausted or frightened child or adult while his opportunity to escape died with the frenetic writhing of a small black line.

"Everybody rested?" he asked, noting that some five minutes had elapsed since they had dropped out of the run.

"Hey, man, not yet," replied Flanders as he continued to gasp for his breath.

"We should rest for a time longer, young man," Peter Stallybrass told him calmly. "We have a long way to go, and to overtire ourselves at the very beginning would cut our chances considerably."

He actually thinks he can make it, Aaron thought, with that arm sweating pain and his slender, intellectual's body. "You're right; it shouldn't hurt to take a few more minutes here."

They sat to one side of the large hall, some leaning against its curved walls, and experienced an almost constant sensation of eeriness generated by the knowledge that they were in a totally alien environment, possibly even under surveillance by the race of creatures who had constructed the ship, until the tension was alleviated by the woman with the bleeding forehead. She made a simple, obviously sensible proposal.

"Since it looks like we're in this together for as far as we're able to go that way," she said, pointing deeper into the ship, "and there doesn't seem to be any chance of help coming from behind us, we might as well get to know one another. My name is Kim Shawlee, I'm forty-nine, from Baltimore, Maryland, and I was visiting the park with two of my sisters and their families. I'm the only one of the bunch who was able to conquer her claustrophobia enough to come down here. Lucky me, huh? Anyone else?"

There was an expected, embarrassed silence while the remaining members of the group looked about to see who, if anyone, would be the first to follow the pale-skinned, dark haired woman's lead. Finally, Doyle, recognizing the therapeutic value of the little confessions, grinned and responded, "Why not? I'm Aaron Doyle, of various addresses, I'm thirty-seven years old, a former deep-sea diver and engineer, and I was here alone, thank God." He looked to his immediate left and to Gloria Thirkell, who sat there.

The red-haired, blue-eyed woman smiled with a little less discomfort and nodded. "All right. I'm Professor Gloria Thirkell, on sabbatical leave from the University of New Hampshire at Durham, where I specialize in the teaching of astronomy. I'm here with two colleagues, neither of whom is among us, though they may have been able to escape through the other doorway." Her light-complexion darkened for a moment, before brightening again.

"Do we really have to tell our ages? Well, let's just say I'm between thirty-five and fifty." In a conspiratorial stage whisper, she added, "That means thirty-eight."

To her left was Susan Leipnitz. "My name is Susan Leipnitz," she volunteered. "I am—was a tour guide here, as this uniform has probably told you, um, oh yes, I'm eighteen, and I'm from Pahaska, which is not too far from here." She sighed. "And I had a lot of friends up there and back in the room."

The silence returned and the man next to her started after an instant and said, "Oh, sorry. I'm James Aymdahle, and this is my wife Kay." The youthful, attractive woman at his side smiled and blushed a bit. She had short brown hair and delicate features, while her husband's hair was black and his face sharply, almost forcefully defined.

He continued, "I'm thirty-four, Kay is a year younger, we're from Castle Dale, Utah, where I am minister to the congregation of the Church of Jesus who worship there. We haven't yet decided to have children. He paused for a moment, as had Susan, and then said in a low voice, "Until today, I was convinced that this craft was an entirely natural phenomenon."

His last statement drew some surprised responses, but they were cut off by the animated comments from the bushy-haired, slightly built man who was next in line. He spoke in a clipped, precise voice that was classically British, "Peter Greyson Stallybrass, here, and I am from Birminham, England, an alien in your midst, if you will excuse the double entendre inherent in that description. I have recently passed my sixty-seventh birthday, my scientific specialty is the field of biology, and, without meaning to minimize the suffering we have all so suddenly been subjected to or the losses we have experienced, I have to admit that this is one of the high points of my entire life.

"To have the opportunity to explore a vast craft of extraterrestrial origin—and perhaps to actually *meet* the beings who conceived and built it—is a tremendous emotional charge for me on both a personal and scientific level. I do intend to 'escape' the vessel, as Mr. Doyle is committed to aiding us, but I shall also absorb every infinitesimal bit of information that I come across while making this 'run' to freedom." His face was as enthusiastic in appearance as his words were in tone, and not once did he mention the broken arm tucked into his shirtfront.

"Oh, sure, the high point of our lives," said Flanders sarcastically. No one responded to his comment, so he coughed and allowed the small girl sitting next to Stallybrass to recite her history.

"My name is Anjanette Palmer, and I will be ten years old in three months and eleven days," the girl said. She still held tightly to Griffin's right hand. "I don't really have a job or anything, and I'm not certain what I want to be when I finish my education, but I believe that it will have something to do with science or the arts. I live in New York City with my mother and spend one month during the summer with my father in Mehetia, which is in what used to be known as the Society Island group. My mother was with me in the ship, but she became ill and had to leave for the surface; I'm sure she made it up all right."

There were some smiles following this impressive recitation from so young a child, and the bulk of the attention shifted to Roger Griffin, who sat as if in a quiet daze until Anjanette perceptively touched his arm. He blinked and looked at her before realizing that he was expected to brief the others about himself.

"Oh, excuse me," he said in apparently normal consciousness again. "I suppose it's a good idea to get to know one another before we move any further into this adventure. I'm Roger Griffin, sixty-six, presently of Tappahannock, Virginia. You could say that, in a manner of speaking, I and people like me are responsible for all of this, since we have helped to stimulate the public imagination with our tales of phantasmigorical invasions and benevolent visitors from the stars. Had we never existed, the public would not have been so eager to investigate this relic, and no one other than those trained for investigation would have been trapped in here."

"Are you a writer?" asked Susan.

Griffin laughed shortly. "So I've been trying to convince myself for more than forty years."

Jefferies allowed his calculated front to slip long enough to admit, "Sure, I've read several of your novels." Most non-Irish people he met seemed to believe that he would read, if anything, unfinished epic poetry during his regular drinking bouts in a local pub.

"Thank you," Griffin said. "There isn't much

more to tell you about myself other than the fact that I attended this tour with my wife, who . . ." his voice broke slightly, and he drew in a deep breath, "who died during the earthquake."

Sympathetic voices responded, but Griffin hardly heard them. He didn't retreat, however, at least not as he had earlier, because now he had to remain in control for the sake of a young girl's life. There would be plenty of time to mourn later, if indeed there were a later.

"Guess I'm next," stated George Flanders, without waiting for the rest of the questions directed at Roger to be answered. "My name's George Leo Flanders, and I'm thirty-five, and I live in Clinton, Indiana, with my wife and four kids, two of each. I'm a salesman for an electronics firm. My family stayed up topside to ride and eat—kids are hungry all the time, aren't they?—so I'm sure they're okay." As an afterthought, he muttered, "Thank God."

A nice, middleclass-sounding background, Doyle thought. I hope that your toughness runs deep enough to allow you to keep up with the rest of us.

"Next?" prompted Kim Shawlee.

"That's me, I suppose," said Patrice Rutherford. She was a tall woman with regular features and smooth, dark skin. "Patrice Rutherford, I'm twenty-four, I live in Winona, Minnesota, and I am studying to become a lawyer."

"Were you here alone?" Kim asked.

"No, I, uh, I'm on vacation with my fiancé. Or I was. I think he stayed in the room."

"Stayed?" repeated Gloria Thirkell. "Was he injured?"

"No. I think he had some sort of emotional breakdown or something. He just *sat* there. Let's go on to someone else, all right?"

"My cue," said the next man quickly. "My name is Daniel Levya, and I happen to be a semi-successful insurance salesman from Hermiston, Oregon. Like everybody else, I'm on vacation with my family, most of whom stayed upstairs to go on all the rides because they didn't want to stand in line." His tone had been almost lighthearted until then, as if he were eager to take the attention away from Patrice's painful memories of her fiance, but now his voice faltered, and it was clear that he had problems of his own.

"I think they're all right, I pray that they are, but I had my son with me here, and when we discovered that the door—the outer door, I mean—had closed during the quake, I went over to check it out and told Earl to stay by the wall panel, where the lights had been turned on. He's just eleven. But he's very smart. I looked when the gas started pouring out through the vents . . . I thought he might have come through this door with everyone else . . ."

"There was another door the soldiers opened," Kim said. "I saw a lot of people going through it into another hall; he could be with them."

Levya managed a half-embarrassed smile. "That's what I'm counting on. He's with them. I mean, he can't be back there."

Though touched by the painful experiences of his companions, Stallybrass couldn't switch off the processes of his mind. "Another group of us free within the ship's interior, perhaps no more than twenty feet away on the other side of this wall. Can we contact them? Do they have anyone among them who knows of our plan to reach the rear of the vessel?"

Rules, who was next in line anyway, answered him, "If there were any park employees with them, Evvy Dunaway, the other tour guide, or any of the maintenance people or even the soldiers, then they would know about the spurs; it's generally believed that they're some sort of emergency structures, so the others would probably try to reach them. If they haven't stayed by the exit door, that is."

"There's a UN man with them," stated Cecil Treacher, the husky Englishman with the rifle. "Rahmahid, my fellow corporal was sent that way by our sergeant."

"And at least one scientist who knows about the timing device we were studying," Thirkell added. "I saw Rupert Weill go through just before I was able to reach this door."

"Then they're probably moving that way just like us," said Levya with a short sigh. "Earl's with them, that's almost positive. He was close enough to beat the gas. How can we get over to them?"

"That's the question," Stallybrass replied. "We've come, what?, perhaps a mile? Well, in all of that distance, I don't recall having seen one doorway or any other sort of exit."

"That's ridiculous," hissed Kenneth Braam, who was still uncomfortable with the situation and likely to lash out at anyone who tried to suggest an answer to any question. "What is the purpose of a ship this size in the first place? And in the second, this can't be a main thoroughfare, because a race so advanced as to build a craft like this wouldn't design such a long stretch of corridor without including some form of transportation other than walking, even if they are ten feet tall. Probably, this hall is nothing more than an atmospheric chamber—"

"We can speculate for the next six hours, Kenneth, but without hard evidence, it won't be any more germane to our present situation than saying that the aliens are thousand-meter-long worms who move about the ship on flying carpets. Why not content ourselves with waiting until we find some sort of opening that will lead us into that other hallway and, for now, we can get on with our introductions so that we can take up the march again?" Stallybrass looked to the girl next to Daniel Levya.

"Elizabeth Rules," she said. "Nineteen, and I work here, as you know. Like Susan, I have a lot of friends in this place, but no relatives." Tall and self-contained, Elizabeth seemed far more angry than fearful at her circumstances.

The next man took his opportunity to speak to them in a low, accented, but quite understandable voice, "My name is Antonio Arbolada, my age is fifty-one. I live in Burgos, Spain, where I am a member of the National Academy of Sciences. The Academy provided the grant with which I came to your country to study this vessel." He smiled, providing a flash of white in the midst of his olive-complexioned face. "I am receiving a much more intimate examination than I expected." He was a small man of intense expression and quick, quiet actions guided by an incisive mind.

His fellow scientist, a bald, pink-fleshed man,

wasted little time on himself or his statistics. "I am Professor Kenneth L. Braam of San Jose, California. I'm fifty-four years old, I have a wife, an ex-wife, a total of seven children and four grandchildren, and I am not at all certain that we are any better off here, in the bowls of this foreign machine, than we would have been had we remained in the outer room." He stared about as if inviting any rebuttal to his comment, but none was forthcoming.

The UN soldier was next. "My name is Cecil Treacher, I'm twenty-eight, and I come from a part of London that isn't covered by the tour trams. I was told about the wonders and benefits of life as a UN soldier at arms by a happy recruiter a few months ago, and here I am. That's all."

That left only three people to identify themselves.

One person was a rather small woman with gray hair and bright, lively brown eyes. She held a wakening young boy in her arms; the child had been rescued from the incapacitating gas by the third person.

The woman spoke, "My name is Frances Claire. I'm seventy-three and not ashamed of it, and without the surgical magic of good Dr. Hirum Thaxter of Saint Johnsbury, Vermont, I never in a million years would have been able to run a mile without dying off six or seven times. Yes, I have a husband and children and grandchildren—in fact, my sons paid for this 'vacation'—but none of them were interested enough to come down here with me except my two daughters, and *they* slipped out of line to run to the rest room and missed the tour."

Frances was obviously trying to joke about her children's luck (good or bad) at being above ground when the tremor hit, but her real concern could be read in her face. She had no more idea about the conditions up there than did any of the others. "They'll get hot meals from the Red Cross, and I have to walk twelve miles to get out through the back door," she said with a smile.

"Is this one of your grandchildren?" asked Kim.

"Oh no; this little fellow is Bobby. He doesn't know or can't remember his last name, but he knows that he is two fingers old." The blond-haired little boy rubbed his red, puffy eyes and seemed none the worse for his exposure to the alien fumes. In a milder tone, Frances explained, "I believe that he's the one who was pinned beneath all that wreckage and saved by Mr. Doyle."

The rest nodded quietly.

Doyle glanced to Thirkell's watch and didn't like what he saw. "It's about time to wind this up, folks."

Con Jefferies adopted his sardonic-and-hedonistic mask. "Should you need to call on me for any reason, just sing out 'Con,' 'Jefferies,' or perhaps 'You Son of a Dog,' which is what most of my acquaintances prefer. I've been around for the past twenty-six years, almost all of them in Clonakilty, Ireland, and, as many of you have already related, I have family here in SpaceWorld, but none of them visited this impossible fantasy with me." He stood and stretched the way a cramped animal would, wondering idly why no more of the group had wives, husbands, or children asleep back there in the yellow mist.

Like Doyle in rationalizing the lack of seriously wounded, Con decided that those who had come below with family members were back there with them, yet, even if they had been given the opportunity to escape.

"We really don't have any more time to waste now," Aaron was saying when Jefferies snapped out of his speculation. "There's still a long distance to cover and our time is getting shorter. We'll stop for rest in another hour or so, but until then we have to keep up a steady, not exhausting pace that can cover at least two miles in forty-five to fifty minutes.

"I know that most of us will feel that we can't keep at it after a few minutes, but with all of the cardiovascular work that our health programs have been performing on us, it'll only be our flab and lack of willpower that we'll be fighting. We can make it, and, if we're lucky, this empty corridor will run like a shot from here, through the neck of the ship where the two main bodies join, and on to the other side."

They weren't so lucky.

Intimidation seemed to affect them all as they walked along the white passage and gravitated naturally into small groups for companionship and conversation.

The intimidation came from the sheer size and church-like silence of the corridor, and it inspired them to speak in voices that were only a few degrees above whispers. Even as they talked, their eyes continued to shift uneasily to the smooth, gleaming walls and floor, as if wondering if they would melt away and leave them somewhere in the more familiar regions of reality. Doyle kept them moving at a steady pace.

"Mr. Athlete up there may like this speed, but if it keeps up much longer I'll have to go back to Dr. Thaxter for some booster work," Frances Claire stated with a tight smile.

Susan Leipnitz, who was walking briskly at her side, looked concerned and answered, "I'm sorry; let me carry the little boy for a while."

Frances looked affectionately at Bobby and knew that it was no time to break the trusting grip that he had about her neck. "Don't worry about me, dear, I'm not nearly so fragile as I look. I'll let you know when I tire out."

Cecil Treacher was no longer certain of his role in this wild affair, since the sergeant was gone—perhaps permanently—and he felt somewhere between annoyed and embarrassed when taking orders from that gung ho civilian at the front of the group. Soon he drifted to the rear. With his rifle clutched diagonally across his chest, he was able to assuage his guilt feelings by telling himself that he was guarding the hinterland.

He found himself next to the broad-shouldered Irish kid and recalled a semi-private conversation he had overheard between him and that Flanders fellow; might as well make talk of it and dust some of the weirdness from this tomb-like corridor.

"Hey, guy, are you the one that claims to be related to Jim Jefferies, the oldtime heavyweight champ?" he asked, not sure how a buck from Clonakilty would respond to a question posed by a former London streetrat.

Con shook his head. "My genes are not so fortunate as that. *My* name is Jefferies, but as far as I know there's no connection with a world champion of any denomination."

Treacher was confused, both by the reply to his question and the mocking tone the slightly younger man employed. "I must have you confused with someone else, then. Sorry."

"Don't be. I know what you mean: the short talk I had with the loudmouth when he was threatening to throw every switch on the control panel, right?"

Treacher nodded.

"I was talking about a relative of mine of undetermined removal named Peter Maher, who was born back in 1869 in Galway and fought from the late '80's through 1908," Jefferies told him. "He fought Bob Fitzsimmons three times, once in '92 and twice early in '96."

Treacher grunted respectfully. This tale had sobered Flanders PDQ, and he felt a measure of that sobriety himself when he considered the fact that this muscular fellow claimed to fight like an illustrious relative. "He must have been something to mix it with a great boxer like Fitzsimmons."

Jefferies cocked a glance at the other with a knowing grin. "In his prime, Peter was a hell of a fighter, but his career didn't exactly peak against Fitz."

"Hmm?"

"In three bouts, he managed one no-decision and was knocked kicking twice. Of course, I didn't bother to tell Flanders that."

"You sly son of a gun!" said Cecil, and they began to laugh together.

The fast walk following the panicked run went on for thirty-six minutes before Doyle sighted the first portion of the long tunnel that did not hold to the beam-straight blueprint. But this section didn't veer to the left or the right; when Doyle got to within thirty yards of the spot, he realized with a start that the corridor turned at a ninety degree angle *straight up*.

"I'll be damned," he sighed quietly, not wanting his flock to hear the pure defeat that he abruptly felt. To come nearly two miles with mounting hopes only to be defeated so completely by the lack of wings was unacceptable to a man like Aaron Doyle.

"Would you look at this?" demanded Flanders, as he trotted to Doyle's side and moved toward the sudden, curved upturn in the hallway. "Shit, I thought you were going to get us out of this mess even if you had to carry us, big man! What do we do now, stand on each others' shoulders?"

"Hold it a minute, George," he replied with a civility that surprised even himself. There was a momentary warmth of satisfaction amid the coldness of defeat when he recalled the other man's first name, which was a facility that he prided himself on. "Don't rush out there until we've had a chance to check out the situation."

"Why, for crying out loud? This ain't the bottom of some giant toilet bowl!"

His sarcasm dug into Aaron like the point of an ice pick, and it was almost by instinct that the angry man's right hand darted out, caught Flanders' shoulder, and spun him about, wide open for the punch that Doyle was tempted to throw. "I said wait! How do you know it isn't a flush pipe of some sort? We're in a totally unexplored environment, you idiot, and we have to watch ourselves at all times!"

Flanders opened his mouth as if to reply, but the aptness of the statement struck him solidly and lopped off any replies for the moment.

While Doyle cautiously approached the verticle shaft, he heard the others gathering behind him, muttering with the same sense of desolation that he felt, and the certainty that he had failed them descended even more heavily on his shoulders. He tried to ignore this sensation as he stood at the edge of the column just far enough into it to look up and see whatever faint hopes he had retained come crashing into his tilted face.

He had had an idea that Flanders had inspired (accidentally) which concerned balancing a man, or maybe two or even three, on his shoulders and getting one member of the group up to the next level, if there was one and it wasn't too damned high. Once up there, the climber could form a rope out of clothing and hoist the others up to another corridor in which they might continue their journey.

His eyes, however, stared up into a lighted cylindrical shaft that soared like a bolt all the way to Heaven.

"Wow!" gasped Anjanette Palmer.

Similar expressions of surprise escaped nearly all of the others as they lined to either side of Doyle and looked up into the emptiness that was equal to the distance that had greeted them outside the first door. They momentarily forgot their position at its bottom.

"Susan, how deep did you say this craft is?" Doyle asked.

"11,403.2 feet," she replied automatically, and the wonder that sprang from the visual confirmation of this fact was brimming in her voice. "In meters, that's—"

"In miles, it's well over two, and I'll bet this well runs every inch of it," he said. "Thanks."

"Mr. Doyle, Mr. Doyle," said Kim Shawlee as she made her way to where he stood. "What are we going to do now? How are we going to get up there?" She had responded well in getting the trapped people to exchange names and histories, but she wasn't handy with solutions in this particular situation.

Before he could answer, Kenneth Braam said, "*Why* we should go up there is a more pertinent issue. What's up there that we don't have in abundance right here?"

"Other levels," replied a voice with devastating simplicity.

Braam jerked around to face Con Jefferies again. "What?"

"More horizontal decks. More than I can count. There." He pointed to the other side of the shaft at an angle that directed his finger to a spot at least three hundred feet above them. "Where the light seems a touch brighter."

Everyone followed his direction to the area that he was indicating. The well was at least fifty feet across, but due to its sheerness and incredible height, the opening to the next level up was very difficult to see, camouflaged as it was by identical coloring in material and illumination. When they knew where to look, they could make out a glowing ceiling like the one they had walked beneath since entering the corridor.

An equal distance above it lay another floor, and another was inset above that one, and on and on in telescoping perspective until they could no longer be distinguished.

"I knew that there had to be other levels and corridors," Stallybrass said aloud, as he had following the discovery that the vessel had half-lifted during the earthquake. "I knew it! This vehicle was constructed by a thinking, rational species, and there is simply no place in such a construction for a tunnel with no exit and leading nowhere."

"Then this is some sort of elevator well through which the aliens could move from floor to floor on their magic carpets, or whatever," theorized Gloria Thirkell.

"Undoubtably," the man agreed, "though I would guess that this is a lesser used, remote one, since it is located so near one end of the craft. And I wouldn't be at all surprised to discover that there is some other sort of automatic conveyance system—perhaps in the walls—to provide less communal travel about the entire vessel. Remember the *Enterprise*?"

"Ah, who doesn't?" Roger Griffin asked rhetorically, with a smile which had been common before the death of his wife but rare following it.

"We must remember that this is more than a spacecraft: it's a *city*, one in which the builders lived while crossing the unimaginable distances of deep space. They had to congregate, as well as be alone, and that requires a lot of room." Stallybrass continued to speculate. "But *where are they*? Why haven't they met us? Certainly they wouldn't have sent such a craft all the way here, equipped and designed as it is without including a passenger load of some sort!"

"Unless it was always meant as a home for us," Braam added ominously. "A prepared travelling cage."

"The thing we need to be discussing right now, people, is how to get ourselves from down here to up there," Doyle interrupted with less soaring realism. "There's no way that we can stack men high enough to reach even to the next level. If we had some of that material that was wrecked in the outer room, we might be able to build a rough scaffold, but we don't and we have to start considering the time."

"How do you suppose the original residents made ascents and descents?" asked Antonio Arbolada.

"Maybe they did have wings," Thirkell said.

"Well, I don't think we're going to make any dramatic discoveries while hovering here at the edge of the shaft like timid mice," Braam stated firmly. He stepped into the circular space at the very bottom of the well to more fully survey its looming interior.

"Professor, don't!" Doyle shouted with an urgency that was purely instinctive. There was something about air currents that he had been afraid of . . .

"Stop being such a jackass, Doyle. I just want to—" The scientist's words ended as if chopped off by an ax and his face dilated in abrupt terror. "Good God!" he cried. His feet were no longer touching the smooth surface of the floor, and the thrashing of his legs as he was lifted ever higher by some invisible agency was horrifying. "My God, help me!" he cried.

"*Kenneth*!" screamed Thirkell.

He began to struggle wildly in the invisible grip. His ascent gained speed with his futile motions so that he quickly went from a foot above the floor to five, a dozen, twenty, and on upward into the merging whiteness high overhead. James Aymdahle had made a short attempt to reach him, but both his wife and Elizabeth Rules grasped his arms to restrain him, and Doyle called out for everyone to stay out of the shaft.

Braam's cries for help evolved into wordless screams as he passed the first level. His hysterical kicking and throwing about of his arms caused him to begin rolling in place in that rising stream near the center of the well. But his rate of climb only increased as he fought to free himself. Within seconds, he was shooting skyward like a writhing, inverted meteor, and he began to move out of their range of visual distinction to become, at first, a blurry shape and then a dark blob against the virgin white of the surroundings.

In no more than half a minute, Braam had become so small as to practically vanish in the heights, but even after the man disappeared from their vision the knife-like agony of his cries continued as he screamed over and over from somewhere high above them.

Chapter Six

It was a bad moment, one almost critical enough to bring to collapse any further efforts to escape the craft.

Kim Shawlee went very quiet as Braam's screams faded, and Doyle saw her pale face become chalk white and her eyes glaze over. He tried to reach her and cut off the explosion of emotion, but she had fallen into the mindless agony of hysteria before he could push through the people surrounding her.

George Flanders, who Doyle had never expected to hold up in situations of great stress, reacted as projected and matched Shawlee's eruption with a string of curses directed at the situation as well as at Doyle, Braam, and anything remotely connected with his delimma. The terror emerging from these two people combined with the somewhat more restrained but no less passionate responses of the rest of the group to create a panic-filled cacophony that had to be stemmed or redirected immediately.

"Shut up!" Doyle shouted. The demand achieved little effect. "Damn it, *shut up!*" he roared with enough power to be heard over the loudest of them.

Susan Leipnitz and Kay Aymdahle shushed Kim with forceful compassion, and the others subsided into whispers and then silence. The little boy was crying with the fear that had been injected into the air by the adults, but Frances Claire swiftly comforted him.

In the sudden quiet, Doyle carefully thrust his head into the vertical shaft and listened for a moment. From somewhere too distant to place, Braam's screams drifted down to him.

"That's a demonstration—an awful, incredible demonstration—of how careful we have to be every instant!" he said. "We are in a functioning, totally unexplored prison here, and *everything* has to be approached with caution. I don't know what caused this, but somehow we still have to get around it."

"An updraft?" asked Aymdahle. "With all this open area—"

"Actually, there should be some form of powerful air currents in action, considering the volume of atmosphere," Stallybrass inserted, "but there's no other evidence of such. To have lifted a fully grown man so swiftly and to such a height, we would have to be in the midst of a hurricane, even here in the hallway."

"Peter, might it be an automatic gravity dampening element?" Thirkell asked.

Stallybrass nodded thoughtfully. Then he stepped a few feet closer to the edge of the well. "Please, everyone, stand away for a moment," he requested.

Those who remained near the upturn hurriedly retreated.

"What are you going to do, doctor?" Aaron inquired.

"In a moment, young man," he replied with a wave of dismissal. When all were safely clear, Stallybrass walked into the shaft without any apparent fear and stopped when he was within five feet of the point where Braam had left the floor. Doyle had to bite his lips to keep from ordering the foolhardy man to stop, and several others drew in sharp breaths. Stallybrass ignored them and dug a handful of silver-colored coins from his right pocket. Dropping carefully to his left knee, he tossed the first of the coins ahead of him in a motion similar to a child playing pitchpenny on a big city sidewalk.

"What's he trying to do?" muttered Flanders.

The coin was an American quarter, and it sailed easily across the emptiness to the dangerous spot until the observers expected it to drop with a plink to the floor. But just as it began a downward arc, it was jerked, as if by invisible strings, directly upward. The coin rose to almost six feet before stopping with only a slight period of deceleration and hanging immobile in the thin air.

"Amazing," whispered Griffin, who was surprised to find himself as enthralled by this small demonstration exhibition as he had been when witnessing a man hurled up the shaft like a shell through the barrel of a huge gun.

More questions flew at Stallybrass, but he paid them no heed and maintained his concentration. He tossed a second coin faster than the first one, and when it entered the field of ascending energy, it flew upward at nearly twice the speed of the first stopping when it approached twelve feet in height. To complete his experiment, the British biological expert stood and threw another coin with all the strength that his injured body was capable of generating, so that it streaked into the flow and sprang up at least thirty feet above the two which were yet hovering motionlessly in the air.

"I understand, Peter!" Thirkell said excitedly. "It's an automatic field that converts the direction of kinetic energy into upward motion!"

"And magnifies it," he agreed. "I know that I didn't have the strength in my last throw to lift the coin that high into the air, or even enough to toss it so far on a horizontal fly."

"But I still don't see . . . I don't understand why it works this way," Patrice Rutherford said uncertainly.

"Allow me," answered Stallybrass. He stepped toward the spot.

"Now just a minute, doctor!" Doyle said quickly. "I don't believe that you should risk yourself this way!"

Stallybrass turned to face him. "Someone has to. There's certainly no way that we can climb to the next level other than via this method, and I have a nebulous idea concerning control of the force, so I am the natural choice."

"But we need you, Stallybrass." As soon as he uttered the sentence, Doyle realized that he had made a tactical mistake; he could only hope that no one had picked up on it.

Stallybrass did. "We are all equal partners in this,

son," he said calmly, but without any sarcasm. "Now, let me try what has to be attempted before we lose any more time."

Doyle nodded wordlessly.

With a short, tense breath, the man took the remaining step to the point where Braam had run into trouble. His right foot came down firmly, or so it appeared, but failed to touch the white floor by a clear inch. Stallybrass could have retreated then; instead, he moved his left foot into position next to his right.

"It's most peculiar," he said clearly, the lecturing instructor now. "Almost like walking on ice. I'm rising, I can still distinguish the sensations of up and down, and I feel as if I could yet pull free if I wished. The rise is quickening." As he spoke, his body floated upward at an increasing speed, though not nearly so swiftly as had Braam's. He reached five feet in just seconds. "I'm going to try something else."

Saying this, Stallybrass breathed in deeply—darting upward with a complementing burst that covered two more feet—and held the air in his chest despite the pain it caused him. His body stopped all voluntary activity, right down to eye movement, and his ascent responded in kind by slowing until he was suspended motionless some dozen feet above the floor. The corridor became eerily silent, as the watchers unconsciously held their own breaths.

Then Stallybrass released his breath in an exhausted sigh that evolved into laughter at the end of it and set him gliding toward the craft's ceiling once more. "Just as I thought!" he called softly down to them. "The shaft converts the external actions of its passengers into vertical lift, even the actions of breathing or speaking, and the acceleration varies with the amount of energy produced!"

"Which is why Kenneth gained so much speed when he started to struggle!" Thirkell shouted up to him.

"Precisely! Watch this!" The man began to wave both hands at the wrists, somewhat in the manner of small wings, despite the pain it caused, and he practically leaped upward; by the time he stopped, he was nearly a hundred feet up the well. "It's easily controllable!" he said.

"But how do you get out of the field?" Antonio Arbolada yelled up to him.

"More experimentation!" he answered. "Mr. Doyle, keep everyone well away from the current while I try another idea!"

Doyle couldn't have moved the fascinated observers away from the shaft even if he had tried, and seventeen pairs of eyes stared fixedly at the strange figure of the ascending man. The pain that resulted when Stallybrass moved his left wrist was strong enough to override even his rapt enjoyment of the developing situation, so he was forced to stop generating upward momentum with this hand. His right arm felt fine, however, and he waved it vigorously before his chest.

The next tunnel-like floor opening was between two hundred and seventy and three hundred feet above the groundlevel surface on which the group stood. In moving himself toward this goal, Stallybrass provided enough energy to assure a rapid climb while keeping his actions limited to prevent an uncontrolled upward plunge such as the one Braam had taken.

As he drew within twenty feet of the eastern face opening and its extension on the opposite side of the shaft, the scientist reduced his voluntary actions at a steady rate and was rewarded with an immediately lessening rise, just as he had expected. By the time the top of his head was level with the second floor, he had apparently stopped altogether.

"Peter?" called Thirkell.

"Watch!" he shouted, and the motion of his jaw and lips sent him sliding quickly upward.

But instead of shooting past the corridor as the onlookers expected, Stallybrass leaned from the near-center of the shaft toward the floor and slipped in one flicker of movement into it and out of sight. The group below burst into a chorus of dismayed cries.

"Quiet!" barked Doyle. "Stallybrass! Are you all right?"

The doctor's face appeared over the edge of the level above, and they could see his joyous expression even from that distance. "Perfectly!" he answered. "I knew that the force had to allow for the passenger to slide out of it at the desired floor. All that's required is a slight leaning action. This sweeps one easily out of the shaft and into the corridor. The levitation feature is absent once on the horizontal."

"What's up there?" asked Doyle. "Are there any signs of activity?"

Stallybrass glanced quickly in both directions, behind into the east corridor and across the well into the west corridor that led toward their destination. "Not a one," he replied. "These halls seem to be duplicates of the lower level . . . although there *do* seem to be doorways in the hall opposite this one. Perhaps over there—"

"How will we be able to get there, Peter?" Gloria Thirkell called. "Will we have to travel the entire length of the vertical shaft and slip out of the down mode?"

"I think not," he said. "Allow me to attempt another trial."

By then, Doyle realized that it would be futile to try to stop the English scientist, so he merely held his breath and watched.

Stallybrass stood at the edge of the corridor directly above them. With a cautious but not fearful step, he placed his right foot into the shaft far to the right of the point where he had been carried by the vertical current; when he shifted a fraction of his weight outward, his foot descended only to a spot that was even with the floor of the corridor in which he had been standing.

"Just as I suspected!" he yelled triumphantly, stepping fully into the shaft.

"Jesus!" gasped Flanders.

"Good Lord, protect him!" whispered James Aymdahle.

While the others stared at the figure of a man apparently floating in mid-air, Stallybrass moved his feet slightly and began a slow circling of the wide, round shaft, remaining only a foot or so away from the wall and avoiding the center where a similar force would have launched him toward the vehicle's roof more than two miles above. His passage was slow, almost serene, because he was applying very little outward motion for conversion. When he reached the opposite side where the well opened into the westbound hallway, he slipped easily into it.

"Bravo!" shouted Antonio Arbolada. "Excellent, doctor!"

A general cheer erupted from the rest.

Beaming, Stallybrass gave a short bow. "There is absolutely no way that a passenger on this craft could fall to his death in the shaft," he said. "We know that an upward flow exists near the center of the well, and I'm convinced that a second leads downward next to it. Between floors, a passenger could not wrench himself from these currents, and on each level, it's possible to direct oneself into another corridor or use the horizontal force to circle to the opposite corridor. I'll be right down."

True to his word, the scientist proved his assessment of an existing downflow by leaving the second floor in a direction that carried him to the center of the shaft. He quickly entered the descending current and drifted to the ground level, where he stepped out and onto the floor as casually as a man leaving an escalator.

"My friends, we have found our means of reaching the next floor," he said needlessly.

There was obviously no reason to remain on the bottom level, so, despite natural apprehension, it was decided that the trapped band would use this amazing, intangible energy to move to the next floor. Stallybrass positioned himself in the shaft just before the grip of the upcurrent as the others formed a single line in the corridor behind him and Aaron Doyle stood to the other side of the group.

He still considered himself to be in charge of the exodus and, as the leader, it was his duty to make certain that everyone made the ascent safely. He called Cecil Treacher to the front of the line.

"Corporal, I want you to follow the doctor up to the next floor," he told the man in a near-whisper while the rest of the group waited nervously behind them.

The husky soldier grinned in a bemused fashion. "I thought I'd bring up the rear, mister, in case something decided to start chasing us, you know."

"That's exactly why I want you to go first," Doyle said. "Stallybrass will show you how to make your way in the current, and once you and he reach the next floor, you can be our protection against anything that might be waiting for us. But don't shoot unless you absolutely *have* to!"

"I don't know, guv—"

"Corporal!" Doyle hissed. "Don't fight me on this! Our time is running out—we've got at least ten miles to go and only five hours to do it in! With you and the gun up there, maybe the others won't be so terrified!"

"Well, if you think so," Treacher said uncertainly.

"Great!" Doyle slapped the man's shoulder and sent him stumbling toward Stallybrass.

The doctor called for everyone to watch his actions closely, and then he stepped into the upcurrent, giving himself an impetus by slowly waving his right arm. When he had reached the second floor, rather than leaning toward the corridor he had originally entered, he shifted his shoulders to his right, which drew him into the circling energy that flowed next to the walls. After just a moment of circling, he hopped into the westbound hall in the same manner as before.

"I'm sure that you can see just how easy that was, and if one of you brave gentlemen will make the attempt, I shall talk you through it!" he stated.

"Sounds like my number," Treacher said. He stepped tentatively into the field.

Treacher followed Stallybrass's directions carefully, with his rifle slung across his back to allow for freedom in his movement. The chunky soldier came through the operation quite well, stumbling only a bit when sliding from the invisible support within the shaft onto the floor of the second level corridor, but instantly snapped his gun into a businesslike position in order to guard the seemingly endless hall while Stallybrass coached the others.

"Perhaps the most important thing to bear in mind," the doctor called, "is not to create too much of an upward motion. This might propell one past the outlet to the floor, as happened with Kenneth."

"Susan," Doyle said with a confident, comforting smile, "why don't you try it next and show the rest of us how easy it really is?"

Fear showed palely in the young woman's eyes, but she was convinced that the ship really was going to launch itself at 10:53 p.m., and after that occurred there would be no hope whatsoever. "Okay," she whispered. With the calm voice of the biologist to guide her, she made the ascent quickly.

The line proceeded smoothly thereafter. Antonio Arbolada was next, followed by Elizabeth Rules, Daniel Levya, the Aymdahles, Gloria Thirkell, and Patrice Rutherford. Frances Claire, who seemed to be a fragile, elderly lady but who was in very good physical condition, stepped up to the shaft with little Bobby in her arms.

"Mrs. Claire, I could take the boy up if you'd like," Doyle said as the woman eyed the towering opening carefully. "It might be better if he becomes upset."

"No, Mr. Doyle, I don't think that would be wise," she answered. "The little fellow shouldn't be separated from me now. We've got each other, haven't we, Bobby? Want to go on a nice slow ride with me?"

The boy grinned and nodded.

"You have to be a very good boy and stay still, okay?" she continued. The Aymdahles had proven that two subjects could travel along the current together without difficulty, but everyone was worried that Bobby might become hysterical and shoot both himself and Frances past the outlet. "Look up there, Bobby," she said. "See the nice man?"

Stallybrass heard enough of this from his position far above them to understand that Frances was trying to fix the child's attention above rather than on the floor that would be moving away from them once they stepped into the flow. He shouted, "Bobby! Up here! Can you see me, Bobby?"

The boy stared up the white expanse until he found Stallybrass' face. He nodded again.

Frances carefully walked into the upcurrent while Bobby was occupied with the man's gentle questioning, and she suppressed the innate rush of fear and shock that each of them had felt when floating into the air with nothing beneath them. Stallybrass did a fine job of keeping the child's eyes focused on him as the two people rose toward the next level, but halfway up Bobby dropped his head to the woman's shoulder. From more than a hundred feet below, Doyle was able to see the widening of the young eyes in surprise when the boy realized that he was no longer on the floor.

The group held its collective breath.

Bobby opened his mouth in a wide, wide smile. "Wheee!" he said happily.

Frances clasped the child tighter, but he remained relatively still, enjoying the view below him, until she twisted out of the current and skated into the west corridor and Stallybrass's hands. The boy laughed in delight at the great game.

"Well, are you ready to make the attempt?" asked Roger Griffin to the young girl at his side.

"I'm not only ready, I'm *eager*!" Anjanette Palmer replied. "You don't have to hold my hand, Mr. Griffin; I know that I can get up there by myself."

Griffin glanced to Doyle and winked slyly. "I was hoping that you would hold *my* hand on the way up."

Anjanette sighed. "Well . . . all right. Let's go!" She practically ran into the shaft.

The two safely made the jump to the next floor. George Flanders, not anxious to try the current, had been allowing others to go ahead of him, but upon seeing these two elderly and the two very young people ascend successfully, he felt compelled to prove himself before the rest. His progress was the most ungainly to date; he jerked spasmodically to get himself moving and then had to freeze motionless to slow the rate of his ride; when he successfully slipped into the circle at the entrance to the corridor, he appeared to be trying to swim through the air toward those who waited for him. He almost bowled over Stallybrass, Levya, and Aymdahle as they grabbed him.

"You're next, Mrs. Shawlee," Doyle said.

The bad cut on Kim Shawlee's forehead had been wrapped with a strip of cloth and had apparently stopped bleeding, but her face was very pale. She displayed none of the buoyancy that had helped to change them from a collection of frightened strangers to a group of friends helping one another out of an incredible trap. She looked from Doyle to Con Jefferies—the only people remaining on the lower level with her—with a touch of panic in her expression. Doyle painfully recalled the way the woman had reacted upon seeing Braam launched screaming toward the roof.

"Mrs. Shawlee, there's really nothing to be afraid of," he said.

She forced a smile. "I'll let you fellows go ahead of me this time," she responded. "I'll make sure that no one is trying to contact us from back in the tour room. I have very sharp hearing."

Jefferies laughed. "I'm a chauvinist, ma'am, and for me it's still ladies first."

Doyle took her arm and gently pulled her toward the shaft. "It will only take a moment and you'll be—"

"Let go of me!" she screamed, jerking her hand free. "Don't touch me! I'm *not* going to do that!"

"Trouble, Aaron?" called Roger Griffin from above.

"Nothing serious, Roger," he answered. "Keep

everyone back from the opening." He looked to Kim, who had leaned against one wall with a hand across her eyes. "Mrs. Shawlee, we can't leave you down here alone. Time is running out."

She laughed in a weak tone. "Remember when I said that my sisters had claustrophobia and wouldn't come down here? Actually, they and their families wanted to go on all of the rides first, and claustrophobia is about the only fear that I *don't* suffer from. I couldn't look at the roof of that other room, and I've felt nauseous ever since we got into all this whiteness. I can't look up that shaft, so you see, I definitely can't go up there without anything to stand on. I'll be all right down here. I'll wait. Someone will send help for us."

Doyle realized that this was a time for firmness; if the woman remained behind, her doubts and fears would infect the entire group and ruin whatever chance they had for escape. "We can't accept that, Kim. You're going up to the next level with the rest of us because that's the *only* way out of this situation. If you can't go with your eyes open, close them."

"No! Oh God, that would be even *worse*! And I wouldn't know which way to lean or when to move!"

"We'll do all of that for you," Doyle told her. "Would you feel better if Mr. Jefferies and I were in the current at your sides and holding your hands? You could look into our faces."

Hysteria was bubbling just below the surface of her eyes. "You'd be with me? Both of you?" she asked.

"I'd be pleased to be your escort, ma'am," Con said with his best easygoing grin.

"He'll be to your right, and I'll be to your left," Doyle assured her.

Kim looked timidly at the shaft. "Will you swear that you won't let me go?"

Jefferies tried a light joke, "On my honor, for what that's worth."

She heaved a deep sigh. "All right. I'll go with you."

"Are you three coming up?" asked Gloria Thirkell from the second floor.

"On our way," Jefferies shouted back.

"Let's go, then," Kim said faintly.

Each man took one of her arms and walked the terrified woman into the shaft. Instead of looking at the vast emptiness into which she was stepping, she stared fixedly into Jefferies' eyes and spoke evenly of her life outside the buried ship.

"I'm from Baltimore, you know," she said. "Lived there for more than twenty years. My sisters live there, too, with their families. I don't have any children of my own—my husband died in an industrial accident soon after our marriage." The trio had already stepped into the current without any reaction from her, and they quickly began to rise, apparently before she noticed any change. "Really, I'd like to visit—uhhpp!"

Con swiftly squeezed her hand and took up the conversation. "Tell me more about Baltimore, won't you? This is my first visit to the United States, and there are a lot of places that I would like to visit, places that I won't have time to get to."

Kim breathed heavily for several seconds, then forced herself to smile and carried on.

The movement went well until the three were just a few yards from the outletpoint, at which time the woman could contain her fear no longer and broke into tears. The circumstances didn't deteriorate too badly, however, as she pressed her face into Con's shoulder and wept to herself. Doyle and Jefferies managed the revolving turn out of the shaft and into the corridor, where Kim dropped to her knees and continued to cry.

"I don't want to be this way," she sobbed. "I want to help, not hold everyone up."

Susan Leipnitz and Kay Aymdahle stooped to her side.

Doyle was more concerned with how much time was left. "What's the time?" he asked of everyone.

"Six-twelve," Gloria answered quickly.

"Damn!" he spat. "We took more than twenty minutes just getting from down there to up here. On your feet, everybody! We've got to get on the stick!"

While most of the group wearily complied, Peter Stallybrass stepped back to the shaft. "I'll catch up to the rest of you in a few minutes," he said.

"Wait! Where are you going?" demanded Aaron. He knew how much he needed Stallybrass.

"We have a companion who's trapped inside the field; I'm going after him."

"Braam? We don't have the time to wait for him! This ship is more than two miles deep. He could be in any one of thousands of floors above us!"

"You needn't wait for us. When I find Kenneth,

I'll bring him to this level and we'll follow after you. I am not abandoning him, Aaron." There was a firmness in the biologist's voice that Doyle couldn't counter with his own forcefulness. Stallybrass continued, "It seems certain that his struggles would have exhausted themselves at some time during the circuit of the shaft, and this would automatically deposit him on a floor. I've been keeping an eye above us during our move up, but I haven't spotted him, which means that he still must be well overhead."

"But Peter, you realize that you're risking your own safety, don't you?" Gloria asked. "We have only four hours and forty minutes left."

"I understand," he responded. "If I reach the ceiling of the vessel and return to this point without finding him, then I'll give up the search. You don't have to wait for me."

"I'm not leaving without you," she stated.

"We could all do with another rest," Con Jefferies pointed out. "Why not give him half an hour, Doyle?"

"No!" Doyle snapped. He looked at the faces that were staring up at him and understood that he was dangerously close to losing their confidence. Time for a compromise, a strategic allowance. "Thirty minutes is just too long, but I suppose we could give him twenty. If you haven't returned by then, Stallybrass, we'll have to leave you behind."

"I insist upon it," the other man said calmly. And, with no further conversation, he stepped into the shaft, glided around the downflow, and vanished upward.

* * *

Doyle was a nervous animal during the enforced break in the run.

Stallybrass's voice could be heard calling from above them for some time, as he shouted the name of the missing scientist into the opposing corridors. But when the shouts had faded from their hearing, the hallway again took on that eerily complete silence that was so oppressive in its stillness.

Everyone but Doyle sank to the floor with their backs against the curving wall. Doyle stayed with the others for a time, but his eagerness to be on with the operation drove him into a scouting stroll in the corridor ahead.

As Stallybrass had said, this hall was identical to the one below except that it boasted huge, oval sliding doors every sixty feet or so. Next to each of these doors glowed a large circle of light at about shoulder level, reminding Doyle of the circles that had raised the doors in the tour room to release the two groups of escapees.

Aaron was tempted to touch one of these panels, just to see if it worked in the same manner, but common sense stopped him: there could be an alien atmosphere on the other side of that metal panel, or a horde of ravening germs, or something even more unhealthy.

As far as Aaron Doyle was concerned, things would be just perfect if this hall stretched the entire length of the ship and delivered them to the southern spur at the rear. Stallybrass, Thirkell, and Arbolada might be burning to see what waited on the other side of the doors, but Doyle wasn't interested. At least he couldn't allow himself to admit he was.

The resting group had become little more than a smudge in the misty whiteness behind him when a chorus of shouts caught his attention. Something was going on back there, and he rushed in their direction.

The source of the noise was a happy event for a change, the arrival of Stallybrass and a dishevelled, emotionally drained, and thoroughly confused Kenneth Braam. He had been found some seventy floors above; as Stallybrass had predicted, physical exhaustion had eased his hysterical struggles, and once he had lost enough external movement, he had slipped from the current onto the nearest level. He was aware of where he was and what was going on, but his overall appearance was of a man who had been hit hard in the back of his head with a shovel.

"Kenneth, did you see anything in the areas above?" Arbolada asked carefully. "Where there any inhabitants or signs of other life?"

"Yeah," added George Flanders, "did you see any way out of this place without having to go ten more miles?"

Braam, who was leaning on Stallybrass for support, stared back at them as if unable to decipher their words for a moment. Then his self-control appeared to return. "Uh, no, I couldn't see very . . . much, very much of anything . . . I was falling and tumbling and all of the openings went by so quickly . . . I didn't see anything."

"Can he walk?" Doyle asked Stallybrass when he reached the group.

"Yes," was the answer. "He seems to be well physically."

"Then let's go or we can forget about even

reaching the second cube, much less the spurs."

This time, no one objected.

The doors drew the attention of everyone as they passed them. Some people, such as Arbolada, were ready to open at least one to examine the room or corridor behind it, but Doyle's strong rejection of the idea and the clear lack of time for exploration prevented this.

They moved at a fast trot, alternating with periods of walking, and the pace effectively ate up the distance. They left the edge of the shaft at 6:23, and fifteen minutes later that area had been lost in the colorless distance that Doyle estimated to be a mile. If they could average three miles an hour—a relatively fast but not unreasonable one mile every twenty minutes—he felt sure that they could reach the rear of the vessel.

Three miles an hour for four hours. It would be a severe test, one that not everyone would pass.

Another stumbling block presented itself only five minutes later.

Doyle was in the lead. Though there was no reason for anyone to "lead" as such, still Aaron felt the need to be at the point, setting the pace for the others and facing first whatever situation arose. He was ahead of the rest when his eyes picked out the trouble that lay only a few yards ahead.

"Oh, hell," he sighed to himself.

Daniel Levya, who was next behind Doyle, overheard. "What's wrong?" he asked, staring into the misty distance and seeing only a uniform white. "I don't see anything." But a moment later his eyes picked up the condition that had produced the subdued anger in Doyle's voice.

The corridor was coming to a dead end.

The long stretch of hallway simply ended in a featureless wall of the same color and material as everything surrounding them, and this sent the hopes of the group on another downward plunge. With one more vital decision to face, they collapsed to the floor to catch their breaths and allow someone with the courage to be reckless to make that decision for them.

"It's fifteen minutes to seven, Doyle," said Elizabeth Rules. She felt none of the wonder of her companions in their spot. "What do we do now? Go back to the shaft and move up a level?"

"If we do so, we'll be backtracking at least a mile and a half," Stallybrass said. His face was becoming progressively whiter and a sheen of perspiration clung to his skin, which was cold in spite of the on-going exertion. "And we have no way of being certain that any of the floors extend any further into the craft."

Doyle's head was spinning with the possibilities he faced. They were cutting the time all too close, as it was, and to add three more miles to their journey, as a return to the shaft would do, would be tantamount to admitting defeat. Whatever he came up with, it would have to be quick. "Do you think that we've reached the point where the two cubes intersect?" he asked Susan, who stood panting nearby.

She shook her head. "Not yet. How far've we gone, two miles?"

"Ten," offered George Flanders.

"More like three and a half to four," corrected Doyle. "I'm good with distances; I can estimate with a fair degree of accuracy."

"Well, the tour room was just south of the midpoint of the eastern cube," she said. "According to the geological surveys, if we've been moving in a straight line we should walk through the . . ."

"The nexus," Gloria Thirkell supplied.

"Okay, the nexus should be wide enough at the mid-point to let us move through it with thousands of feet to spare, and three miles is just about two-thirds of the way to it."

"Then this isn't the outer wall of the first cube," Doyle said slowly. "It's just a damned wall!"

"We've got to go back," Flanders added forcefully. "What other way is there?"

"Sideways," Con Jefferies answered.

"You mean through one of those doors?" asked Braam, who had gradually regained his composure after his rescue by Stallybrass.

"There are plenty to choose from," Jefferies said.

"But what proves that there's not a noxious atmosphere on the other side?" Braam asked. "Or hordes of bacteria to which we have absolutely no resistance?"

"This reminds me of a conversation that was held back in the tour room," Con said with disgust. He walked away toward the nearest door on the north side of the hall.

"Kenneth, he's right," Stallybrass pointed out. "We've been taking chances since the first touch on the activated control panel, and by now we've certainly been exposed to alien infection, if we were meant to be. I'm of the opinion that any door we are not physically ready to enter will not open to us."

"I'm of the opinion that you're as crazy as a son of a bitch," muttered Flanders.

Doyle stood from his crouched position like a savage warrior ready to do battle. "That's enough! We simply don't have the time to retrace our steps and start all over again at the shaft. Those of you who want to try that can move down the corridor. But don't leave yet! I'm going to open one of these doors, this one closest to the end of the hall, and if you're a safe distance away, you'll be able to see if I'm overcome by fumes or heat or anything."

"That's an excellent suggestion," Stallybrass said. He and the others moved about twenty yards away from the door Doyle had chosen, the last on the corridor's northern side, and left Aaron and Con Jefferies alone to test the glowing wallpanel.

"You'd better get back with the others, Irish," Doyle said while he eyed the panel.

"Not this time, boyo," Con replied. "If you pass out, you'll need somebody to drag you back to the shaft."

"This is no time for false heroics, man."

"The way I see it, this is the time for anything we feel like trying, since it's hardly likely that we'll get a second chance. Besides, if you and me tear it, old Georgie there can get the rest out safely."

Doyle grinned slightly. "Okay, hardhead, but don't say you weren't warned."

With seventeen members of the group waiting nervously sixty feet down the hallway, Doyle took a last breath and placed his right palm against the lighted plate. He wasn't certain whether or not he expected the mechanism to react to his touch, but either way, he would have been startled. And he was. The door began to move with eerie silence.

Unlike the doors in the tour room, this one moved horizontally into the left side of the frame. The interior was completely dark.

"Christ," whispered Doyle, staring into the arched opening that was at least fifteen feet high at its peak and twenty feet wide. "Do you feel any difference in the atmosphere, Jefferies?"

"I don't think so," Con answered. "No, temperature's the same; I don't smell anything . . . maybe a little mustiness."

"Yeah. Well, I guess we should go inside and see where we are. Still volunteering?"

Jefferies stepped to one side. "After you," he said.

Chapter Seven

Before the men could step into the yawning darkness, Cecil Treacher broke from the group down the corridor and trotted up to join them. He had unslung his rifle.

"I think I should go inside first," he said, "in case something is in there already."

Doyle had little faith that anything that could design and pilot a vessel this size across thousands of light years could be stopped—or even threatened—by Treacher's rifle. But even if the weapon was no longer anything more than a pretense, he couldn't take that away from Treacher at this point.

"Let's go in together," he said. "Three sets of eyes will give us better protection than one."

"If we could see what we're supposed to be watching for," Jefferies muttered.

Doyle stepped into the open room carefully because he wasn't sure that the floor within was even on the same level as the hall. His foot came down upon the same smooth surface at the proper point, and he stepped fully into the blackness.

"Hey!" he shouted loudly.

"'Scuse me, sir, but who in the hell're you yellin' for?" asked Treacher.

"Quiet!" Doyle hissed. He repeated his shout.

An echo faintly answered.

"We're in another cathedral," Con observed. "I wonder where the light switch might happen to be?"

The three men moved to the sides of the open doorway and began running their hands over the walls. They had no way of knowing if the designers of the craft had placed devices for controlling the light system near the doorways, of course, but it seemed logical that some way of providing illumination would be located near the entrance to the chamber. Unfortunately, their groping fingers found nothing.

"As much as I hate to say it, friends, we may be forced to go through this stretch blind and holding onto one another's shirttails," Aaron sighed.

The other men and women had congregated at the doorway by then, and Elizabeth Rules suggested, "Why don't we just try another door? We don't know if this one leads anywhere at all."

"That makes sense, Aaron," Gloria Thirkell added.

"Sure, we won't waste anything but time," he said, angry at the continuing frustration he was encountering. He walked back into the corridor, with Jefferies following.

Cecil Treacher, the only person remaining in the room, whispered a curse from the days of his youth and squeezed the trigger of his automatic rifle, almost without realizing that he was doing so. Fire erupted from the barrel with enough energy to briefly illuminate a scene of polished metal, but no one had opportunity to consider the vision as the four shells that had been released in the short burst crashed into the ceiling—or some surface over head—and began caroming about the interior of the room.

"Outside!" Doyle shouted.

Treacher dived into the hallway and, along with the rest of the group, flattened himself against the northern wall. The ricocheting bullets whined within the blackness for what seemed to be an eternity, with the staccato noises painfully reaching those in the corridor like repeated blows. Actually, it was only seconds before the shells lost their velocity and either smashed against the walls or spun into the depths of the chamber. When silence returned, the refugees held their breaths until little Bobby began to cry. Frances Claire took the boy from the arms of Patrice Rutherford, who had carried him for the older woman during most of the preceeding run.

"That was the damned stupidest stunt I've ever seen!" Flanders screamed at the verge of hysteria. "You could have killed us, you dumb jackass!"

"Man, it was an accident—" Treacher began.

"It was irresponsible!" countered Flanders. "You're supposed to *protect* us!"

While others rushed between the two men to

quell the argument, the man who should have been at the fore in dampening the hostility instead gazed into the open room with growing wonder. A pure white light was appearing above him. The lighting system of the vast room had been triggered somehow by the burst of gunfire.

By then, the nineteen people trapped in the alien ship should have become inured to the incredible dimensions of the rooms they were travelling through, but none of them could look into this new chamber without feeling their hearts almost stop. Treacher and Flanders forgot their confrontation as everyone moved past them to join Doyle in the doorway.

Stretching before them was a room that soared hundreds of feet overhead and at least a couple of thousand to the east, which meant that most of the doors that they had passed on the northern side of the corridor during their long trek had led to this same room. It was far larger than the tour room, which had seemed so amazingly huge only a few hours earlier. But, unlike that room, this was no empty cathedral.

Silver pipes, as thick as Doyle was tall and as reflective as glass mirrors, filled the almost unbelievable volume of the chamber in all manner of coilings, jets, loops, and towers. Empty, the room would have provided the space needed to launch and fly a small plane; packed with glistening metal as it was, a climber with a thirty-foot ladder would have been able to reach the ceiling by scuttling up to the horizontal pipes overhead and then scrambling upward from there. No other form of structure was visible among the winding, jungle-like recesses, and cool light that radiated from the walls as well as the ceiling eliminated the shadows that the network might have created. Some of the uppermost pipes were invisible to the visitors due to the cancelling effect of their reflective surfaces.

"I didn't know that the Grand Canyon had been moved indoors," Roger Griffin said in a near-whisper. He and the others stood with eyes turned upward for several silent moments.

"This must be the plumbing for the whole ship," Flanders speculated. "I mean, the pipes . . ."

"That's probably right," Braam agreed.

"No, you're wrong," stated Griffin with certainty. He had been pushed to the edge by the death of Maureen and held in the depths of shock by the continuing flight for survival, but now, in this awesomely vast room, the sense of reverence that he had felt upon crawling into the vessel was returning in strength. He was living his own fiction. This was Asgard, and gods lived here.

"Right, I guess you know all about it because you write that science fiction shit," George said.

Roger was too enveloped in the moment to notice the antagonism. "I'm sure that there is some type of plumbing system in this craft, but this is the heart, the engine, this is where the power, oh God, the *lifeblood* originates! The energy that flows through these pipes brought the ship through space and placed it here, to wait for us."

"I wish it'd missed," Flanders sighed. "This can't be an engine. There aren't any wheels or belts or . . . or any moving parts at all!"

"But it is."

As they talked, the group moved deeper into the

room, still gazing at the tremendous dimensions. All had momentarily been removed from the immediacy of their circumstances—all but one.

Kim Shawlee was not claustrophobic, as she had truthfully told Aaron Doyle, but her present problem was just the opposite of that which had affected Carol Palmer, Anjanette's mother. Above ground, practically every piece of material on the mountain was devoted to the outward expansion of the human race into the limitless eternity of space, and this as much as anything had driven Kim beneath the earth in an effort to escape the trappings of a "happy outing" that she had not wished to be a part of in the first place.

The tour room had been a trial, of course, but the knowledge that thousands of tons of soil rested on top of it had countered her panic enough to allow her a modicum of self-control. The hallways were painful ordeals, but nothing that she couldn't handle. The levitation shaft had been pure hell, and that had proven to her that even the pressures of survival weren't able to subjugate the paralyzing weakness within her.

Now, while all of those about her were marvelling at the gigantic surroundings, Kim felt the demons clawing at her knees with their debilitating fingers and the lightheadedness that preceded a fainting spell was floating from the back of her neck toward the front of her skull. The air above her was packed with coiled metal, but that rational realization did nothing to ease the terror of knowing that the roof up there was so *high*, so far, far above her . . .

Unnoticed, Kim Shawlee slumped against the wall to her left, the same wall that had stopped their progress in the corridor, and pressed her face against the smooth metal.

"Since we have literally nothing to go on when speculating as to the propulsion of this craft, you could well be correct, Mr. Griffin," Peter Stallybrass said. "Whatever drove it across the void has to be a process totally beyond anything our science has been able to devise."

"But pipes, Peter?" asked Kenneth Braam.

"Why not?" The biologist surveyed the west wall. "It seems that they all feed into—or draw out of—the chamber beyond this wall. I wonder what's on the other side?"

"Here's another door," said Susan, indicating a duplicate of the entrance to the room just a few feet away. It even had a glowing panel on the right side, apparently activated by Treacher's inadvertent gunfire stimulus. The young woman stepped toward it.

"Wait a minute, Susan!" Doyle said quickly. "You'd better let me open it."

"Superman," muttered Elizabeth Rules. "Protect the little girl."

"You want to open it, Miss?" asked Jefferies casually. He received no response.

Doyle herded everyone away from the door and positioned himself safely to one side of it. He fully expected to find another vast, dark cavern on the other side, since it made no sense to place a door to another well there—though there were all of those pipes. When the door reacted smoothly to his touch, sliding upward this time, he realized immediately that every idea that he had formulated concerning the area beyond would have to be tossed aside. A brilliant red glare poured through the opening before the door was fully up; it dazzled Aaron's eyes as he leaned around to search for its source.

"I'll be damned. It looks like the heart of a volcano," he said.

Before him for at least a mile stretched a virtual sea of radiant crimson matter, boiling and spitting like fresh lava in its bed, though Doyle couldn't be sure that it was even a liquid. The chamber that contained the glowing material was vertically cylindrical, and far in the distance, he could make out the other bank of the pool.

Located in the center of the sea was a round column of the same white metal as the walls. It rose up out of the inferno and thrust through the room's ceiling, which, surprisingly, was only fifty feet or so above Doyle's head. Running from the column both into the red material and upward into the roof were pipes identical to the ones in the room in which he stood. The surface of the boiling pool was about a hundred feet below the floor on which the group nervously waited.

"Close the door, you cretin!" shouted Braam. When Doyle continued to stare at the vision of Old Testament Hell before him, the scientist leaped toward the panel.

Doyle had heard him, and without taking his eyes from the fiery sight, he reached for the control to the door. Braam collided with the much heavier man just as the latter touched the panel, and he went to the floor hard, just in front of the descending plate of metal. He shouldn't have had any difficulty in catching himself and regaining his feet, but rather than sprawling on the floor, Braam's palms hit something a fraction of an inch above it and slid from beneath him if they had touched a sheet of ice. With shock coating his face, Braam shot forward toward the mouth of the volcano.

"Aaron! A force field!" Stallybrass yelled.

But Doyle's trained reflexes responded to the emergency even more swiftly than Stallybrass's cry. He dropped to his knees, caught a fistful of Braam's trouserleg, and jerked the struggling man back into the room just a couple of seconds before the door slipped quietly into place.

"Another force field!" Stallybrass repeated excitedly. "It's obviously designed to allow inspection of the matter in the chamber, perhaps even to reach that central column for whatever reason. Kenneth, this is the second time that you've accidentally revealed to us a mode of transportation!"

"What do you think the material is, some sort of propulsive fuel?" asked Gloria Thirkell.

"Obviously. There must be other collections of fuel overhead, perhaps dozens, into which this column is connected to mix and manipulate various elements to create energy. This fuel chamber might even extend completely through the depth of the vessel, and all of these corridors could be simple, seldom-used serviceways!"

"I thought that these creatures must have some more efficient method of travel," Antonio Arbolada stated. "Perhaps to associate, to *meet* with one another these hallways are fine, but to walk about such a huge ship would be inefficient, even if they are many feet tall."

"And what good does all of this theorizing do us?" demanded an irate Braam. He got to his feet.

"That fuel in there has to be radioactive just to provide enough power to move this thing, and we've all been irradiated with a lethal amount!"

"For God's sake, Kenneth, we don't have time to wrestle over every possible danger we encounter!" Thirkell almost shouted. "From the beginning, you've been bitching about temperature and atmosphere and infection, even though it has to be obvious to you that whatever automated intelligence controls this craft is preparing for these contingencies. If the power source were dangerous to us the door wouldn't open; it's as simple as that! For one reason or another, the pool has to be monitored and inspected by the occupants; thus the force field."

"Right," Doyle said quickly. He was glad to bring an end to the frightened, pointless conversation. Maybe he *was* already dying due to exposure, but he was going to go out making an effort on his own behalf. "It's at least a mile across that thing in there, so we're going to have to double our pace to work our way around it. I'm checking the doors across the corridor, but if the rooms over there are just the same as this one, we'll need to get on our way immediately."

Without awaiting any arguments from the others, Doyle exited the huge engine room, crossed the hall, and palmed open the first door that he reached on the southern side. The lights were on in this chamber, and a glance told him that it was identical to the one he had just left.

"The engine must take up the major portion of this cube," he called back to the others. "I can't tell how far around the core the room extends, but it's south of the central point, so this should be the shorter way around. Don't stand there! Come on, let's go!"

The group hurried across the hall to join him, with Kim Shawlee weakly bringing up the rear, but they travelled only a little more than a hundred yards before coming up against another in the seemingly endless collection of walls. This one had no exits.

"Damn! what do we do now?" Flanders asked of no one individually.

"There were three doorways in the tour room," Stallybrass pointed out. "We took the center door, which undoubtably was designed to service the engine rooms. The southern and northern doors must have led around this place."

"Earl was in the group that went through the north door," Daniel Levya said. "He's probably already in the second half of the ship."

"He may be, my friend," Stallybrass said encouragingly. "Perhaps he has already found the exit."

"God, I hope so," Levya said.

"Well, even if we go back to the tour room, we won't be able to get in," Susan said to Doyle. "If there's no other way out of the room that opens into the fuel pool, we'll be trapped right here until the ship lifts off."

"There's *no* way?" Flanders asked. "We're stuck between right here and the front room?"

Doyle was sweating, though the moderate temperature of the manufactured atmosphere had remained unchanged. After a moment, he popped his right fist into his left palm with a loud noise. "What's the time?" he snapped.

"Seven-twelve," answered Gloria.

"Seven-twelve, seven-twelve," he repeated nervously. "All right, ladies and gentlemen, we've got one way to go: across the engine pool."

"What?" Braam exploded.

"That's crazy!" Elizabeth Rules cried. "It would be suicide! That stuff down there is red hot!"

"I felt the heat!" Doyle replied. "It's bad, but we can stand it. The energy field runs across the pool with at least a hundred feet to spare, and if it runs all the way to the center column, there's a good chance that other lines extend from there to the far side. We've established that the field leads to the central column in order to allow the passengers to inspect the room, so I'm betting that there are fields that lead from the other side of the column to the opposite wall."

"Yeah, betting our lives," muttered Flanders.

Rage flooded through Doyle, and he roughly shoved the heavyset man by the shoulder, sending him staggering back. "Goddamnit, Flanders, put up or shut up! Nobody's forcing you to come along! Why don't you and your buddy Braam chooch your butts back into the ground floor hall and hide your faces in a corner, if you can find one!"

Con Jefferies stepped up to Doyle's side. "You have to control yourself," he told Flanders. "You're not facing anything that all of us aren't," he said in a low tone.

"That's right, Irish, but I'm trying to do something about it! Nobody stood around arguing when the gas was spewing out of the ceiling; this is the same situation. Come with me or stay here, but, I'm warning you, don't stand in my way!" He spun about and jogged to the nearest engine room door.

Jefferies looked to Flanders and Braam. "I believe that the next decision is yours, fellas."

"Hell," spat Flanders, "if we were outside, mister . . ." He followed Doyle and most of the others toward the door.

After a moment, so did Braam.

Doyle confidently touched the palmplate. The door slid upward to reveal the same furious scarlet vision as had the door in the other room. He placed one foot over the edge of the floor and felt the invisible resistance of the force field.

"It's there," he stated with a smile. "I'll go first to test it, and the rest of you can follow. Mrs. Claire, if you and two or three of the other women go together, maybe the little boy won't be so frightened. And you, Mrs. Shawlee, if you go with them and move on your back, watching the ceiling—"

"I'm not going," Kim said quietly.

Doyle merely stared at her.

"I can't go out there! I'll fall!" she asserted with the first touches of panic. "You'll all fall into the fire and be burnt up!"

"Kim, you made it up the shaft, and you can do this," Frances told her in a comforting tone. She reached out to take the woman's hand.

Kim danced away, and her eyes were like those of a trapped animal. "Oh no, no, you can't trick me! You'll drop me! I'm not going out there, and none of you can make me!"

"For crying out loud," Flanders moaned.

"Kim, you can't stay here!" Gloria Thirkell said firmly. She and several other people moved toward the terrified woman, but this only forced Kim to flee deeper into the room among the countless pipes. She was crying now.

"Get away from me, all of you! Don't touch me!" she shrieked.

"But you *have* to go with us!" Peter Stallybrass said.

"Mrs. Shawlee, listen to them!" Anjanette Palmer added.

"Leave her!" ordered Doyle. "We don't have time for this!"

"You cold son of a bitch!" Elizabeth cried.

"It's her choice! Maybe trying to go this way *would* kill her! But it's the only way, and we've got to take it while we have the opportunity!" Doyle stepped again onto the transparent plane that was created by the ship. "Watch how I do it and follow!"

Doyle slipped to his knees and then leaned forward over the furnace-like opening. Even though the watchers knew what to expect, they still gasped openly as he stretched out on nothing above the roiling, hungry maw of the craft's energy source.

"It feels smooth, like glass, just the way standing in the shaft did!" he told them. His body jerked a few inches into the chamber. "The motion principle is the same: action converted! Here I go!" With an awkward thrashing of his arms, he shot away from the door and into the void. "I'm swimming!" he called, almost happily. "It's so easy!"

Doyle allowed the exhilaration of his flight to shut out the doubts and fears that had been plaguing him, and he thrust the failure that was Kim Shawlee completely away. He *was* flying, like no other human being had ever done before him, except in dreams, and that stirred emotions as primitive as the will to survive. It was much better than the standing, upward motion of the shaft.

His state of euphoria didn't last very long, however. The boiling morass even now might be needling withering rays of deadly radiation into him, but in any case he knew that it was throwing heat up at him in a steady cloud that was much worse than he had expected. He felt his skin reacting as if he were at a beach on a hot day, and even the air was more difficult to draw into his lungs. But he couldn't let them know that.

"It's no trouble!" he called. "A little warm, but damn it, we can take a little heat, can't we?"

The line of force in which he was moving was rule straight, and it was headed for the central column, as he had figured it would. The heat was strong enough to cause him to quicken his swimming motion so that he could cover the half mile or so faster. When he had slipped to within thirty yards, he had to stiffen and slow his passage so that he wouldn't smash into the white tower that was rising before him.

Aaron's vision was excellent, but it wasn't until he reached this point that he was able to make out a fairly wide ledge composed of the same material as the column and ringing it like a lip. Then he saw a great number of recessed panels in the column itself containing what were obviously mechanisms for monitoring the activity inside it. With a smooth economy, he reversed his body's position and glided to his feet.

The gauges meant nothing to Doyle, so he instantly turned back in the direction he had just come. At that distance, the doorway was considerably smaller and the intense faces that were framed by it were mere impressions. He waved to show them that he was okay and then shouted, "It works fine! Just like the shaft! I'm going around to the other side to see if there are other force fields!"

After a moment, the faint but distinctive voice of Stallybrass drifted back, "Please be careful and hurry!"

Waving again, Doyle quickly moved to his right along the ledge.

The column was large in its own right, something around two hundred feet in diameter, and the recessed indicators were located at regular intervals about its skin. Aaron had to wonder just what use these readings were to the builders of the craft. Were they bits of information that couldn't be transmitted to some central monitoring station? How often were the readings taken during a voyage? Once? A thousand times? What sort of power generator could turn out the kind of energy needed to conquer interstellar space and yet remain so completely controlled that a biological entity could visit it this way without sustaining damage? Or, indeed, was this the engine, as Griffin said, or a dumping area for used—and harmless—fuel residue?

So many questions without the prospect of a single answer. If he had had a spare decade and a bilingual guide, maybe he would have been able to understand the incredible machine in which he was trapped.

Since he had no reference points to work with, Doyle had to estimate when he was on the opposite side of the column. When he experimentally dipped his foot over the edge of the metal lip on which he stood, his welcome reward was the now-familiar sensation of a functioning force field beneath his shoe. Of course, the ledge might have a field all around it as a safety measure.

Squinting, Doyle was still unable to make out any trace of a doorway on the wall opposite the column, which was not unexpected considering that white on white did not make for a distinctive outline. However, he did think that he noticed widely spaced smudges of light that would be the glowing panels belonging to those exits that he was searching for. But the radiance of the ceiling and the red glare of the molten sea made this an iffy observation.

After all, the field stretched in that direction for some reason.

Before he returned to the original spot on which he had landed, Doyle took several coins which had somehow remained in his pants pocket throughout the chaos and dropped them on the ledge to mark where he had paused. Then he trotted around to the landing point by moving about the metal lip in the same direction in which he had begun. The open door that he had left behind was an indistinct but welcome vision, and had much more emphatic outlines than the possible openings on the far side.

"It's all right!" he called to the waiting group. "There's a field on the other side, and we can float to one of those doors over there! Start moving!"

Doyle watched as the procession began, and he was somewhat surprised to see Roger Griffin and little Anjanette Palmer sliding along the invisible pathway before any of the others. The writer had seemed to be almost catatonic since the discovery of his wife's body, but something—maybe it was the realization that he was at the heart of this marvelous machine—apparently had snapped him out of his daze. He laughed aloud as he swam clumsily over the ocean of molten lava, and when the girl began to breathe heavily in the hot air, he rolled over to shield her against the radiance and they completed the crossing in that position, slipping lightly onto the ledge at Doyle's side.

Treacher came next, a prudent fifty feet behind Roger and Anjanette, and he was quickly followed by the Aymdahles, Patrice Rutherford, Susan, Elizabeth Rules, Gloria Thirkell and Peter Stallybrass together, Frances Claire and Bobby and Daniel Levya in the largest single group, Antonio Arbolada, George Flanders, Kenneth Braam, and Con Jefferies in the rear. There were no extremely difficult moments, though many found the landing at the column to be hard to negotiate and all were surprised by the heat from the pool.

"Everyone's here and ready to jump to the other side, I see," Aaron stated.

"Everyone but Kim," Elizabeth said.

He ignored her. "It's . . . seven-twenty-eight, which means that we don't have a single minute to waste," he said while glancing at Gloria's watch. "Follow me."

In a tight and nervous line, the group moved behind Doyle around the column and to the point where he had left the coins.

"See those patches of light?" Doyle asked.

"Only barely," admitted Stallybrass. He was sweating profusely, and despite the crimson glow he looked quite pale.

"Those must be the palm panels at the sides of the other doors," Doyle went on. "I'm going to slide over to the nearest one and make certain that it opens before any of the rest of you follow. You can see me from here, so don't follow until I give you the signal." Without awaiting discussion of the plan, he stepped into the field and was on his way to a target at least half a mile away.

Doyle was at a point about halfway to the door before any of the waiting people at the column heard the cries from behind them. It was Susan who first picked up on them. Moving carefully along the ledge, she returned to the landing spot and saw, in the still-open doorway that they had abandoned some minutes before, the screaming figure of Kim Shawlee.

"Dear God in Heaven," she whispered.

"Don't leave me here!" Kim's frantic plea rolled weakly across the intervening space. She was crying hysterically. "Don't leave me behind!"

"Come on!" the young guide responded. "You can make it!"

"Help me, please help me!"

Susan wanted out of that vast prison as much as any of the fleeing people, perhaps more so than some of them, but she didn't pause for a second thought when she saw the terrified woman begging for support in crossing the bubbling pool. Susan placed one foot into the field and started to push herself away from the column when a large hand dropped on her shoulder and brought her to a startled halt.

"I believe this is my job, sweet'eart," said Cecil Treacher with a grin. "I'll pop back there and bring the lady over."

"But I can—" Susan began.

He shook his head. "My duty. Can't let any of you take unnecessary risks, and all that. It won't take me long." The man raised his voice so that it would carry back to Kim. "I'll be right over to escort you, ma'am! Just wait right there! Don't move!"

"Hurry!" she screamed.

Everyone at the column had heard the shouted conversation, and they began to crowd around to see what was going on behind them, leaving Doyle to continue his journey toward the second door alone. But Susan realized that their excited presence would only increase the panic that she could recognize in Kim, even at that distance, so she explained the situation and asked them to return to the far side of the shaft. Only Jefferies remained with her to watch Treacher's mission.

The heavy-shouldered soldier was nothing close to graceful in his flight above the radiant pool, but he crossed the area in a surprisingly short amount of time and landed next to Kim. He took her hands in his own and, in a calm, reassuring manner that Susan had not known him to possess, quieted Kim's hysteria. After another minute of soothing talk that was too faint for the guide to hear, he wrapped his arms about Kim's shoulders and began the return voyage to the tower.

"I'll be cracked and reshelled, but I didn't think

that our military buddy had such a fount of human kindness within him," Con Jefferies said with sincerity.

The crossing went smoothly for half of its length, with Kim lying on her back, eyes firmly pressed shut, and Treacher providing the locomotion; but again the woman's raging fears overcame her most desperate efforts at self control. While Cecil was staring toward the column and sweating with the combined effects of the heat from below and his propelling motions, Kim began to weep heavily. Her sobs swiftly escalated into open cries of panic and a thrashing of all of her limbs that doubled and the tripled the speed at which they were moving.

Treacher attempted to calm her with words, but they had no effect. A vision of an emptiness overhead and the yawning maw of Hell below engulfed the woman's brain, searing away her rationality and reducing her to the level of a beast. Treacher caught her legs with his own and pinned them together, but his actions only served to heighten the blaze of terror that resided in her deepest self; she fought him savagely, so that his advantages of size and strength were negated by the sheer emotion that she was broadcasting and her convulsions continued to increase their rate of speed.

"If they hit the tower going that fast, they'll be *killed*!" Susan cried.

Jefferies made no reply, but he leaped from her side and into the field with his intentions fully obvious to her. She tried to clutch his arm, but he was gone before her fingers could close about his sleeve.

Jefferies realized that Susan's prediction was on

the mark: if the two slammed into the wall of the column or the lip that ran around it, their bodies would be broken like unprotected eggs. The only way that he could see of countering the speeding pair was with a physical force that was moving at a faster pace in the opposite direction. He began to flail his arms and legs madly in an effort to match and surpass their speed before he collided with them.

It took only an instant, during which Susan stood and watched transfixed. The two people hurtling toward her were still struggling wildly with each other when Con, also thrashing in the air, plunged into them like a human cannonball. The sickening sound of bones striking other bones came to her ears clearly, and the lungs of all three were emptied of breath in simultaneous, bellowing groans. For a flashing, broken second, the three formed one huge boulder of humanity, and then they shot away from one another.

Susan expected to see the bodies fly about like billard balls and leave the relatively narrow channel of energy in which they were moving completely, but her Earth-educated mind was not in tune with the otherwordly physical laws that applied within the ship.

The kinetic field would not allow them to leave it in the middle of the crossing. Instead of spinning away into the far reaches of the room, the trio slid to the edges of the field, were trapped there by the same force that was moving them, and began revolving inside a great, transparent cylinder that was at least forty feet across. Jefferies' impetus was overmatched by that of Treacher and Kim Shawlee, which meant that his direction was reversed and he was abruptly shooting in a wide spiral toward the column along with the other two.

Susan screamed and dropped to the ledge. She had no way of knowing where any of the three would strike the column, but it seemed certain enough that all of them would do so at a killing rate of speed.

Though stunned and hurt by his collision with Cecil and Kim, Con retained the presence of mind to wrap himself into a tight ball and stop all the motions of his body that were at his command. He couldn't see the rapidly approaching tower in his spinning flight, anyway, so he squeezed his eyes shut.

The Irishman hit the wall of the column some six feet above the lip in a downward arc, with his bowed back taking most of the impact. There had been no time to draw another breath after losing his first in the explosion of the collision, so he couldn't cry out or even grunt when he struck. He dropped from the wall to the ledge and actually rolled again into the force field before Susan grasped his left leg and dragged him back. His consciousness was nothing more than a shower of colored lights inside his ringing skull.

Susan's screams brought the rest of the group charging around the tower, and James Aymdahle and George Flanders acted more out of instinctive self-protection than plan when they threw their arms about Treacher's limp body as he slammed into them. The three were knocked violently against the column, and the soldier's head struck the unyielding metal with the force of a weight dropped from a distance onto a hard floor. The sound was awful. All three tumbled to the ledge.

Kim Shawlee was conscious and screaming insanely as she soared toward the stunned crowd. Her maddened struggles multiplied her speed as she approached. There was no hope for the woman, even if she had been within reach of the stretching hands of Patrice Rutherford and Roger Griffin; the angle of her arrival took her not into the impenetrable face of the tower, but off its right side, so that she spun away from the metal like a ricocheting bullet.

Somehow, Kim resisted the call of unconsciousness, a call that might have saved her life by ending her struggles, and the watchers could only gasp in astonishment as again she flew away from the column, now at almost a right angle from her approach.

The design of the conveyance field was ingenious, and it provided limits for those utilizing it in the manner for which it was intended, but Kim's hysteria, her lack of understanding of how the effect operated, and her terrible luck in merely rebounding from the tower rather than striking it fully as the men had took her beyond the safety measures. She was tossed like windblown flotsam away from the column and out of the paths of energy.

When she first left the field, there was a fleeting moment during which she seemed to be balanced between worlds, with the grip of the frightening energy countered completely by the eternal reach of gravity, so that she actually appeared to hang in the nothingness that was some forty yards from the horrified people on the ledge until reality reasserted itself. Kim had stopped struggling in that fraction, so when she fell toward the boiling sea beneath her, it was with an almost serene grace. Her face was turned to the watching people, enabling them to witness the strange look of disbelief in her eyes and the way she tentatively reached out for them.

"Jesus Christ!" Flanders gasped.

Susan turned her face away, while Anjanette cried and buried hers in Griffin's arm.

Kim didn't look down until a second before she plunged into the crimson pool, and that left time for only one short scream. Her feet entered the liquid, and this incited a brilliant burst of white light that seared into the unprotected eyes of the men and women on the tower. With pained cries, they turned away from the flash. By the time their vision had cleared, no trace of Kim Shawlee remained in the seething morass.

"She's dead," Patrice Rutherford whispered in disbelief. "The field didn't stop her . . ."

"There was nothing that could have been done to help her," Stallybrass said. "How are the men?"

Treacher was unconscious at the feet of Aymdahle and Flanders, neither of whom had been injured by the collision. Jefferies was still on his knees, but he was alert and slowly regaining his breath and composure.

"This one will live," he assured the rest. "I just hope to God I'm not responsible for what happened to that poor woman."

"You're not!" Susan said quickly. "If you hadn't slowed them down, they both would have been killed when they hit the tower!"

"Yeah," he muttered, "I made a hell of a lot of difference, didn't I?" He stared at Treacher, who was resisting attempts to revive him.

As the awful impact of Kim's death ebbed from the stunned spirits of the group, their normal responses to the circumstances slowly returned and they could hear the distant shouts from the opposite side of the vast chamber. They had completely forgotten about Aaron Doyle during the tragic events of the moment.

Doyle had reached the opposite wall while their attention had been diverted, and the active door-panel that he had touched had opened another way through the body of the vessel. Standing in that doorway, he had witnessed the fall of something into the red pool and the bright explosion that had followed, but he didn't know what had created the activity. His shouts were almost desperate questions to that effect. Finally, the people that he had left behind reappeared around the body of the column and they told him what had occurred.

"Jefferies is okay?" he asked.

"As well as normal!" Con yelled back. "But the corporal is out cold and looks to be committed to staying that way! He's not bleeding, but you'd better bet that he's sustained a fractured skull!"

"Just wonderful," Doyle spat, resisting the nearly overpowering urge to punch the object which happened to be closest to him. "Well, there's nothing we can do to help him now except bring him along. Jefferies, if you feel up to it, you and Flanders take his arms and bring him across first. There's another corridor over here, and if we have any kind of luck to speak of, it'll take us straight through to the other side."

By the time everyone had crossed into this next doorway, it was seven-thirty-seven. Three hours and twenty-four minutes had passed since the beginning of the earthquake, three hours and sixteen minutes remained until the projected liftoff of the craft, one of their number was dead, and they had not yet reached the midpoint of the double-bodied ship.

Chapter Eight

The hallway was blue.
Every area the group had encountered since leaving the tour room had been uniformly colorless except, of course, the red glare of the engine room they had just left. But the long corridor that awaited them after their second crossing of the hot sea was a light blue. Almost sky blue.

And there were no doors. The corridor ran into the distance, as did all the others, but as far as they could see there were no side exits. At least the cool whiteness of the ceiling was a contrast to the blue walls, something that had been lacking everywhere but in the engine room.

"All right, I don't know what this hallway is or where it leads," Doyle said, hoping to mask the group's near exhaustion from themselves.

"That goes without saying," stated Braam, fully himself once more.

"All I *do* know is that it runs to the west as nearly as I can reckon, and it's sure to get us closer to the other end of the ship," Aaron continued. "Any luck with Treacher?"

Peter Stallybrass was kneeling next to the big soldier, trying to revive him. "He's coming 'round," the doctor said. "I can't say how badly he was injured, of course, but I would not rule out a fractured skull."

"He'll get the best of care once we've escaped this place; let's go." Doyle turned toward the long, blue corridor.

"Just a minute," James Aymdahle said swiftly. "We've just lost one of our number! A woman's dead! Are we going to leave without so much as saying a word for her soul?"

"You're the preacher," Doyle responded with intentional venom. "I'm concerned with those of us who are still living, so why don't you take care of the dead?"

Aymdahle stared into the gigantic room he had just crossed, and while the others began to move westward once more, with Jefferies and Braam assisting a still-fuzzy Treacher, he looked into the hissing ocean that had claimed Kim Shawlee. There was no sign of her body, but to Aymdahle the body was only a portion—and an insignificant one—of the total being.

James knew Doyle would have said that the woman brought the tragedy upon herself, through her uncontrollable, irrational terror. But Doyle had never known or understood the awful depths to which fear could claw within the soul of a victim.

He, James Aymdahle, knew, and he had been trying to forget for most of his adult life.

Are you with us, God? Here, inside this foreign machine that so many people are convinced was built and flown by another race of intelligent creatures? Did your Son die for their deliverance, too, and can it be that I have been wrong all these years? Are we not the Chosen because we are the Only? Why must that poor woman have met with Hell in all this madness, away from her family and her proper life?

"James," said his wife, touching his arm, "we have to go now. They're leaving us behind. We can pray for her when we're outside."

Wordlessly, Aymdahle made his break with the soul who had been engulfed by that vision of eternal punishment and with his wife ran to rejoin the others.

Everyone behind Aaron Doyle had by that time become convinced that the man was inhuman . . . not because of the way he had so coldly dismissed the loss of Kim, but because of the pace that he set for them to reach the other side of the craft. Clearly they were not yet halfway to the spurs though they had wasted more than half of their precious time, and doubt was growing that they'd get there in time. The possibility of death aside, they knew that they'd need an incredible amount of luck to ensure even the opportunity to escape, and luck was one element that was in short supply.

Only Doyle himself seemed unaffected by the pace. Frances Claire had gone far beyond what anyone would have expected of her seventy-three-year-old body, even with the genius of modern medicine working its wonders, but the time had long since passed when she could carry little Bobby. Her breath was ragged even when she rested, and she was deathly white.

Anjanette Palmer, though young and healthy, was still a child, and her strength had been almost exhausted by the effort of keeping up with the longer strides of the adults.

Roger Griffin, with whom Anjanette had allied herself, looked very tired, and Peter Stallybrass was obviously in ever-increasing pain from his injuries.

Half the others were exhibiting symptoms of advancing exhaustion. Twelve miles was a very long race to run.

Aaron hardly noticed the ebbing reserves of those he was leading to safety. His early life had been hard, and he had learned that those who were most fit to survive a situation survived; there was only so much that even a leader could do to help those less ready to meet the challenge. He was not in the same taut condition that he had maintained while working in the oceans of the Earth, but he was fit enough to cover the distance that stretched before him in the time allotted.

Maybe the ship *wouldn't* launch itself skyward at ten-fifty-three p.m.—it had only been a guess put forth by that Irish guy, anyway—and maybe he and the rest would have to turn around and start back as soon as they discovered that the "spurs" were nothing more than racing stripes, but he was still going to be sure that he and those strong enough to follow him would be in the position to take that desperate gamble when zero hour arrived.

Doyle was so intent upon accomplishing his single purpose in life that he would have passed by the element that possessed the power to assist him in the run were it not for the small, dark scientist from Burgos, Spain. Antonio Arbolada lurched forward to catch Doyle by the shoulder and pull him to a stop when they encountered it. The hallway had remained featureless until that moment.

"It's not time for a rest!" Doyle said angrily as he turned to face Arbolada. "You people have got to understand that our *one* chance of surviving this is to push ourselves to the limit of—"

"No, no rest," gasped Arbolada, his complexion made even darker by his exertion. "This, I believe we should investigate . . . the door."

Doyle stared at the wall to his right in sudden realization that there was another doorway there. The corridor stretched seemingly to infinity ahead, but this was the first, and to his knowledge, the only exit from the tunnel. At its side, a familiar panel glowed coolly at shoulderlevel.

"It's probably just another room like the one on the other side of the engine," he said. "It monitors or converts the energy produced in there somehow."

Arbolada leaned against the curving wall beside the outline. Behind the pair, sixteen other men, women, and children staggered toward them, with Frances and Stallybrass nearly a quarter of a mile back; it was seven-fifty-three, and the group was exactly at the midpoint of the vessel.

Arbolada shook his head as words escaped him for a moment. Then he found his breath, "This appears to be the only door. In the other corridor there were many, many doors into the rooms. The systems of this craft all seem to be functioning well, even to giving us air to breathe, and I cannot believe that the inhabitants were forced to walk such great distances. I believe that this portion of the craft is the propulsion unit visited only on occasion by maintenance groups and this floor was not used for regular traffic. Perhaps these long corridors are designed to be travelled through slowly, so that some process—decontamination suggests itself—can take place, rendering exposure to the engine fuel harmless.

"If the second portion is the . . . living area, perhaps where the aliens lived while exploring other worlds, perhaps where they now reside, then there would be more methods of travel there. I feel that this could be an outlet to one transit system."

"You sound like Sherlock Holmes deducing a subject's childhood traumas by scraping the soles of his shoes," Doyle observed.

Arbolada smiled. "If I am wrong and there is no help beyond the door, at least we will be together in one group and rested."

Doyle decided to wait until everyone arrived before he opened the door, but he hadn't realized that this would take an additional five minutes. The time was put to good use by those who settled onto the floor while he paced nervously before them.

Con Jefferies sat heavily next to Cecil Treacher, not exhausted but thankful for the respite. "How are you coming along now, Major?" he asked the other man.

Treacher's dark face was becoming redder with

the exertion, and his wideset eyes seemed very puffy, though the rear of his head had hit the column wall. He turned to Jefferies upon hearing the question, but there was no recognition in his gaze and he said nothing in reply.

"I said, are you feeling better now?" Jefferies repeated.

"Oh," Treacher grunted. He looked away from Con and allowed silence to fall again. When it seemed that the question had slipped completely from his mind, he added, "Got an ache in my head. Where did the underground go?"

"The what?" asked Con.

"The underground."

"Christ," sighed Jefferies, "go back to dreamland, Colonel." He turned to Aaron. "Doyle, we've got to find some other way to travel, or some of us," he indicated the few who were still staggering toward the spot, "are not going to make it to the far end."

Doyle nodded. "It had to be expected. The older members just aren't able to go all the way. They've surprised me by lasting this long."

"You icehearted bastard," Jefferies whispered with anger overflowing his tone. "Only the fit survive, and the casualties are not to be given a second thought, right?"

"Don't turn into Elizabeth Rules on me, Jefferies," Doyle replied. "This is no time for that sort of talk."

"I suppose it isn't, not while you're so wrapped up in saving your own butt."

"Be realistic, man."

"Certainly," Con responded with more emotion

than he had intended. "I guess that being trapped inside a machine built on another world and waiting to be shot from Earth to God knows where is realistic."

Aaron's patience was swiftly deserting him, as well. "It's *happening*, isn't it? And I didn't see you lagging behind to help Stallybrass or Frances Claire!"

"Please, this will not help our circumstances," interrupted Arbolada.

Doyle turned away from the pair angrily and remained quiet until all the group was assembled. While the last arrivals leaned against the walls or kneeled on the floor, gasping for breath, he explained Arbolada's theory to them and summarized their position.

"This corridor runs for as far as we're able to see, and it may well take us straight to the other side; but if we keep to it, there's a damned sure chance that we'll have to run the entire way. On the other hand, if this does lead us to some sort of interior transport system, as Arbolada thinks, we could reach the other side of the craft in a matter of minutes. The question is: do we continue the way we're going or gamble on opening the door without knowing where it will lead us and what kind of atmosphere it contains?" He waited, not expressing his own opinion.

"Certainly, there should be no danger in trying the doorway," Stallybrass said in near-exhaustion. "Whatever's behind it shouldn't prove deadly—"

"Or so you say," Braam broke in. "Don't forget, we've lost one of our number already."

THE ASGARD RUN

"It sounds as if you're voting against opening the door, then," Doyle said.

"I didn't say that," Braam disagreed quickly.

"But you haven't said much of anything in a constructive vein since we got into this, have you?" Without awaiting an answer, Doyle went on, "Is there anyone who objects to trying the door?" No one spoke. "Okay, it's settled."

Stepping up to the panel, he touched it and watched as the blue panel slipped silently upward. A wave of the cool light with which they had all become familiar flooded outward and allowed them to look into the room beyond.

Their sensibilities had been battered and strained almost to unacceptable limits during the trek through the vessel, so it was understandable that they expected to find yet another vast chamber stretching regally before them. This expectation made their surprise all the more sharp. The room into which the door led was no more than thirty feet wide by fifty long, with a thirty-foot ceiling. In contrast to the engine room—and even the tour room—this area was practically claustrophobic.

Doyle took a step into the room, swiftly surveying it and spotting three more doorways on the far side. The entire area was bare of any sort of furnishings; the only exception was a series of grayish, painting-like outlines at irregular points along both the white walls to either side of the group. There were also several piles of gray-colored ash littering the floor next to the walls, as if small fires had once been kindled there. Aaron walked to the nearest outline and began to examine it.

"Looks like we've stumbled into the art room," muttered Daniel Levya.

"No, this isn't paint," Doyle said. "It's—it's material of some kind." He touched the strange design, which extended from the floor to a point about four feet above his head, and found that it definitely was not a thin layer of coloring. In fact, it was at least a half inch in thickness, and it rubbed away on his finger. The outline had a pair of long projections for its lower half, two more extending from its upper portion, and a rounded, differentiated half-globe at its top.

"It's clothing," Doyle concluded.

"Clothing?" Flanders repeated skeptically as he and the others moved into the room at Doyle's side. "Pressed against the wall?"

"Futuristic coathangers," Jefferies suggested. "Or, should I say, ancient coathangers?"

"I don't understand," Elizabeth Rules said. "Why would they build a room just to hold a few sets of clothing? And why does it fall apart when you touch it?" As if in illustration, she pulled lightly at an "arm" of one of the outlines, and it crumbled like a collection of densely packed dust to drift about her feet.

"As to the second part, we must remember that this vessel has been encased within this mountain for tens of thousands of years," Stallybrass said as he examined one of the piles of ash. "The fantastic condition of most of what we have encountered has tended to make us forget that so much time has passed. I would guess that the walls interact with the clothing in some fashion to hold it in place, but the material has been affected by the passing centuries and has degenerated into what you see now. These clumps of powder must be the remains of other suits. As to why a clothing room is located here, I'm open to suggestions."

"They're uniforms," Jefferies said with the instinctive certainty that he had displayed at the control panel in the tour room. "These were kept here so that the inhabitants could put them on before entering the engine area."

"That's wonderful," Braam sighed bitterly. "Even with their advanced technology, the designers were afraid to get too near the power source without protective clothing, and we danced through as if it were a walk in the sun. We're probably so thoroughly irradiated that we'll be dead within minutes."

"Dear God," whispered Frances Claire, her tired face flushing with fear.

The fiery rage glowed in Doyle's eyes, but he kept his voice controlled, "Maybe we're dead, Braam, and maybe we *aren't*. An educated intelligent man such as you should be leading us, not crying up your sleeve. We're here, and we have to deal with that."

Braam said nothing, and the room fell silent.

"It's getting late," Gloria Thirkell finally said. "It's six minutes after eight."

"All right," Doyle responded. The cool anger was gone from his voice, but the resolve remained. "We're faced with three doors again; seems like the aliens had a strong inclination toward sets of three. Any votes?"

"The middle," said Anjanette.

The others turned to stare at her.

"We took the middle door in the tour room, and

it brought us this far," she explained.

"Through the middle of the engine and all of the—" Braam mumbled.

"Shut up, Braam," Roger Griffin advised the man wearily.

"The middle door, then," stated Doyle. "Any objections?" None were voiced, so he pressed his right hand against the glowing panel and took a step back to await the opening of the door.

Nothing happened.

Doyle hit the panel a second time, more forcefully, but the only response to his action was a slight modulating of the cool white color of the control panel to a darker, somewhat reddish tone. This color change had not been seen in the panels of any of the other doors they had seen.

"Come on," Doyle whispered to himself, practically punching the dull-ruby radiance. He felt sure that they were about halfway through the vessel with a little more than two hours of escape time left, and he didn't want to be stopped by a malfunction at this point in the effort.

While the rest waited anxiously at the center of the three doors, Con Jefferies, also worried about the psychological effect of a locked passage on the group, walked to the lefthand panel a few feet away and pressed it firmly. The color changed in the same fashion as the center panel, but the door remained as resolutely closed as had the one before it. Seeing this, George Flanders decided to try his own luck with the panel on the right side but was no more or less successful than the first two.

"So it all ends here," sighed Elizabeth Rules,

"just because we don't know the right combination to get out."

"It can't be a question of knowing a combination," Doyle said firmly. "There's nothing different in this panel than those we've already opened! It's a simple pressure plate, that's all."

"So far as we know," added Kenneth Braam.

"No matter, it's still a long walk," Elizabeth said.

"Just a minute, I feel something!" Anjanette said, letting go of Griffin's hand and stooping to the floor, where she pressed both palms against the smooth surface. "The floor's shaking."

"She's right," Susan Leipnitz said as she did the same.

"Damn, all we need now is another earthquake," Flanders said in a voice filled with honest dread.

By then, half of the group had gone to their knees to assure themselves that some sort of vibration was running through the floor.

"It's getting stronger," observed Jefferies. "We'd better get ready."

Doyle shook his head and spoke with uncharacteristic uncertainty. "I don't think it's a quake. It's getting stronger, or maybe *nearer*." He placed one hand against the doorway which had remained shut following his touch of the pressure plate, and a sudden realization struck him. "It's not the earth that's trembling this time. Something inside the ship is moving."

"But what?" asked Gloria.

Aaron stood and looked at the unmoving door. "We should be finding out in a few seconds."

Before any other questions were asked, the vibration in the floor stopped altogether and the center door began to slide open. Again the assembly was startled by the size of the room into which they peered, and again this surprise was due to the comparative smallness of the area rather than its vastness.

After the double-chambered door had slipped completely into the ceiling, the group saw a room that was much larger than the average dining room in an American home but still almost claustrophobically close in relation to the gargantuan scale of the vessel. Quietly, the group stepped into the room and stared at the unusual way in which it was furnished.

Where most of the other rooms they had passed through had been largely empty, this chamber of roughly seventy feet by twenty-five feet was almost filled by a double row of couch-like furnishings that lined either side. The "couches" were brown, apparently made of some material resembling very substantial foam rubber, and ran from the open doorway all the way to the rear of the room.

There were "hills" in the design of the cushiony objects that created rises in the material extending almost to the twenty foot high ceiling and practically separating them into a dozen cushioned valleys on each side. The couches sloped sharply upward from the somewhat narrow central aisle until they reached a height of about four feet; then they levelled out like conventional beds until they met the walls, which were padded with similar material. Only the radiant ceiling was free of the cushioning.

"A bedroom?" Stallybrass inquired dubiously.

Doyle slapped one hand down on the absorbant

brown material. "No, if my guess is correct, this is one of those interior modes of transportation that Professor Arbolada has been expecting to find since we left the tour room. It's my guess that this is equivalent to our notion of a subway car."

"It was moved here by our activity at the touchpanel?" asked the Spanish scientist. "And it moves throughout the remainder of the vehicle?"

"Why not? Twelve miles is a long way to get around by foot, and even if those force fields were set up all over the ship, the crew would still need a faster way of moving from place to place, wouldn't they?" Doyle pointed to a portion of the interior wall just inside of the doorway to its right. "And I'll be extremely surprised if that isn't the control panel that guides the car."

They all turned to stare at the indicated board. Recessed in the padded wall was a large panel that consisted of numerous tiny pressure points glowing with a wide variety of colors, dozens of lines of black script which were nothing more than indecipherable scribblings to the group, and a knob-like projection at its very center. It was clearly active.

"The vibrations we felt were caused by this car, as you called it, arriving from somewhere else in the craft," Thirkell stated.

"Almost certainly," Doyle answered with a triumphant smile. He felt that he had finally discovered the way out of the trap.

"Then there are probably two more coming in," Jefferies said. "I felt a faint trembling in the floor even after this door had opened."

"Ditto," said Flanders.

"On a craft of these dimensions, three independent conveyance systems must be required, with junctions so that the travellers can switch from one to another," Griffin said. "Or maybe the builders just enjoyed supplying everything in threes."

"There are undoubtably hundreds—perhaps *thousands* of these cars available to the controlling computer brain, all able to move through the various tunnels at the same time," Stallybrass observed.

Doyle's exuberance appeared to be boundless. "Don't you understand what this means? We won't have to *walk* the rest of the way! Or float! This car can carry us anywhere we want in a matter of minutes! We're going to get out of this!"

"I don't know if we should tamper with the equipment," Braam said tentatively. "After all, we can't read this control board."

"Trial and error!" Doyle replied. "We *have* to go this way; our chances of running six miles in two and a half hours are slim at best, and it's damned certain that some of us will not be able to make it that far."

"Even our direction of travel will be guesswork," Arbolada pointed out. "My wristwatch contains an electronic compass, but it has ceased to function within the craft. I agree with Mr. Doyle: the risk is necessary if we are to have any opportunity of reaching the other side."

"Do you think we should all go together?" Jefferies asked. "With three cars here, it seems likely that our chances of finding the exit would be greater if we split up."

"I don't like that idea," Anjanette Palmer said quickly.

"Naturally, it's up to the individual," Doyle answered, "but there's at least one other group wandering around in here somewhere already, and even if a few of us stumbled across the spurs, we couldn't return to guide the others. The chances of finding each other again would be extremely poor."

His explanation drew several nods and words of accord, but before the decision could be approved, Daniel Levya stepped away from the group and back into the uniform room. His face was a flushed mixture of fear, embarrassment, and resolve.

"I'll stay here and guard the rear," he said with a weak half-smile.

"Guard? What the hell are you talking about?" asked George Flanders.

"Go ahead. If you make it all the way, somebody can come back for me."

Doyle walked swiftly through the car to join the man. "Daniel, you just heard that it would be almost impossible for us to find one another again if we split up. Either we all escape or none of us does, all right? Come on." He took Levya's left arm.

With surprising ferocity, Levya jerked free. "I said I'm staying here!" he nearly shouted. "Leave me alone and go ahead with your plan. I'll be okay."

Doyle started to respond, but Griffin spoke first, "I believe I understand, Mr. Levya; it's your son, isn't it?"

The rage in the man's face drained instantly to be replaced by deep pain. "I shouldn't have left him back there . . . I should have stayed . . ."

"Mr. Levya, if he didn't reach the second door and escape before the gas overtook him, there was nothing you could have done."

"I could have *stayed* there with him! He's only eleven, Christ, he's our *baby*—"

Flanders actually laughed aloud. "He's a fast little kid, right? It's a cinch he's with the people who made it through the second door and on his way to the spurs right now."

Levya squeezed his eyes shut and nodded intensely. "I know he is."

"Then come with us," Doyle said.

Levya's nod immediately became a harsh shake of refusal. "I'm going back, back to the shaft, and I'm going to check every floor of this ship until I find him."

"There isn't time for that," Peter Stallybrass told him. "There are hundreds of floors, in addition to the fact that, by taking the center door in the tour room, we've surely come an entirely separate path from the other group. We went through the engine of this vessel, but the doors to either side of ours undoubtably led around it to the north and south, possibly even allowing them to travel faster than we. Mr. Levya, there's a good chance that your son is *ahead* of us!"

"If he is, then he's got an opportunity to get out; if not, I'm not leaving him inside this goddamned piece of alien machinery! I'm going to look for him, and I thank you all for your concern, but there's nothing that you can say to change my mind."

Doyle finally understood how the love of one person for another could override even the instincts for self-preservation, and he silently shook Levya's hand before turning back to the transport room.

"Let's go, people," he said.

Flanders stepped into the doorway. "What are you talking about? You're not going to leave the jerk here, are you?"

Startled faces shot incredulous looks at the man. Roger said, "He's made his choice. We can't argue with that."

"Don't give me that baloney," grunted Flanders, reaching out as if to grasp Levya, who moved away from him. "This is suicide, and we can't let him do it without even trying to stop him!"

Doyle's left hand darted like a striking snake and snagged Flanders by the collar. "Shut your mouth and get back in the car," he ordered tightly.

Flanders looked shocked by the opposition he was encountering. "But it's ridiculous! There's no chance that he'll be able to find anybody in a ship this size, and it's crazy to *want* to stay in here, isn't it? How can we leave him?"

"By getting inside the car and using that control board to launch it. You can come along or go the rest of the way alone."

Flanders dropped his hands to his sides. "No, no, I want to go, but I don't understand . . ."

Doyle roughly shoved him into the transport room. With a last nod to Levya, he grasped the large central knob on the control board and gave it a twist to the right. It moved smoothly, denying the many centuries that it had waited unused, and the doors began to slide downward.

"Goodbye, Mr. Levya!" Susan called. "Good luck!"

Daniel raised his hand in farewell and remained

that way until the door had shut him away from their sight.

"I suppose we should climb onto the couches before we start," Roger Griffin said as he stooped to help Anjanette to do so. "Knowing the size of this vessel, the transport system will have to move pretty fast just to get *anywhere.*"

"I doubt that we'll be forced to deal with the usual problems of inertia," Stallybrass said. "I'm forced to suspend my natural skepticism in these circumstances, and I would be quite surprised if this car isn't equipped with some sort of stasis arrangement."

"Then why the extensive cushioning?" Thirkell asked.

Stallybrass smiled and awkwardly worked himself onto one of the deep couches. "I couldn't say, so I shan't take any chances."

At the control board, Aaron was faced with another in the long line of choices that he had encountered since the escape from the tour room. He had hoped that if they did come upon Arbolada's theorized internal transport system, the control equipment would be laid out so that he could decipher it. Ideally it would be arranged in a schematic pattern with flashing lights designating where the car's location at that instant and where each selection would deposit them.

The board most resembled an elevator panel, with varying colors instead of floor numbers. Naturally, this gave Doyle no hint as to where a blind decision would take them or even in which direction they would be travelling. If they were at junction of the halves of the craft, as Doyle figured, any trip would take them west and closer to their goal, but if the initial selection failed to get them to the spurs, they could well be as lost as Doyle had ever been beneath the waves of the oceans. The brimming optimism he had experienced only moments earlier suddenly threatened to desert him.

"Any suggestions?" he asked Arbolada, who stood next to him.

The smaller man shook his head. "None beyond guesses. If we had time and trained personnel, it seems likely that we could interpret the written language, but we have neither. I might point out that it is possible that the locations are listed in increasing distance from this spot. But it is just as likely that these relatively few lights may indicate nothing more than various floor levels."

"Where did you learn to offer such encouraging words?" Doyle sighed. "Since we don't have any better method of selection, I'll start with this top lefthand corner and work my way down; maybe that'll keep us moving in one direction, anyway. Everybody ready? There may be a hell of a takeoff when I hit this."

Arbolada scrambled quickly onto the deep cushioning, and, with Doyle himself stretching to reach the panel from a seated position, only Cecil Treacher was left standing—rather forlornly—in the aisle. Con Jefferies jabbed his shoulder lightly.

"Climb aboard, man," the young Irishman advised.

Treacher stared vacantly at him. "Isn't it time

that we found the way out of this place?" he asked.

"That's exactly what we're trying to do, General. Get on the couch."

The soldier responded by working himself between two of the rubbery hills, saying as he did so, "You know, I feel like my feet are wrong. Do I have them on backwards?"

"Jesus," whispered Jefferies.

Aaron reached up and touched the first glowing point with his right forefinger.

The room trembled for no more than a tenth of a second and then launched itself toward the east with the explosive power of a rocket blasting beyond the Earth's atmosphere. Screams filled the car as each rider was slammed deeply into the cushioning in the direction of the doorway by which they had entered. The acceleration was so tremendous that they felt as if the springy brown material were reaching out to envelope them. Patrice Rutherford, who had been perched on the edge of one valley, was rolled by the powerful force away from the couch and onto the floor. Flailing desperately, her body slid along the smooth surface from the front of the room to the firmly shut doorway, where she crashed into the metal with terrible force.

Doyle was pinned to the wall next to the control panel just as surely as if the flat face of an invisible five-ton locomotive had been rolled against him. His back was sinking into the padding deeply enough to be totally beneath the surface level of the wall covering, while his cheeks were drawn to either side of his face in a ghastly unnatural grin.

Despite the pressure, he didn't lose consciousness. Believing that something had gone completely wrong with the operation of the car, he tried to move his arm enough to touch the control panel a second time. It was like attempting to reach through concrete. He swiftly turned his attention from the panel to the effort his chest was making to draw in the breath that had been squeezed from him so abruptly.

As with all extreme episodes, the flattening pressure seemed to last for an eternity, but in fact only a few seconds passed before the car suddenly stopped. But only for a moment. The redirection of the vehicle took just enough time for them to breathe once before their helpless bodies were tumbling back into the padding, though on the opposite side.

The blackness that had been stretching out to grasp them from behind filled their vision as they fell, facefirst this time into the couches. The foamy brown material engulfed them so that they were instantly beyond the reaches of air or even light. On the floor, Patrice bowled from the door to the front of the car.

As swiftly as the crushing forces had afflicted them, they vanished. With a brief flip at the end of its journey, the car dropped into total immobility, which allowed the trapped people to pull free of the smothering padding and fall to their backs with ragged gasps. No one had breath for cries or screams, but the room was filled with the sounds of their desperate battle for air.

"Oh, God, that . . . that was *terrible*." Elizabeth Rules said weakly. "Did it take us to the other side?"

"This *can't* be right," added Braam angrily. "The

acceleration was too much, too brutal! I don't care, even if it is designed to convey the ship's crew all about the interior, this type of speed is deadly! There must be some sort of stasis system that we didn't implement."

Roger Griffin was in the same cushioned valley as the much smaller Anjanette Palmer, but he had managed to avoid falling upon her during the mad ride, and now he was frantically trying to make certain that she was not injured. "Do you feel all right?" he asked, ignoring the blood that was streaming from his own nose. "Are you sure?"

Anjanette had not yet drawn enough air into her lungs for speech, but she replied with a definite nod of her head.

Griffin turned his attention to the rest of the assembly, "Is anyone else hurt?"

"My legs are bad," Patrice Rutherford said, with tears rolling down her cheeks. Peter Stallybrass stood unsteadily and then stooped to examine her.

It was quickly established that Patrice had sustained at least one broken leg and probably other fractures. As gently as possible, Doyle, Jefferies, and James Aymdahle raised her to one of the couches.

The reminder of the people in the car had fared better because they had managed to stay in the foamy cushioning, but a number of minor injuries had been incurred during the violent trip. The most seriously hurt person was Frances Claire. Though she had suffered little visible damage during the ride, the trials of the past hours had been especially hard on her. She was at the point of almost complete exhaustion.

Her breathing was irregular, her skin waxen and bathed in a light sheen of cool sweat, and a slight trickle of blood could be seen at the corner of her mouth. Thirkell, Stallybrass, and Susan made her as comfortable as possible, while Kay Aymdahle took care of Bobby, who had come through the ordeal with no evident injury.

"I'm afraid that she won't be able to survive this much longer," Stallybrass whispered to Doyle after leaving Frances. The two men had stepped near the doorway. "She just isn't able to withstand the strain any more."

"At least she won't have to walk any more," Aaron replied. "With a couple of the girls on either side of her, maybe she won't have it too bad on the next jump."

"Who says there has to be a next jump?" asked Jefferies. "We may be at the rear of the ship now."

"I doubt that we've come that far, but standing here won't tell us anything." Doyle turned to the control panel, only to find Roger Griffin and Anjanette already there.

"Does this control the door?" Griffin asked, his hand on the panel's large central knob.

"That closed it," Doyle said. "I turned it to the right."

Nodding, the writer twisted the knob counterclockwise and stared at the doorway in what had become a ritual among the group. Doors had been closed to them throughout their journey, hiding the future from them, or perhaps protecting them from it; each time one of the huge sections slid aside or overhead, the potentialities of what waited behind it were literally endless.

The door slid open, and they were confronted with a return to the vastness that they had encountered early in the adventure. Only the engine room approached the incredible expanse of the area they now faced, and the total volume of even that place was rendered practically inconsequential by the seeming endlessness of this new discovery. The room seemed to be round and more than a mile across. It was shaded in the soft, ethereal white light that appeared to be favored by the designers of the vessel. And its ceiling was so far above them that its misty recesses might well have been the deep sky that the trapped people had left behind when they descended into the mountain. In fact, it resembled the elevator shaft on an immensely broadened scale.

Several members of the group wandered out into the huge space with their necks craned back and their faces wide with awe.

"As a writer, I should have a comment appropriate to the situation, but I'll be damned, I can't think of a thing to say," Roger whispered.

"I wonder if one can acquire a permanent disability from being overexposed to bewildering majesty?" murmured Stallybrass.

"Gaping paralysis," Thirkell smiled, but she didn't take her eyes from the intimidating sight.

"What do you suppose those things are?" James Aymdahle asked his companions while pointing to a number of large globes of a slightly darker white hue which were suspended, apparently by some invisible energy, throughout the air above them.

The globes were entirely featureless and served no obvious purpose other than as possible decorations, despite their considerable size. Hours earlier, the fact that these strange objects were floating so easily overhead would have been cause for wonderment, but now the negation of gravity was almost commonplace.

"I have neither the data to make a realistic assumption nor the bravery to chance a guess," admitted Stallybrass cheerfully. He was so enthralled by the circumstances in which he found himself that there was no room for fear.

"Professor Thirkell?" asked Kay Aymdahle.

"Don't look at me," she responded. "Why not try the man who's been involved with this sort of thing for most of his life?" She pointed to a still raptly staring Roger.

"I believe," he said from somewhere deep within his creative heart, "that this could be the recreation area." George Flanders parted his lips to make a derisive comment, but Jefferies stopped this with a shake of his head. Griffin continued, "It's my guess that the same energy that operated in the shaft and the engine room is in effect here, and if we walked out into the central area, we'd be able to soar up there like birds. The inhabitants might gather here to commune with one another, maybe to have sexual union, but most of all they come here to play. Those globes up there could be places where they alight to look down on the rest of earthbound reality."

"Makes sense to me," Con said quietly.

"I want to try it!" Anjanette stated with a burst of elation.

She understood the precariousness of their situation and the fleeting amount of time that they possessed, but the child that was an integral part of the adult intellect had tasted the ultimate joy of flight already. She imagined herself gliding, soaring, and swooping through the alien atmosphere above her head, if only for a few precious moments, and she realized that this opportunity would soon be lost to her forever. Still gazing upward, she took a step toward the center of the great hall.

"Whoa, no time for that right now, little lady," Aaron Doyle said in the tone of an adult laughing at the irrationality of a child. Kay Aymdahle caught the girl by the shoulders.

"But I'll only take a minute," Anjanette said futilely.

"More important matters face us," Doyle continued. "We've got to decide if this place is anywhere near the escape tunnels."

"Peter Pan will have to wait," Flanders told the girl, grinning.

Peter Stallybrass took a fortifying breath before readjusting his broken arm to a more comfortable position. It had suffered greatly during the ride in the car. He was still in awe of a mechanism that could provide a fresh, breathable, *alien* atmosphere throughout its huge body after millennia of burial.

"I'm inclined to believe that we're still a considerable distance from the rear of the vessel," Peter said. Before any questions could be voiced, he explained, "The transit room was in motion for only a few seconds, certainly no more than a quarter of a minute, and no matter what its speed, it could not have covered six miles in that space of time. Also, if you look you can see a large number of doorways identical to this one arrayed throughout the room, leading in from all directions, it would seem. I find it hard to believe that we are more than a mile into the body of the second portion of the craft."

"Okay, does anyone find fault with that theory?" asked Doyle. "No takers, then? Next problem: do we try to cross this room to another door and check out what's behind it, or do we just get back into the car and punch the next button on the panel?"

"Like hell, I don't want another ride like that one," Flanders said.

"Well put," added Jefferies.

"We'll have to use the transit system for the rest of the way," Gloria Thirkell said. "Even if we have to strap ourselves to the couches somehow, at least it'll move us along the line. Walking, we wouldn't have any chance at all."

"It's a hit or miss method of travel," Aaron reminded them. "We can't even be sure that we'll be moving west with the next selection. But I agree that we have to risk it."

The group had turned back toward the open car when Stallybrass halted them with a word. Doyle might have been the actual leader of the escape attempt, but everyone recognized the towering mental presence of the British scientist and paid heed to his observations.

"As Professor Thirkell stated, there are some of our number who have literally no chance of reaching the exit by foot, but I must add that there are some who may not survive being subjected to the stresses of that great acceleration for much longer.

Mrs. Claire, certainly, and others... but why shade the facts? I sincerely doubt that *I* can withstand the ordeal again."

"Peter!" gasped Gloria. "Your arm?"

"There's also been some internal injury. Hemorrhaging. And the condition has been deteriorating since we left the tour room."

"I'm sorry, I didn't know..." she said.

"So what's the answer?" Flanders asked. "We can't leave anybody else behind!"

"Perhaps this car is only a... what might be called a 'service' vehicle that isn't really designed for the average crew member. One of those others could be better equipped for our use, with contour seating or other useful alterations. I realize that we don't have the time to check all the other doors, but if we opened one, it seems to me that there would be an excellent chance of finding one of the more numerous passenger vehicles, if they exist at all."

"What time is it?" asked Doyle.

"Nineteen minutes after eight," Gloria replied. "We have two hours and thirty-four minutes."

"I'll check the door over there," Doyle said, indicating the glowing point nearest the left side of their position. It was a good hundred yards away. "The rest of you wait here in case that car is the same as this one. We won't have to move Patrice or Mrs. Claire."

"I'll go with you," Con said.

"No, stay here with the rest. I don't expect any trouble, but you should be here to get everyone back in the car in case I don't get back. I'll wave for you to come ahead if necessary." Doyle started off at a fast trot.

He kept his eyes fixed on the slightly bluish radiance of the wallpanel next to the closed doorway as he ran, and the pervasive misty whiteness of the surrounding area subtly worked to convince him that he was moving through the heart of a drifting cloud. When this eerie sensation began to affect his balance, he had to shake his head to clear it of random fantasies.

He also seemed to feel a weak but constant attraction toward the center of the vast room, as if the little girl's urge to fly had activated some aspect of the chamber that was now reaching out for a corporeal forms to cast into its great heights along with the frolicking ghosts of its builders. He didn't enjoy the feeling.

Doyle quickly reached the second door, but when he touched the panel the scene that had taken place when he summoned the first transit car was repeated. Over two minutes passed before the trembling in the floor ended and the door slid upward to reveal an almost exact copy of the car he had left behind.

"Sorry, old man," Doyle mumbled. He turned to the group that waited behind and waved his hands in a negative fashion over his head, shouting, "No good! It's the same!"

"Right!" Jefferies' voice answered faintly. He and the others began to move back into the car.

Doyle started to walk in that direction, already debating with himself about which destination to choose next and how he might be able to discover if the jumps would bring the group any nearer the western spurs, when he decided to give Stallybrass a second chance. It was possible that the "service cars", as the biologist had termed them, were all located together and the passenger vehicles could be found further around the perimeter of the room.

Of course, he had no time to check the dozens of doorways, but he impulsively decided to make one more investigation, this of the next car positioned to the west. Without alerting the others, he sprinted to the panel, summoned the car, and swiftly looked within when it arrived.

It was the same as the first two, which reinforced his bias against doing anything on impulse.

"You took your time getting back," George Flanders said when Doyle entered the car and shut the door. "Read any good books along the way?"

"I was looking into another car, just to be sure," Aaron replied.

Stallybrass looked to him hopefully.

He shook his head.

"We'd better be on our way, then," the scientist said. "Everyone is prepared."

Doyle slipped onto the couch next to the control panel, positioned his left shoulder firmly against the rear wall, and reached across his chest with his right hand to touch the second gleaming dot in the selection column. The room was instantly on its way to the indicated point.

Goodbye, thought Anjanette. Maybe in my next life, I'll be a bird.

Chapter Nine

The second ride was no more gentle than the first, though less damage was done to the passengers because they were prepared for the extreme acceleration.

The speculation that was voiced by several of the group that the car must contain some sort of system for either slowing its speed or cancelling the terrible forces produced by its acceleration and deceleration seemed logical, but the most intense examination of the panel by Doyle, Thirkell, Stallybrass, and Braam failed to locate any such protective capability. It was clear that if they were determined to ride, they would be forced to pay for the privilege in new bruises and strained muscles.

The best method of protecting against damage during the high velocity trips seemed to be to lie longitudinally between two of the cushioned "hills" while bracing oneself to either side with tensed arms. Of course, not all of the riders were physically able to do this, and a number of them collected together in the "valleys" to firmly hold one another and hope that they weren't bounced off the couches by the abrupt turns, climbs, and dips of the vehicle.

The second stop of the car revealed even less of interest to the fleeing people than the first had. As far as Doyle could tell, the new arrival point was nothing more than a junction, sort of a train station where passengers from one car could switch to perhaps fifty others which undoubtably ran throughout the vast ship.

This discovery could have led to another period of discussion and debate among the members of the group concerning whether or not they should try another car, but Doyle realized that, with no more hard information than the meager amount they possessed, any argument would have done nothing more than consume their ever-eroding stock of time. He quickly got the party underway again before anyone else decided to study the possibilities.

The third stop showed them only what appeared to be a janitorial room; it might have been of interest, but offered little help. The fourth time the car's doors opened, it was to the sight of another seemingly endless corridor with hundreds of branches leading away into the depths of infinity. Even if this hallway offered a transit force field, no one bothered to find out because it would mean leaving a swift mode of travel for a much slower one. The blind search continued.

The greatest problem facing the group was their

inability to tell which way they were moving. Arbolada's compass gave fluctuating readings whenever he keyed it in on his watchface as it was cut off from the Earth's magnetic field within the ship, and their instinctive reactions couldn't be trusted due to the dazzling speed and the way the vessel altered direction. It even rose and dropped through dozens of floors in seconds. At the velocity with which the car moved, they could have been standing at the rear of the ship in only minutes had they been able to send it to a definite goal and bypass the stops they were making.

The fifth arrival brought them to a hive-like collection of relatively small cells stacked cliff-dwelling style in the face of a wall. There the riders were allowed to catch their breaths and check for further physical damage before the next jump began. Susan Leipnitz was standing and exercising her cramping legs when she noticed that the UN soldier lying on the couch across from her was still as death.

"Corporal Treacher is unconscious," she said, after checking on him. "Isn't that dangerous so soon after having hit his head as hard as he did?"

"It could be extremely serious," responded Stallybrass, making his way toward her. "Is the fellow breathing?"

"Yes, but fast and shallow."

Several people tried to revive the husky young man, but their efforts brought no response.

"He definitely has sustained a grave head injury," Stallybrass said. "Unless we get him to a medical unit soon, it might prove fatal."

"We're doing the very best we can to get him out

of here, doctor," Doyle replied coldly. "Time?"

"Eight-thirty-seven," Gloria answered.

"We can't waste any more time here. Jefferies, Flanders, you two get on the couch on either side of him and make sure he isn't thrown around too much during the trips. Be especially careful of the rifle."

"Aye, Admiral," Con said.

The sixth stop yielded nothing hopeful, simply because none of them could even guess what the open space before them represented. It could have been a gigantic meeting hall somewhat like the birdroom, a sleeping chamber without any form of bedding, an empty storage area, or any of a hundred other things. Doyle chose not to investigate further and sent the car barrelling along to the next destination.

As the continued use of the transit car apparently failed to bring the group closer to freedom the spirits that had been so high at the discovery of the system began to fall once more. Treacher was still unconscious, and Frances Claire was barely able to hold on to her senses through the on-going ordeal of the terrible acceleration. Her moans of pain following each trip were pathetic reminders of her failing condition, but most difficult for the other passengers to endure were her weak sighs of dread as they prepared for another fast journey in the car.

Little Bobby had been alternately enthralled and horrified by the wild careening of the vehicle during its first trips, but as the routine of a brief spurt of motion followed by a slightly longer period of rest became established, the boy seemed to retreat into himself and the safety of Kay Aymdahle's arms. He made little noise at all by the time of the sixth stop.

Stallybrass's condition was also deteriorating, though he said nothing about it. His one concession to the pain and weakness that wracked him was to station himself next to the doorway of the car, opposite Doyle, so that he could examine each new area without having to leave his place of rest.

Patrice Rutherford bore the pain of her broken bones stoically from her position near the front of the vehicle with her teeth set and her inner self praying that it would all be over soon.

The earthquake had hit at just after four in the afternoon, meaning that the men and women had been underground in the buried spacecraft for more than four hours; the urgency of their circumstances had forced aside their rising hunger and exhaustion, but a great thirst was slowly clawing its way into their throats. Despondency could now be recognized as one of the primary enemies that Doyle faced in his sworn dedication to lead the others to their one chance of escape.

The minutes seemed to pass at a dozen times their normal rate.

Seldom more than three were spent anywhere the car stopped, but these began to mount as Doyle, fighting a faint hysteria to which he would never admit, continued to punch the glowing dots on the control board. They had paused at the indecipherable sixth area at ten minutes before nine; half an hour later, they seemed to be no closer to the rear of the huge vessel.

But this atmosphere of approaching doom was swept violently aside when the car jerked to a halt at a point over a mile higher and ten miles away from the tour room.

"Does it appear encouraging?" Stallybrass asked.

Encouraging? Doyle thought sadonically. Does he mean is there a sign shaped like an arrow pointing west and saying, "This way out?" Aloud, he answered, "It's a door."

Stallybrass struggled from his prone position on the couch to peer out of the car where the leader of the refugees stood. For a brief moment, his self-control slipped and the pain that was now coursing regularly through his body escaped as air whistling through his clenched teeth. But this weakness exhibited itself for only an instant.

"One door?" the biologist queried while slowly standing.

Doyle stared upward. "One hell of a big one. Thirty feet high at least, fifteen across. It's set in a recess just a little larger than itself. There are no other features in the compartment."

"So I see," Stallybrass said, joining Doyle in the comparatively small cubicle.

"Are we staying here?" called Elizabeth Rules from within the car.

Doyle scanned the well-lighted blue room once more and replied, "I see no reason to. This place looks like an anteroom to a prison." He started to return to the transit vehicle.

Stallybrass raised his right hand. "A moment, if you please, Aaron. This may bear deeper investigation."

A tone of frustration—perhaps even of building defeat—permeated Doyle's response, "Doctor, I shouldn't have to remind *you* that we have, at most, an hour and a half to locate the way out of this industrial asylum."

"And how can we say that this is not that doorway?" Stallybrass asked, with biting logic. "Aaron, in every other place we've stopped there were a number of other doors, sometimes thousands other than the one by which we entered. Every other place we have visited was freely open for visitation, yet this tiny room seems to be accessible only through this single route. What makes this area so exclusive? Can we even open that door?"

This isn't the way out, Doyle said firmly to himself, though he wasn't able to produce a single rational argument to the scientist's theory. The seconds of their lives were running from them much more swiftly than falling grains of sand, and he could have carried the smaller man back into the car under one arm. But Doyle understood that his untested psychic revelations could not automatically override the trained instincts of a man like Stallybrass.

"I suppose we can spare a minute to try the door," he said.

"Probably won't take that long," the other man muttered as he approached the radiant white spot on the wall to the right side of the long-sealed door. "I would be extremely surprised if this isolated entrance responds to anything of less physical impact than a nuclear reaction."

Stallybrass touched the glowing plate and was not surprised.

The other doors in the craft had opened smoothly and without delay at the contact of human hands.

Now, at the first brush of Stallybrass's fingers, nothing at all happened to the closed door, which perversely pleased Aaron Doyle. The scientist touched the panel again, but still there was no response.

"Let's go," Doyle ordered.

"Another moment," Stallybrass replied absently. Then he hit the illuminated point forcefully with the edge of his closed hand.

A groan came from somewhere far below them. It was an expression of pain that originated in the heart of metal that had been forged millennia before. Under normal circumstances, the door would not have responded to the touch of any creature other than one of a number it had been programmed to react to, and this number certainly did not include anyone from a world other than that of its birth.

But the craft was not operating as it had been designed. A control defect, that had been responsible for the extensive malfunctioning of the ship's program had insinuated itself as far as the locking system of the room before the humans reached that area, and the door went against its design to obey the command of Peter Stallybrass when he pounded his fist into its pressure panel.

The mechanism made grotesque noises that would have seemed more appropriate to an aged wooden structure, but it did open. While the scientist, Doyle, Con Jefferies, and Gloria Thirkell watched, the metal separated from its long union with the floor and inched upward until it exposed a huge, angled tunnel beyond. Set into the tall ceiling of this new corridor was a pair of fiercely brilliant bands of red light.

"The hall to freedom?" asked Jefferies.

"I wouldn't let myself be carried away with enthusiasm," Doyle said.

"Notice the lighting system, Peter," Thirkell pointed out. "That is not at all like the fluorescent lighting we've seen so far. Actually, it almost looks . . . malignant."

"Possibly a cleansing radiation of some sort," he answered. "It could prevent contamination of the chamber that lies beyond. Or it could be red just because the crew liked that color. Kenneth will be wild with anxiety. I'm going to investigate."

"Um, I don't mean to sound like Kenneth," she whispered, "but do you think it's wise to expose yourself to that without knowing its nature?"

Stallybrass smiled. "We may be no more than ninety minutes from destruction, so I've decided to give in to every facet of my curiosity. Aaron, I intend to follow this tunnel to its end; if you feel that the rest of the party's best interests would be served by continuing now, please do so, though I would appreciate ten minutes to explore, if you can allow it."

"Ten minutes isn't much," Jefferies said, "and, as the man said, this could be the spurs. One of them. I'm going in with him."

"Hell, what can we lose?" Doyle asked with a bitter laugh. He didn't feel up to adding the cheap but realistic kicker, "Our lives?"

After Doyle explained the stopover to those waiting in the car, most agreed that there seemed to be a chance that they had stumbled upon the possible exit from the craft. When the group left to explore the recesses of the corridor, only Frances, Bobby, Treacher, Patrice, and the Aymdahles remained behind. James expected no trouble, he said, but with the English soldier soundly unconscious he felt that one of the men should stay behind with the injured.

Perhaps none of the investigating party believed that this hall would lead them from the vessel and from there out of the side of the mountain range, but they all fervently hoped so. In any case, the tunnel was worth a quick check simply due to its apparent isolation. They kept close together beneath the cool but strangely threatening red strip lights, and their walk lasted a surprisingly short time: after moving forty feet inward, turning sharply to the left, and then traveling another sixty feet, they came upon a second door, this the image of the first.

This door was not programmed to resist entrance, as the previous one had been in its fully functional state, and it slid up obediently. The room beyond was not freedom, but it literally stunned the breath from each of the onlookers.

"My lord, it's more than I might have dreamed," Stallybrass managed to whisper only after long moments of complete silence. "It's the aliens themselves."

The chamber was enormous, but size had little impact on the people at that stage. What caught their eyes, reached into their souls, and wrung every drop of belief from them were the rows upon rows of transparent cases filled with greenish fluid and the bodies of what had to be the designers and crew of the foreign craft in which the humans stood.

Silent again following the awed observation made by Stallybrass, the party moved into the bright white room to look more closely at the creatures inside the containers. They were giants, of course, averaging between ten and twelve feet in length as they floated in the liquid, and each exhibiting four limbs attached to their long, capsule-shaped trunks.

While the general morphology of the aliens had been startlingly close to that of humans to that point, the appearance of the creatures' heads wiped away similarities. There was no visible neck. The heads were long in proportion to the forms, with peaked skulls and no evidence of any kind of hair. They were narrow and extended to either side even beyond the "shoulders," and the side portions appeared to be structurally so designed with bone and organic function rather than just fleshy extensions.

In spite of the aliens' size, the overall impression was one of a certain delicacy. The limbs, both longer and thicker than even Doyle's arms and legs, still seemed too thin to competently support the round body and unusually heavy head.

Through the green-tinted fluid that filled the compartments, it was difficult to determine the color of the aliens' flesh, though in glancing at the long rows of boxes it appeared that each of the individuals was of the same general hue. The only clothing in evidence was a loose garment wrapped around each form. There were no obvious signs of variation from one individual to the next, including external sexual characteristics.

"I knew that they had to be here, somewhere," Stallybrass said with reverential emotion spilling from his voice. "This craft is simply too large to have been an automated probe. There had to be some further purpose—some intricate plan behind such an awesome expenditure of energy and resources. And here they lie, preserved perfectly after all these centuries of sleep."

"But . . . how many are there, five hundred?" Thirkell asked. Her thoughts were tumbling over one another in their eagerness to be expressed.

"At least that," Braam said. "Maybe eight hundred."

"With so many individuals included in the mission, is it realistic to believe that this was a mere exploratory journey? I know that this may sound like dialogue from a bad science fiction film, but there are enough aliens in this chamber to create a viable, permanent colony. They must have been planning to *live* here on Earth for a long time."

"Lucky for us something went wrong with the programming," Flanders observed wryly.

A foreign look of anger erupted in the eyes of Peter Stallybrass. "Lucky?" he demanded. "My friend, if this vessel had carried out its mission upon reaching our pathetic world, we humans might have been soaring throughout the Universe right now, rather than grubbing about in the thoroughly ordinary planets closest to us! With the knowledge these beings possess, we could be immersed in Newton's infinite ocean of discovery rather than fingering pretty shells on the shoreline!

Luck? Whatever it was that caused the machinery of this mission to fail was undoubtably the saddest blow ever to be received by the human mind!

"And the only blow to overshadow that is the fact that this treasure of advanced technology and understanding is destined to be taken from us before we can dip our fingers into so much as the dew it exudes! We've *got* to observe, catalogue, photograph with our minds every detail we encounter!" The biologist's face, which had been pale due to his injuries, was now flushed with passion. His eyes seemed afire with excitement, his veins distended. "We have to record this and deliver it to those outside so that we may understand what the heavens have given us. So imprint all of this, *everything*, in your memories! The sights, sounds, and smells! Had they survived, these people might have saved us ages of ignorance and death!"

"Or they might have wiped us out like minor vermin," Flanders countered with devastating precision. "Me, I'm glad they're dead."

Doyle tapped his fingers against one of the long, clear boxes and found that it felt somewhat like hardy plastic. "*Are* they dead, doctor? You said that they were sleeping in preservation; maybe these are suspension cabinets of some sort."

Stallybrass drew in a short breath, and his eyes grew even brighter. "You could be right! Thirkell, Braam, we have to attempt to revive them! We could establish communication, I'm certain, in a matter of days, perhaps hours! And the things we could *learn*! Look for controls, all of you!"

"Hold on, there!" Doyle said loudly before anyone could move. "We can't afford to get involved in something like that right now! Time is running out, people, and we can't be sure that they're alive, even in suspension."

"They must be!" Stallybrass asserted. "Light speed must have been a barrier even to their science, and this is the way they circumvented the great chunks of time that are inevitable in interstellar flight!"

"Then why design a craft with so much volume apparently devoted to recreational activities, if they were going to spend the trip unconscious?" Roger asked. He was only slightly less excited than Peter. "Maybe the trip didn't take hundreds of years, or even decades: couldn't it be true that this sort of suspension was necessary only during certain periods, such as launching and landing? Or why couldn't it be that they were so easily bored that even a few weeks' travel was a hardship to them?"

Even the dour Braam was swept up in the enthusiasm. "But it's just as likely that all of the recreational facilities were designed for use *after* landing on the planet, to be used while they established their colony and prepared the world for those to follow!"

Aaron broke through the billowing conjectures of the trio. "I don't care what the reason for any of this was; all I know right at this moment is that our main priority is to escape from this ship! And that doesn't give us time to stand around debating their origin, why they came, or how they got here! We've got to get going again!"

Stallybrass whirled on Doyle like a fencer attacking an opponent. "Then you should know that the only way you will get me from this room before I am prepared to leave is to *carry* me bodily through that tunnel!"

"If it comes to that—" Doyle began in response.

"Shut up!" Jefferies' shout cut through the atmosphere of charged emotions like a knife. He stood deeper in the room than any of the others, at least fifteen yards in among the tall rows of cabinets, and it was clear from his intense expression of concentration that he was listening to something.

For a moment the chamber was silent to the ears of the rest of the group, and then Flanders said, "What's the matter, kid? Smelling for ghosts?"

"*Shut up, damn you!*" the young man repeated, his eyes threateningly wild. He waited where he stood for a moment longer and then darted through the crisscrossing lines of containers toward a point even further from the entrance. When he was a good two hundred feet from them, he stopped and stared at something that was hidden from their eyes by the cabinets; in spite of the distance, the look of sheer horror in his face was as clear as the keen, high-pitched whistle of shock that emerged from his throat.

"Oh, no! It's . . . oh *Jesus*," he whispered just loudly enough to be heard by them. Then he began to stagger backwards, never taking his eyes from the vision that had captured his frozen attention. He moved like a man with only minimal control of his own body.

"What in heaven's name is wrong?" Stallybrass asked. He started to walk toward the stunned man.

The alien craft had been incompletely activated by the power of the earthquake, and its already damaged control center had sent out a number of messages to various parts of the interior, some of them contradictory. At least one order had reached this, the suspension room, with enough power to produce a result.

Before the disbelieving gaze of the group of humans, something rose into the air some twenty feet in front of the retreating Jefferies. It was this vision that changed the people who experienced it beyond anything they could have imagined.

It was a sort of hand, but not the hand of a human being.

As large as the face of a brief case, the "hand" contained seven digits, including two that extended in opposable lines to the remaining five. It bore no trace of hair or nails, and it was light yellow. It was attached to a long but relatively slender "arm" of the same shade, and it hovered in the air above the cabinets with a slight trembling that spoke at once of its present weakness and its potential suppleness. While the eyes of those away from the spot were glued to that hand and followed its motion as it dropped to the top of the cabinet nearest it, Jefferies' attention was still clutched in a paralyzing grasp by something only he could see.

The creature to whom the hand belonged sat up.

Stallybrass shrieked piercingly in a cry that was filled with a consuming pleasure. "They're alive!" he shouted with wonderous passion. It was as if he had been delivered directly from the mouth of Hell by an all-benevolent God. "We can meet them! They live!" Now unaffected by his injuries or his exhaustion, he raced among the transparent containers toward the awakened alien even as Jefferies stumbled away from it without averting his eyes.

Doyle might have said something cautionary to the scientist at that instant; he was never sure thereafter. But even if Stallybrass had heard him in the mad welter of voices, he would have paid no attention. Nothing else in his entire life had approached that moment for importance, and he would have rushed in to the meeting even if he had known that contact with the alien would infect him with a fatal extraterrestrial virus.

He charged to the point where the clearly confused and unsteady being was slowly rising to its feet. Jefferies snapped out of his trance enough to grasp the older man as they passed one another and wrestle him against a cabinet.

"Get your hands off of me, you animal!" Stallybrass cried. "I have to talk to them!"

"Think about it!" Jefferies shouted back. In spite of his youth and strength, he was hard-pressed to hold the man. "We should stay away from it, at least until it's fully recovered from the suspension! It might not even be able to live in this atmosphere, and the control computer might flood the room with gasses that are poisonous to us!"

Stallybrass continued to struggle.

Jefferies' words seemed to be prophetic. The creature had reached its full, imposing height by then, but it stood swaying desperately with its huge hands held before a "face" that contained six spider-like eyes and two other openings that were partially covered by flaps of flesh. Something definitely was wrong with the alien, though it was impossible for the humans to know if the difficulties had arisen from the awakening process or the strange atmosphere in which it found itself. One possibility seemed as likely as the other.

After the initial period of total shock and inaction, the ten people who had remained near the entrance to the room were gripped by the undeniable reality of the moment, and they began to move toward the giant. As unlikely as it might have seemed to them, the alien was surviving in the Earth-styled atmosphere. At least, no one could detect any change in the air or temperature of the room.

The fleshy coverings of the creature's face had ceased their frantic trembling, and this led Thirkell and Braam to believe that somehow the alien had voluntarily stopped breathing without causing itself any physical harm. Stallybrass was still too involved with breaking free of Jefferies' grasp to speculate on anything.

"Maybe we *can* communicate with it," Gloria said. "If it can understand us, through direct mental contact or whatever, we can get it to stop the launching of the ship."

"And get us out of here," added Flanders.

"What an opportunity," Braam gasped. "No one in history has been offered a chance like this!"

"Just be careful and go slow," Doyle warned them as they walked into the collection of cabinets. "Just because they're more advanced than we are, we can't be sure they're any more cordial."

The confrontation was filled with promises, and thoughts of safety or revulsion were rapidly vanishing before the towering impact of the realization that this would be the first meeting with intelligent, technologically advanced aliens in the entire history of the human race. The creature had not yet shown any sign of recognizing the small intruders into its world, but due to the boundless drive of Peter Stallybrass, if nothing else, such a meeting could be only seconds away. There were rays of glory dawning even in the dull soul of George Flanders.

"Great Lord in the Sky!" shouted a man's voice from behind them.

The group spun about to find Cecil Treacher standing in the open doorway. There was a drunkenness in his stance and an obvious wildness in his eyes. A thin red stain had trickled from his right ear, and the cold, deadly Converse rifle was in his hands. At his side, James Aymdahle was seemingly attempting to direct the husky soldier back into the corridor; when he paused to look at what had so startled Treacher, the evangelist's mouth opened in a soundless cry and he literally dropped to his knees in amazement.

"It's him, Old Beelzabub!" laughed Treacher in tones of madness. "Come to get me, big 'un? Ready to try it, slip it in? The fires of Hell must have burnt every hair out of your arse, forker!" The soldier took several weaving steps into the room.

"He's still got the gun!" Aaron hissed. Shoving by those who were behind him, he raced through the maze of containers in a desperate bid to reach Treacher before the inevitable occurred. His frantic rush was not fast enough.

"Bit into a live one here, you great buggery bastard!" the injured corporal roared. Holding the deadly rifle butted to his hip with its muzzle directed upward, Treacher ripped loose a long burst of gunfire that rattled shrilly into the once sacred reaches of the chamber.

"Get on the floor!" screamed Jefferies as he dragged Stallybrass down.

Everyone in the room dropped except Treacher, who was caught up in his mission, and Doyle, who was leaping to stop him.

The first shells in the automatic stream shot above everything to sing off of the ceiling, but Treacher's addled mind was still sharp enough to draw the line of fire downward at his intended target. The alien moved its massive head slowly, so slowly in response to the ragged noise that it hardly had opportunity to see the creature that was killing it before the bullets tore through the pale yellow body. Large chunks of flesh exploded from its back in a cloud of pink blood. The opening nearest the bottom of the head grew wider as the flaps pulled away from it, and a low sound, akin to the sounds created by an orchestral bass, rolled into the air, dragged in low agony from the depths of the creature's huge body.

Stallybrass screamed.

Treacher's smile continued to cut through his face as he brought the gun back from its initial sweep to throw another gush of death into the alien. This knocked more flesh and blood from the chest area as it forced the creature into a backwards stagger. When the head dropped into the line of fire, most of the uncomprehending features were ripped away in bloody fragments. The alien dropped heavily to the cold floor, leaving no hope that it had survived the assault.

Treacher had time to send dozens more shells into the clear cabinets nearest him, and though the transparent material resisted the attack with greater strength than even thick glass, six of the containers were shattered before Doyle pitched into the man's legs and brought him sliding to the floor. A final round of fire skidded with terrifying noise across the floor, but no one was injured by it and the gun spun out of the soldier's hands.

"You stupid son of a bitch!" Doyle shouted in a white rage. He clutched the front of Treacher's uniform and dragged the dazed man to his feet. "Don't you know what you've done?"

"Don't hit him!" Gloria Thirkell called. "He's hurt, he has a concussion, possibly a fractured skull!" She started to run toward the two men while the others stared about in stupefied horror.

Forcing himself to release Treacher, Doyle dropped the soldier back onto the floor and stared at the destruction the brief attack had wrought. Green liquid was pouring out of several shattered containers, whose occupants had been mutilated almost as badly as the roused alien. Suddenly the chamber was filled with death and despair, even though none of the humans had been hurt in the chaos.

"What was that thing?" asked Aymdahle from his kneeling position.

"That was the owner of this place," Doyle heard himself answering. "It was someone you didn't believe existed—a creature that might have shown us the way out. And I think it was our last hope."

Chapter Ten

There was nothing more to be gained from the preservation chamber.

The alien was definitely dead, as were those in the shattered cabinets, and a brief reconnaissance of the rest of the room turned up no other revived creatures. Thirkell made the suggestion that the group remain in the chamber to await the arousal of another of the crew members, but even she was not really in favor of this, and the idea faded quickly.

After a few moments devoted to speculation on what might have happened in that room, the group of men and women returned through the corridor. Stallybrass, who might have offered resistance a few minutes earlier, left meekly and had to be helped back to the car. The fire that had flared so brilliantly behind his eyes when the meeting with the alien seemed imminent appeared to have died along with the creatures that had been taken from him.

Those who had remained in the car were anxious for an explanation of the sounds they had heard, but the lifeless manner in which the replies came spread discouragement throughout the group. Only Treacher returned to the transit vehicle happily; he laughed mindlessly about his victory over "Old Nick" and even sang a snatch of a childhood ditty dealing with another lad who had overcome the Evil One. Then he climbed onto a couch, slumped against its padded wall, and began to mumble in a low, rapid tone to himself, pausing occasionally to laugh loudly.

At nine-thirty-six, Aaron Doyle dispiritedly pushed the next of the glowing dots and sent the vehicle on the way to its next stop.

Two more fruitless stops ate away another five minutes of the time left to them. Giving in to his growing desperation somewhat, Doyle abandoned his progressing line of choice at the control board and went directly to the final smudge of light, reasoning that this command might take the car to the very farthest point that was possible to reach in the craft. But the destination of the last light seemed to be only a huge communal bathing area, empty of water or bathers.

Another random selection did no better for the searchers. When the car arrived at the fifth spot following the disaster at the preservation chamber, it was thirteen minutes to ten.

Only an hour and three minutes remained before the theorized deadline.

Doyle was reaching for the central knob to open the vehicle's door when a fragment of the recent past crashed into the present with the roar of a thousand wars and again turned the world upside down. Although there was every reason for the group to expect at least one more major tremor, when the final shock of the day rolled through the mountain range and caused the alien craft to shudder madly, no one could recognize the event as anything other than a traitorously early launching of the vessel.

They were tossed about inside the padded vehicle as brutally as they had been during the first quake, before the ship had turned on its side. Their cries mixed with the sounds of millions of tons of shifting earth, and they bounced about the cushioned room like beans in a child's game. The tremor lasted for three and a half seconds.

"No, not yet!" Doyle screamed as he tried to stand and reach the knob that would open the car's door.

"Have we launched?" Kenneth Braam asked in the general din of cries and questions. "What happened?"

"I thought you said we had an hour!" Elizabeth Rules shouted in rage at Gloria Thirkell.

Con Jefferies found himself in the aisle with the bodies of Susan Leipnitz and Cecil Treacher tangled on top of him. Bobby was wailing piteously, and Kay Aymdahle was crying, "Why won't it stop?"

Treacher sat up and said in apparent good humor, "I think my head is filled with cold water. You know, I don't believe I could live through another of those."

We're on our way Out There, Roger Griffin thought with a strange amalgam of terror, joy, awe, and anger. Will it be what I've believed for so long? Is there a galactic community?

"Make it stop, Mr. Griffin!" Anjanette screamed. "Make it stop!"

Only Antonio Arbolada realized that they were still beneath the mountain. "My friends! Please, stay calm! Calm yourselves!" Only after several repetitions did his words have any effect. "I do not believe that we have been . . . *lanzamiento*, uh, thrown into space! I believe that we are yet upon the Earth!"

"Please listen to him!" Stallybrass added, though there was little strength in his voice.

"*Terremoto*!" Arbolada continued. "We have undergone another earthquake! The craft is still on Earth!"

This possibility was eagerly seized on by the people in the car. Within moments all that remained from the previous eruption of emotion were the cries of little Bobby and a distraught Kay Aymdahle.

"It must have been another tremor, like the one in the hallway!" Gloria agreed.

"We've still got a chance, then?" Flanders asked.

"They're right," Doyle said with certainty. "Let me get the door open to find out where the hell we are and—"

"Wait, don't open it!" Jefferies shouted from the door. "Don't you feel the vibrations? Either we're moving again, or the quake is still going on!"

His observation was swiftly confirmed by the others: there was a steady sensation of activity, though it seemed controlled and relatively faint, not at all like the insanity of the quake or the danger of the speeding car.

"Something's been activated by the shock," Thirkell ventured, "or maybe this means that the ship is preparing for a launch."

"We've got to find the way out, then," Doyle said. Ignoring the cries of the others, he turned the knob to open the door.

Their location was one of the seemingly endless areas of congregation provided for the crew, as was obvious by the vastness of the room's dimensions, its openness, and the eerily beautiful display of moving, transmuting, and dazzling colors hovering like a cloud of dreams at its center. In spite of the precariousness of their situation and their own physical injuries, the watchers awed wonder swept over them all.

The room—thousands of yards across, hundreds of feet high, circular, gold in color, and gradually sloping like some titanic basin toward its center—was not apart from the basic plan of the vessel, as its hundreds of other doorways testified. It seemed to be designed for easy access, but no one could even guess at the meaning of the glorious and stunning mist at its heart.

The mist was of no single hue—its composition seemed to be of all visible shades of the spectrum—and it moved as if the colors were the bloodflow of a living entity at least five hundred feet across and extending three-quarters of the way to the ceiling.

could have been an example of the aliens' most impressive art form. It might have been a manifestation of the malfunction which had caused the vessel to bury itself so long ago.

Or it might have been a living brain.

All these thoughts and many others less lucid flooded through the minds of the observers. As they stared at the spectacle, little Bobby suddenly leapt from the arms that held him and ran out of the vehicle, overcome by a wave of fear. Screaming for a mother who had died in the initial shock of the earthquake, he ran blindly toward the room's center.

"Grab him, Aaron!" Gloria said as Bobby darted past the big man's legs.

But before Doyle could react, the boy was fleeing deeply into the tremendous room.

Those who could run tumbled out of the car after him. They didn't know what the glowing vision in the center of the chamber was, but they knew that it could be extremely dangerous and perhaps deadly. The cold certainty that they all would be facing death in only an hour was shoved aside by the present crisis. Bringing Bobby back to their number would not raise any new hopes of escape, but they couldn't allow the child to face his last moments alone.

Bobby had come through the many ordeals virtually unscratched, and now fled the longer-legged adults who lurched after him with their sore bodies and injured limbs, his terror multiplying his speed. Their shouts only increased the panic that gripped him, and the sight of them stumbling along with arms outstretched offered no reassurance. They weren't his parents, and this place wasn't his home. He wanted to go *home*.

Doyle and Jefferies led the pursuit. They would have overtaken the boy long before he reached the distant central illusion had it not been for the fact that the hysterical child instinctively shifted the direction of his run according to the dictates of his panic. The men found their superior speed useless as they clutched at the dodging boy and lost him. The air currents, previously so gentle, were suddenly raging torrents, and the howling they produced shrouded the shouts of the adults and heightened the insanity of the moment.

Everyone except Stallybrass, Treacher, Frances and Patrice left the transit car to help Aaron and Con, but Bobby slipped away from all of them and sprinted in a direct path for the mysterious image at the central portion of the room. Jefferies was nearest the boy at that instant, and he leaped into the air in a final grab for him, falling heavily to the sloping floor as Bobby reached the kaleidoscopic vision and ran into the mirage.

There was no change in the writhing tower of light, no evidence that the child had ever approached it.

"But what *is* it?" asked Susan as she stared into the glistening display. "I thought, back at the car, that it was some sort of glass tank filled with electrical equipment." The powerful wind almost drowned her words.

"It's a field, like the one that runs across the engine room!" Gloria shouted in reply. "It encompasses the lights but allows solid objects to enter or leave it!"

THE ASGARD RUN

"Then we have to go in and get him out!" James Aymdahle stated.

He had been a quiet presence throughout most of the journey through the craft, but the sights he had been exposed to in the suspension chamber had affected him profoundly.

"Where did he go in?" he asked frantically. "Here?"

"Just a minute!" Doyle said. "Nobody's going into that stuff before it's checked out! All of you, stand back!"

Carefully, ignoring the wind that was tearing at his hair and clothing and the steady vibrations that were growing under his feet, Doyle stepped up to the face of the dazzling exhibit and looked directly into it. It was a storm caught in a bottle, with every shade of every color that he had ever seen flashing inches from his eyes. Each color twisted as if in physical torment while it lived on the edge of the storm. Doyle pushed his right hand toward the mist.

There was no heat and no sensation of cold. The storm might have been only the ghost of an actual event for all the effect that it had on the space it occupied. He forced his fingers closer to the surface, holding his breath. He touched the storm—or what should have been the storm—only to feel nothing against his flesh. He shoved his hand deeper so that it actually sank into the vision and the vibrant colors ran like liquid about his wrist, but the only indication that he had broached the boundary was the sensation of a slight, pleasant coolness. His hand was gone from his eyes right just as if it had been painlessly amputated.

"I don't feel anything inside!" he shouted to the rest. "In fact, I can't even feel the wind in there! I'll look for him!" And he stepped into the whirling tide.

There was a moment of darkness when Doyle's face moved swiftly through the edge of the storm, but as soon as he had been completely enveloped he found himself again able to see. A convulsive breath rushed into his chest.

Doyle was standing in another world, a world he had left behind for the love of a woman named Glynna, a world in which the sun was dim and often blue or green and death could be as near as the self-contained environment strapped to one's back. It was the world he had known under the seas.

Choking on what should have been salt water, Aaron spun on one foot and abruptly found himself again in the midst of the gale in the golden chamber. At least, part of him was back there; the defined surface of the trapped storm still shot up from the floor of the room to close over every portion of his body other than his head and neck, which protruded beyond the border of the phenomenon. To the startled people waiting for him in the room, Doyle seemed to have been beheaded and mounted on a wall.

"It's okay!" he assured them, moving fully into their line of vision. "The lights have an effect on the mind! When you go through, you seem to move into another world, like something from your memory! I was back under the ocean!"

"Could you see the boy?" Griffin yelled.

"No! The image restricts your vision to itself!"

"Then we'll have to grope through it to find him! You'll need all of us to help!"

"I don't know—"

"In the name of God, we have to find him and get out of this place!" Aymdahle shouted passionately. "We can join hands or spread out or whatever we have to do!"

"That's right!" George Flanders agreed with an enthusiasm seldom displayed during the ordeal. "If we go in together we can rescue the boy!"

Doyle had no chance to object because the group moved almost as one toward him. There was no plan in their action, only a sense of urgency that told them they had to be somewhere other than this chamber when time ran out.

"Wait here!" Roger ordered, taking Anjanette by the shoulder just as she was about to enter the field.

"I want to help!" she cried. "I can find him!"

"Anjanette, don't argue with me! I can't let you take a chance like this! Wait here, and I'll be out in a moment!" The writer waited no longer but turned to the flashing wall, drew in a breath, as Doyle had done before him, and charged into the alien essence.

"You'd better come back!" Anjanette screamed at him through her tears. "You'd better!"

The storm, as the people discovered almost immediately, was based within their own minds and linked directly to the artificial brain of the craft itself. Doyle had been extremely perceptive in describing the effect of the phenomenon in externalizing certain portions of their thoughts, but he had not realized that the mechanism went beyond an illusionary level. This was a place designed for *creative* experience.

Doyle returned to the ocean when he joined the others in the search for Bobby. He tried to see through what he believed to be a facade formed by the twisting of light rays and locate the child within the enclosure. When that effort failed, he changed his approach; ignoring the surrounding vision he walked forward with both arms spread wide in the hope of encountering Bobby somewhere between that spot and the end of the field.

While the water he appeared to be moving through was not real and he was not in danger of filling his lungs with it, his mental self was interacting with the advanced technology of the ship. The ocean, what he knew of it and how he responded to it, were facts actually rushing into the craft's memory banks in preparation for a reconstruction of the environment he chose. Doyle was accomplishing this purely by chance, without the active cooperation and awareness for which the equipment had been built.

George Flanders expected to find himself in another world due to what Doyle had told the group, so he was not upset to be surrounded suddenly by his home in Indiana. That was what he wanted desperately, to be at home with his family, his wife, Evelyn, and his sons and daughters . . .

When he thought of them, they appeared, right there in his living room, but there was no joy in their faces, only the constant masks of tolerance and poorly hidden disgust.

"I'm sorry," he cried. "What do you want me to

say, what do you want me to do?"

For some reason, Daniel Levya suddenly materialized in George's home, and he was standing at the front door, opening it while he motioned to George with a friendly smile.

"Get out!" Flanders screamed. "I'm not going to stay on the ship! I want to get away, like everybody else, to get home to my family!"

But the escape that Levya was offering was more of an alternative than Flanders realized.

Gloria Thirkell was no longer in the ship according to her perception; instead she was back in the ages of the great thinkers of human history, interviewing them. Antonio Arbolada found himself in the suspension chamber once more, though now all the aliens were alive, awake, and eager to impart to him all that they knew of the Universe beyond his small solar system. Susan Leipnitz discovered the exquisite reality of a lifelong fantasy, as a number of her fellow searchers were doing at the same moment, but Kay Aymdahle was forcing herself to claw her way through a cavern bursting with gigantic spiders and slugs, the two creatures she most feared in actual life.

And all of them were mixing reality with their dreams.

Roger Griffin was walking on a bridge. Below him lay the galaxy in its stardusted immensity, overhead was a wonderfully blue sky decorated with mountainous white clouds. There was no beginning or ending to the bridge, and though he felt an elation unlike any other he could recall, he had no idea why this particular image had been snatched from his mind. It corresponded to nothing that he knew, either in experience or invention.

His steps on the somewhat aged wooden bridge made a comforting rhythm, and several moments passed before he realized that someone was following him. Turning swiftly, he found himself staring into the face of a young man he had never met before, but he was also a young man Roger knew as fully and intimately as he knew himself.

"Hi, Roger," the man said cheerfully. "Or should I call you Dad? Or Brother?"

"Eric," Griffin responded in near-breathless wonder. "Eric Hudson from *Pursuit On Theta Gamma*! But—you aren't real. You're a character..."

"I didn't exist until you wrote your first novel, Roger. Now I'm alive not only here, in this psychic cloud, but also in the minds of everyone who's ever read that book. Strong as half a dozen gorillas, quick as a cat, hedonistic as you always wanted to be, I guess I really am *you*, in a magnified version. We all are, to a certain extent."

Gasping, Griffin looked about to find hundreds of men, women, children, and intelligent non-human creatures stepping out of the clouds and surrounding him with eager questions and comments. Roger was overwhelmed. He recognized every one instinctively, even those who looked nothing like the cover and interior illustrations that various artists had supplied for his works. And they were all so vibrantly *alive* and joyous at finally meeting him.

"Don't be nervous, old boy," Hudson laughed from his side. "We love you, even those of us you saw fit to kill off! We've been waiting for this meeting for years!"

Emotion flooded through Griffin, bringing tears to his eyes and tightening his throat. "My God, oh . . . oh, my children," Roger cried. He and Maureen had been unable to have children, but the constant pain of that reality vanished as he rushed forward with arms spread to embrace them.

"We've always loved you because you first loved us, Roger," Hudson whispered.

Peter Stallybrass had not been physically able to join the others when they rushed from the transit car to catch Bobby. He was very near death, and he accepted it with calm sadness.

But when he heard the wind suddenly increase to near hurricane velocity and the awestruck comments from the others concerning the mysterious light display, he dredged up enough strength to prop himself in the doorway and view the phenomenon. When he witnessed the disappearance of Bobby and Doyle even his open mind was strained to accept it. But the sight of Doyle's partial reappearance forced him to believe he had begun to hallucinate.

After the others entered the field, leaving only Anjanette behind, Stallybrass called her back to him, straining to be heard over the roaring winds. She swiftly repeated what Doyle had said about the interior of the field.

"Then the activity somehow draws memories from the minds of those who enter it?" he asked the girl.

"I guess so," she answered. "But I don't know how or why."

"It must be another recreational device, perhaps even tied in to the computer that runs this craft. Think of what we might be able to discover in just a few minutes in there!"

"We don't *have* a few minutes!" Anjanette cried. "We have to find the escape hatch!"

"Yes, yes, of course. Run back to the field, but don't enter it, do you understand? We wouldn't want you to become lost in there, as well." Stallybrass watched the girl as she hurried back to the very edge of the phenomenon, and then he nodded to himself, as if arriving at a final solution. Fighting the pain, he turned back inside the car and limped to where Frances Claire lay, unconscious but obviously still suffering from her many injuries. "Wake up, my dear," he said, shaking her gently. "The others still have some chance of escaping, but I fear we have passed that point."

Cecil Treacher had drifted in and out of consciousness following the short battle with Doyle in the suspension chamber. When awake, it was obvious that he had no real understanding of where he was or what was happening. So the other members of the group had decided that the best they could do for the man was to allow him to relax in the thick cushioning and keep him from being tossed to the floor during the high-speed transfers. He had taken no interest when the others left the car, but seemed fascinated by Stallybrass's approach to Frances.

"Hey, old man, what are you doing?" the soldier asked, sitting up.

"Nothing that concerns you, lad. Go back to

sleep." Peter carefully helped a confused Frances to her feet. The elderly woman hardly had the strength to breathe any longer, and a stream of fresh blood bubbled from her lips with each exhalation.

"You going on a date, gaff?" Treacher inquired.

A smile rose from somewhere to flash across Stallybrass' face. "Yes, son. I suppose that we do have a date together."

"Is this a nightclub? I sure could use a pint. I think I got a quid somewhere on me."

"It's no nightclub. You just wait here and you'll be fine in a few minutes."

Working as hard as he could, Stallybrass helped Frances from the car and into the billowing atmosphere of the golden room, patting her shoulder to comfort the quietly weeping woman. They didn't take the path followed by those who had gone before; instead, both understanding that they could not withstand even one more trip in the vehicle, moved to the right as they left the car, swiftly leaving Treacher's sight.

"Have a time, gaffer!" Cecil called after them. "Drink one for me, won't you? And tell them Treacher is still at his post, leading the way!" He laughed shrilly, holding the sides of his head in his hands and rolling into an almost fetal position. "Treacher's at his post and God is in His Heaven and all's right by me! I think I'm dying! Mother! Where's the goddamned key? I can't find it!"

In a high, breaking voice he began to sing a song he had learned in school twenty years earlier.

James Aymdahle had gone into the storm determined to find the frightened child, carry him out, and then break from this hellish prison before the most terrible event that he could imagine took place. But his resolve weakened swiftly before the parade of images that were stolen from his thoughts and played out before his eyes. He wandered through scenes from his childhood, as well as lands that he had never consciously constructed, and his steps carried him into revelations about himself that were beyond any form of self-analysis. He had known that other men had such darkness within themselves, but he had never suspected that *he* . . .

These disturbing sights were brushed aside, however, when he entered the temple.

It was a large, ancient building that had been designed and built in the days when craftsmanship was taken for granted; Aymdahle knew that it stretched high above his head even though the dim light in the silent room was concentrated at the front of the long aisle in the area of the pulpit. A man stood in that globe of light . . . he even seemed to be emitting it, and though his back was turned and he was far ahead of James, the evangelist could tell that he was a tall, slender man whose very presence exuded benevolent strength.

"Hello!" Aymdahle called out, and the word echoed through the dark reaches of the temple. The man appeared not to have heard him. "Who are you? Can you help us?" The man remained turned away from James.

He was desperate now and growing more so by the second. The noise of his running feet on the hardwood floor sounded to him like the chattering of Treacher's gun back in the suspension room, where it now lay. As he ran frantically toward the pulpit, he realized that *this* was his race to safety, not the trials he had been going through out there in the belly of the machine.

"Who are you?" he screamed again.

The space seemed to expand even as he crossed it, so that he remained a steady distance away from the man. He ran and called alternately, unsure as to whether he should approach this silent icon, but after both his energy and his passion had begun to ebb he stopped his futile chase and slipped to his knees on the smooth floor.

"All right, damn you!" he shouted in rage. "If you won't help me, then you'll go up with this ship, too! We'll be condemned together!" He dropped his face into his hands, feeling his sense of impotence and fury begin to boil into his fingers. He was not afraid of death. He never had been afraid of dying, especially since he had entered into the fold of the protected. But he was terrified of *not* dying when the ship lifted.

"James," said a quietly authoritative, yet tender voice.

Aymdahle raised his eyes to find the man now standing directly before him. But he was no longer dressed in modern wear. The man wore a robe and sandals, and his beard and hair were so familiar . . .

"It shall be well, James," the man said.

"My Lord," Aymdahle whispered reverently. "My Holy Savior."

The man extended his right hand to James, who stood slowly before him. The glow that had shown about the pulpit in the midst of the darkness now surrounded the two. As James allowed his devotion to flow in the words of worship that he was unable to constrain, the penetrating light began to gain in power until within moments it was a white fire that shut away the figures at its heart and blazed like the very sun in the retreating darkness of James Aymdahle's world.

And it continued to grow.

"Something's wrong," Eric Hudson said.

The wonderful hubbub that had engulfed Roger Griff on finding himself in the living sphere of his imagination suddenly dropped into silence. Griffin, his face flushed with joy, looked to his first important creation quizzically.

"Someone else in the field is overdoing it," Hudson explained as he raised his face into the soft breeze like an animal sniffing for scents. Of course, he had the sharpened senses of an animal in addition to his great speed and strength. "It's a man, a fanatic, and he's broadcasting almost pure psychic energy. With the computer amplifying his emissions, this could get extremely dangerous."

"Maybe Roger should leave the field," Diane Prentiss, from *We Regret to Inform You...* observed.

"What? I don't understand," Roger said. "What's wrong?"

Hudson jerked his thumb over the side of the bridge, and the characters who had grown out of the author's life's work began to step over as casually as if they were moving into another room.

"No time to explain further, Rog, you've got to move out and get behind some closed doors before things go into recyclic reaction. We'll alert everyone else in here and see if we can shut down this

Aymdahle's broadcast system, but we want you safe first," he explained.

"James is causing it?"

"Bingo. Halohead himself. He's trying to create a *Divinity*. Look at that." Hudson pointed off the right side of the bridge where the blackness of the Milky Way melded into the vivid blue of the atmospheric sky. A stark, colorless light was beginning to radiate from an empty point where the panoramas met, and its strength was washing out the hues of Griffin's reality the way a projected slide can be outshone by a naked bulb. "That's going to get bad fast, and the damage to your corporeal form could be fatal. Diane will show you the way."

"But the others who came in with me—"

"We'll take care of them; don't worry."

"And little Bobby?"

Hudson grinned and thumped his own chest. "Delivered to you personally, I promise."

Roger felt it all slipping away again, just as it had when he had looked into Maureen's still features. "But I can't leave you now! You'll come with us, won't you?"

"Not this time. But everything will be fine. We can't die, you know, not as long as we're alive up here," Hudson pointed to Griffin's head, "and in those thousands of other skulls that you've indoctrinated."

"I won't leave you behind!"

"So you'll be taking us along. Just remember, somebody has to get out of this thing to write it up for the rest of the world, and who's better than you?" Still grinning, Hudson stepped over the side of the bridge as had the hundreds of others before him and began trotting along the skyway in search of Bobby. "Take him away, Diane."

The tall young woman took Griffin's arm and began to lead him along the bridge as the brilliance to the right continued its even increase. "Listen Roger," she said eagerly, "we've really got to do this again sometime, because I've got a million questions to ask and at least that many things to tell you."

Griffin heard her, but he couldn't tear his eyes from the glowing fireball behind and the casual manner in which Eric Hudson was jogging apparently into the eye of its energy. Hudson seemed to feel the attention being directed at him, because he stopped briefly and turned to face him.

"Oh, and Roger," he shouted, "the earthquakes have really screwed up the automatic systems of the ship and did severe damage to the rear compartments, so be careful! The spot you want to press in the transit vehicle is in the lefthand column, sixth from the bottom! That'll deliver the car to the aft sector on the right floor, and the doorway to the spur should be flashing red by this time in the countdown, since it hasn't been secured! You'll have to reach it on your own, I'm afraid, but you can do it! *Adios*!"

And then he was gone into the spreading brilliance.

The whiteness grew like a rampaging beast.

The flood of colors that had wrapped the field earlier were seared and blown from the storm by its advance, so that there seemed to be a miniature sur evolving within the golden room. But there were no eyes to view the spectacle: Patrice Rutherford and Cecil Treacher were unconscious, and Frances Claire and Peter Stallybrass were gone.

Just before the transformation of the display was completed, Antonio Arbolada staggered out of it, led by a portly young man who was entirely unknown to him. Before the Spanish scientist could ask anything of his guide, however, the latter had merged with the field and was gone.

In quick succession, eight more of the thirteen people who had vanished in the seething mass of color reappeared, each directed by an individual who was unknown to him or her, and their states of confusion were monumental and identical. Roger Griffin was the last to return from the influence of the effect, led by an attractive young woman who immediately disappeared in the same manner as all the guides before her.

"What's going on here?" Aaron Doyle demanded over the wailing of the wind and an urgent new note that seemed connected with the ever-heightening whiteness. "Who were those people and where did they come from? The man who brought me out said that there was some kind of danger from the light!"

"I can't explain it now!" Griffin shouted back. "They were telling the truth, and we have to get in the car and close the doors before the crisis is reached! Hurry! Where's Anjanette?"

"Here you go, Roger, the Kiddy Corps has arrived!" said Eric Hudson as he stepped from the now solid white globe with Bobby in his left arm and Anjanette clutching his right hand. Both youngsters were ecstatic. Anjanette ran quickly to Griffin, and Kay Aymdahle rushed to take the boy from Hudson.

"Thank you, Eric! You've saved us all!" Griffin literally yelled.

"Who, me? We both know who I *really* am, don't we, Rog?" Hudson answered.

With the speed of a whip, Doyle's right fist jabbed out and closed on a large clump of Hudson's shirt. "Now *I'm* going to find out!" he exclaimed. "What's going on?"

The younger man's eyes narrowed slightly, though the smile never left his lips. "My friend," he said in a low voice that somehow carried through the combined cacophony of the wind and the shrieking menace within the field, "you have approximately one hundred and fourteen seconds to live unless you get your tail into one of those cars, because that nutcake back there is going to destroy every living thing in this room with his religious emanations. That's not enough time to begin explaining my existence to you." Using only the thumb and forefinger of his left hand, Hudson easily pulled Doyle's clenched fist free of his clothing, "So I advise you to get moving. Until next time, Rog." Like a shadow, he slipped back into the energy that had formed him. Doyle could only stare in shock.

"I saw my mother in there!" Anjanette cried excitedly. "Well, not really my mother, but I went in—I had to find you, Mr. Griffin, so I did—and the computer that controls the ship reached into my mind! My mother is alive! I *know* she is!"

"That's marvelous!" Griffin responded. "Right

now we have to get into the car! We have less than a minute and a half!"

The two broke into a run for the open doorway, and the rest of the stunned group followed them. Doyle twisted the door into the closed position as soon as the last person, Kay Aymdahle, wearily entered.

"James?" the woman said, her eyes scanning the extent of the car. "Wait a minute, he's not here!"

"Mrs. Aymdahle," Griffin said, "I'm sorry. Your husband is still in the field. Actually, he's causing it; his fervent religious beliefs are being magnified by the field's own energies, and this is going to lead to a dangerous cyclic explosion any moment now. We have to send this car on its way."

"You shut up!" Kay screamed. "We aren't going to leave him!"

Kay dropped Bobby into Susan's arms and pushed past Griffin to leap onto the couch next to the control panel. Before anyone could stop her, she twisted the knob. The door had opened only a crack when the people within the car were made witness to the terrible cataclysm that was unfolding just outside their protective cell.

The white light that had been dazzling to the eye seconds earlier was now a burning tidal wave of energy, and it burst through the opening with such power that the vision of everyone within was seared into agonizing blankness. The whistling noise that accompanied the light had swelled to a piercing blast of pain that cut to the center of their minds. Blinded and deafened as they were by just this momentary display of the destructive power, they would have been destroyed by it in a few more seconds had not Doyle seized the knob at the instant the door broke its seal.

His fingers closed about the rounded device despite his blindness and he turned it in the reverse direction almost by reflex. The door stopped moving and then slid shut, blocking out the withering radiance and reducing the sound by about two-thirds.

"We can't go back for him!" Doyle shouted to the group. "We've got to get away from this place!"

"James!" Kay wailed.

Susan Leipnitz had been looking away from the door when the light flooded in, so her vision, while affected, was not so badly impaired, and this allowed her to glance around the car.

"There are others missing, too!" she cried. "Elizabeth went with us after Bobby! And where's Doctor Stallybrass? And Mrs. Claire?"

"They must have gone into the field to help us and been caught too near the energy to be brought out by my people!" Griffin said.

"They went on a date," stated Cecil Treacher, but his ramblings went unnoticed in the atmosphere of panic.

"If they're not in here, they're outside, and we can't open the door again!" Flanders said frantically. "Let's go, man, now!"

Doyle's eyes had cleared enough for him to pick out the dots on the panel next to him by that time. Aymdahle had created his own end through the fervor of his convictions, so little pity could be spared for him; but the women, Frances and Elizabeth, had trusted him to bring them out of this madness, and he had failed them. Stallybrass was gone, as well, and the group might not have reached this far toward safety without his brilliant mind and great courage. If they were down there, in that erupting chaos, could they still be alive? Could anyone save them?

His duty was to the living.

"They can't be helped," he said in a burst of emotional anguish. "We have to go on. I'm activating the car."

"Aaron, wait!" Griffin's memory had abruptly returned completely to him. "I know how to reach the spurs! It came to me in the field, from the computer!"

"Well, what do I do?"

"It's the sixth selection from the bottom in the lefthand column! That will take us to the rearmost compartment, and the spur is located on the other side of it! Left side, sixth up!"

"And it's an escape hatch?"

"My God, I don't know!" Realization raced through Griffin like a numbing fluid. "I didn't ask!"

Doyle cursed. "It's all we have, so everyone get ready! Make sure that Patrice is protected!" His vision was almost normal by then, and as the others hurried to the protection of the couches, he stared hard at the control panel. Sixth from the bottom, left side. Just another point of light, but it had to be the right one. Something awful was about to occur in the golden room, and he didn't know if they'd have another opportunity to find the escape route. "Ready?" he asked. "Now!"

The internal systems of the ancient technological wonder functioned to their full capacity once more and hurled the group of frightened people toward their destination. While they were yet in the grip of the awesome acceleration, a massive explosion rocked the room they had just fled, but it wasn't until the car had reached its next terminal that the shockwave was able to overtake them with a final taste of the incredible power of James Aymdahle's obsession.

The blast tore the double-chambered door from its mooring and forced it inward, allowing the tremendous energies that had fuelled it to flash inside the transit vehicle and bath the two people in all of its power. Had they been irradiated by the power a second before, when it had existed primarily as light and heat, before the moment of transformation, the pair would have been incinerated. As it was, they were largely unaffected by the radiance and protected from the fury of the explosion by the metal of the car itself, though they were knocked unconscious by the combination of the two.

Peter Stallybrass awoke first. There was a harsh ringing in his ears, and, if anything, he felt even worse than he had when he and Frances had left the first car to hide in the one directly to the right of it. He had known then that Doyle and Thirkell and the others would not have agreed to leave him behind as they continued their wild search for escape, so he had counted upon hiding out until they departed. Frances would not have survived another high speed trip any more than he would have.

By trial and error, he had discovered how to open the door to the vehicle just enough to allow him to peer out and eavesdrop on the activities of those at the central field in the room. While most of their words were lost to him in the rising noises, he was able to understand that James Aymdahle's blind devotion had incited some sort of malfunction within the system. When the others returned to their car, he closed the door to his, hoping that the field would not be totally wrecked by the intrusion of the novices into the effect.

Frances would be able to spend her last hours in far more comfort through the intervention of the phenomenon, and he'd have the answers to all the questions he had formulated since his first conscious thought.

But the explosion promised to have ruined that.

When he first realized that he had survived the blast, he thought that he must have been blinded as well as deafened, because he was lost in darkness. After a short time, however, he caught sight of a weak, multi-colored glow from somewhere near the front of the vehicle and understood that the lighting system, rather than his eyes, had been destroyed.

Crawling painfully to where the door had been blown away, Stallybrass gazed at the incredible devastation that Aymdahle had created: the ceiling, which had been alive with soft radiance, was completely dark; the countless doors to the countless vehicles servicing the room had been blasted open to expose, variously, the empty cars and the even more desolate passageways that had contained them; and, worst of all, the glistening captured rainbow that had been a huge, vibrant field was now reduced to a mere parody of it former self, a ball of muted colors no more than three feet high by ten across. It was the feeble light from this that allowed Peter to survey the remains of the room.

He sighed and lowered his face.

When Stallybrass opened his eyes again, he was startled to find that the glow that was seeping into the vehicle was perceptibly brighter. His desperate eyes sought out the source once more and confirmed the fact that the field had strengthened in the few seconds that he had been in the open doorway. It was now as tall as a man and correspondingly broad.

"Frances, it works!" he shouted joyously, though his own voice was an unintelligible roar within his head. "We can go into it!"

His delight brought him to his feet, and in the steadily more visible interior of the vehicle, he found Frances Claire and carefully awakened her. He didn't understand how she had lived through the last trial.

"It's all right now," he whispered without realizing that he was speaking.

Frances moved her lips weakly in the half-light, but Stallybrass heard not a syllable.

"Hearing's gone!" he shouted, happily for all of the seriousness of the statement. "That doesn't matter now, though, if you'll come with me!"

It was obvious that Frances didn't understand what was occurring, and it was almost as clear that she didn't know where she was anymore. There wasn't much time left to either of them.

Stallybrass shouldn't have possessed the strength to lift the woman to her feet with his one arm, just as she shouldn't have been able to walk from the transit car while leaning against him. But the two friends, who had met only a few hours before, drew from one another and gave freely the energy that was needed to make their way down the long slope to the burgeoning field of color. Maintaining their bond of mutual strength and trust, Frances Marian Lawson Claire and Peter Greyson Stallybrass stepped arm in arm into the brightly shining heart of the future.

There were so many questions to be answered.

Chapter Eleven

The shock wave caught up to the vehicle carrying the thirteen refugees just after it stopped at its final destination and before Doyle could recover enough to open the door. It was in no way comparable to the rumbling catastrophe of the earthquake and did no significant damage to the people in the car, but it made them realize the monumental power of James Aymdahle's obsession.

"Good thing we were in here!" George Flanders said. He had come through the entire ordeal virtually unscratched, and now he confirmed his on-going good luck by standing and finding no new injuries. "That guy must have gone up like Little Boy over Hiroshima."

"Mr. Flanders, please!" Susan Leipnitz whispered tersely from his side. She pointed to a distraught Kay Aymdahle at the front of the vehicle.

"That was her husband, you know."

Flanders coughed in embarrassment. "Sure, kid, sorry."

Doyle stretched himself cautiously as he stood before the control panel. "So this is the place, right, Griffin?" he asked without turning away from the board.

"According to the information I was given, the door to the spur lies just across the room," answered Roger. "I can't guarantee that it's an escape tunnel, of course, but where else can we go?"

"Time?" Doyle called.

Gloria Thirkell glanced at her watch, which had survived the long trial intact. "It's late, Aaron, I have twenty-four minutes after ten. We have twenty-nine minutes left."

"Let's hope that this room isn't very wide," muttered Doyle. He knew that he could get through even a mile-wide chamber in half an hour, but there was the crippled Rutherford girl and the generally poor condition of almost everyone else to take into account. He forced himself to smile enthusiastically. "This is the last run we'll have to make, so let's see what we're up against, shall we?" He dialled open the car door and looked out.

"Damn!" yelled Flanders as the room was revealed. It was near the opening.

It was at least half a mile across and five decks deep, but this alone was not what was so disheartening. The last quake, which had apparently caused the automatic systems of the craft to increase the airflow to dangerous levels, also appeared to have centered most of its destructive power on this rear portion: the huge chamber had been packed with equipment of all types, entirely beyond the imagination of the observers. Now this equipment was scattered about the wide floor in a state of destruction; the overhead lighting system had been knocked out; and, most discouraging, columns of fire had sprouted from countless rents in the piping and floor and walls where exotic gasses had mixed with the synthetically produced Earth atmosphere and blazed like gargantuan torches.

"We'll never get through that," Kenneth Braam observed darkly, his eyes reflecting the towering flames.

"He's right," Kay Aymdahle said. "That's an inferno! We should have stayed in the other room!"

"No, we can make it," Doyle said firmly. "There are open stretches of hundreds of yards in there, and we can always go around the fires and the larger chunks of machinery."

"But we can't even *see* the other side!" she countered. "Do *you* see a red, blinking light on a door out there anywhere?"

"We could work our way around the room next to the wall, and we'd be sure to pass the right door that way," Gloria Thirkell said.

From the back of the group, Con Jeffcries spoke up, "That would take too long! We have time for one shot, and I'd bet that, since the spurs are located at the very rear of the ship, the doorway is directly across from us! We've got to decide right now: how are we going to go?"

"Across!" Doyle said. "That's where I'm headed! If anybody wants to try another direction or use the car to retreat back into the body of the ship, it's up to you!" This tactic had worked on several occasions earlier, and he hoped that it still possessed the power to move them.

There was a brief discussion, one filled with fear and uncertainty, but the pressure of the time kept it short. After a moment of wrestling with their anxieties and terrors, all of the passengers except Patrice Rutherford and Cecil Treacher agreed to follow Doyle's bid. Patrice was still unconscious, as she had been through much of the desperate latter portion of the escape attempt, and Treacher was lying on one of the couches, watching the proceedings with no evident interest. Aaron stepped to the side of the young woman.

"What about her? I guess we'll have to leave her behind," Braam said.

Doyle curled his lips back from his teeth as he looked at the balding scientist with unadulterated disgust. "You keep away from me, you son of a bitch!" he warned in a tone that was heard only by the other man. "I don't know why you're here! I can't understand how Stallybrass could have been incinerated back there, or even Aymdahle or Elizabeth . . . I can't make myself see the justice of their deaths while you, who fought us every step of the way, who wanted *everyone* to go back into the tour room, you stand here ready to escape! I won't have you in my life, Braam, so don't bother to worry about how Patrice will be taken care of. Just look after your own ass, the way you have been since the minute you stepped into this ship!"

Without waiting for a response from the stunned

man, Doyle stooped to Patrice's side and lifted her easily into his arms before standing as if she weighed nothing at all.

Due to the severity of her injuries, the rigors of the high-speed journey and the numerous shocks that had passed through the car had left her unaffected, but this gentle action seeped through the pain into her mind and caused her to stir. "Gerry?" she whispered through dry lips.

"Just relax," Doyle answered softly. "You're okay now."

She smiled and settled back into that insulated state that separated her from the consuming pain.

Despite the dark, flame-broken atmosphere that awaited them, the vehicle emptied quickly after Doyle left with Patrice in his arms, but Jefferies, who was in the rear of the group, realized that someone was being left behind. He stepped back into the car.

"Hey, Treach, aren't you coming along?" he asked.

The English soldier raised his head from the cushioning.

"We're leaving, understand?" Jefferies added. "Escape time, home free, and all of that. Come on."

"What's your name, boy?" Treacher said thickly, as if his mouth were filled with pudding.

Jefferies sighed. "That couldn't matter less right now, laddy, just come on." He reached down to take the other's arm.

Treacher pulled free and lay back on the couch. "I think I'd rather sleep here. Turn out the light."

"Hell, man, we don't have time for this!"

Treacher laughed. "None of us have any time,

turtle, it's too late. There's ice cream in the air tonight." Saying this, he smiled at something Con was unable to see and dropped his head onto the thick cushioning.

Jefferies knew with a sick certainty that Cecil Treacher would go no further after coming so far. To be sure, he carefully turned the man's face toward his and gazed into the open yet sightless eyes.

"Isn't he coming?" asked Flanders from the doorway.

"Not tonight," Jefferies said hoarsely. He closed the soldier's eyes and walked from the vehicle.

Flanders started to follow, but suddenly the vision that he had experienced in the golden room —Daniel Levya returning to the depths of the monstrous vessel in search of a lost son and beckoning to George to go with him—sprang into his mind. He was on the verge of freedom now, further along than seven of his original companions had managed to get; maybe all he had to do was cross this last room, open one more door, and walk out alive and whole, something that he had not really believed possible at the beginning of this thing. He was *that* close.

And he would go back to a family that treated him like so much excrement stuffed into a suit of clothes.

Back in the first hallway, when everyone had been exchanging their histories, it had been easy to lie, to say that his wife and kids had remained on top to ride and eat; that way he hadn't had to admit that for one of the few times since he had married he'd gone against their wishes to do something that *he* thought would be entertaining. The Saucer had seemed like nothing more than a dull, stultifying museum to them, certainly nothing that they wanted to waste a vacation on, and when he had insisted on going, the blowup of all blowups had taken place.

Which was why Evelyn and the kids were now in Orlando, Florida, while he stood in the interior of an activated alien vessel poised on the verge of a trip to the stars.

He couldn't have faced that humiliation, the admission that he had as much say in the running of his life as the family dog, so he had invented the story about having them along. No one would have to know that his demands had lost out to the lure of Disney World. Would it really be worth going back to that? He *did* love them, after all, apparently more than they loved him. But if this ship were preparing to leap back into eternity . . . might that not be preferable to his existence as an oversized, loud-mouthed coward? Who could know what it might be like up there?

George stared at the body of the English soldier. You and me for the stars, bud? he thought.

On the other hand, if he did escape, he would be one of the most unique people in history, a man who had made a run through a vessel from another world and lived to tell the tale. This realization rushed through his body like a wave of pleasant heat. A claim like that could lead to television, maybe even books and a movie about him. A claim like that could easily change a Nobody into a Somebody.

"So long, Limey," he said to Treacher's corpse. "I

got places to go!" He rushed out of the car to catch up to the others.

At first the pathway through the room was clear and straight, lighted in flickering crimson by the many fires blazing fiercely throughout it. The destroyed machinery formed ragged and hazardous mountains all about them, but Doyle in the lead with Patrice in his arms always found a way through the debris. The disrupted air circulation caused the burning gas jets to whip wildly in every direction, creating the first real barrier to their escape.

"How do we get around *that*?" shouted Gloria Thirkell as they drew up before a literal geyser of flame that was shooting from the floor seventy feet ahead of them. Piles of machinery and shattered flooring on either side of the fire locked them into a valley-like trench.

"We backtrack!" Braam answered. The fire and wind formed a terrible roar that was difficult to speak over. "We'll have to find a place where we can slip through to the other side of this rubble!"

"But that will take at least five minutes!" she responded. "We have only twenty left!"

"What must be done, must be—"

Doyle interrupted the shouted conference, "This metal must be a highly advanced alloy," he said, indicating a collection of plates that had been ripped from the floor when the titanic machine that had been affixed to them was toppled by the series of quakes. "And it's got to be heat resistant! Get a long piece of it to use as a shield! With a man at each end to hold it up, we can crouch down behind it, sidle along as close to the perimeter as possible and get through that way!"

"Buy, Doyle," Braam began, "the wind is whipping that flame around like—"

"Did you hear me, Thirkell?" Doyle shouted.

She nodded and pointed to Flanders, Jefferies, and Arbolada. "You three, give me a hand with this!"

The group used the unsteady illumination of the fountain of fire to select a chunk of metal nearly four feet wide and twelve long. Though the plate was over three inches thick, they were startled by its weight when they began to separate it from the pile.

"This stuff doesn't weigh as much as balsa!" Jefferies said as he effortlessly lifted an end of it with one hand. With the knuckles of his other, he rapped the panel sharply. "Hard as steel, though!"

"We should hope that it is a non-conductor of heat!" Arbolada noted.

The shield's lack of weight allowed the three men to handle it without difficulty, Jefferies taking the lead, Arbolada the center, and Flanders bringing up the rear. The group ducked behind the plate and began to move quickly in the direction of the burning jet, which was being twisted about by the high winds like a flaring whip.

They made good time in the beginning. Bobby was terrified, but with Kay and Susan holding him between themselves, he was in no danger of breaking free as he had done in the golden room. As they neared the base of the fire, the air temperature rose steadily, but the men holding the plate weren't able to detect any corresponding rise in the metal's temperature.

THE ASGARD RUN

Halfway past the fiery obstruction, the group reached its closest point to the blaze, about thirty-five feet from its base. Here, the air smelled like acid, but Doyle gambled that in spite of the discomfort, no one would suffer severe or permanent damage from the heat, if it got no worse. Nearly as difficult to tolerate was the monstrous noise created by the flaming column.

Doyle was near the head of the procession, still carrying the apparently lifeless Patrice Rutherford. At regular intervals he braved the certainty of singed hair and blistered flesh to peer over the top of the barrier and gauge the unpredictable gyrations of the flame. Suddenly he realized that the blaze was about to vent its full power on them at the command of the cyclonic winds.

"Get down!" he shouted.

Gloria Thirkell, behind Doyle, responded with, "What did you say?" It was clear that no one else had been able to hear him over the noise.

The fire was heading straight for them, blown almost parallel to the floor and perpendicular to its point of origin, like a blazing scythe. To guarantee immediate reaction, Aaron released his hold on Patrice just enough to slap the metal shield out of the hands of the three men while bellowing, "Get down and hold your breaths!"

The plate thumped edge-on to the floor, and Doyle yanked it into a diagonal angle against the machinery behind them. The startled group ducked behind the plate as the flaming jet splashed over them.

It didn't last long, not more than half a second, but for that crystalized instant, the entire world was fire. The flames clawed like a rabid beast trying to sear the bodies of the huddled people.

The makeshift lean-to deflected the direct bursts of the flame and the incredible insulating qualities of the metal kept the group protected. Although the temperature behind the plate soared with the blast of flame, it was mild compared with the intense heat licking the other side.

The column was gone within the second, driven in a different direction by the winds.

Though there were a number of other blazing leaks in the chamber, none were so dangerously situated that the group had to approach so closely again. When they had put the tower of fire some seventy feet behind them, they dropped the plate and resumed their agonizing progress to the other side.

Eighteen minutes remained until the deadline.

When they were two-thirds of the way to the opposite wall, Doyle's eyes widened as he spotted the glowing outline of a huge doorway in the distance. A moment later his spirits sagged at the sight of a long, high ridge of rubble that had once been a battery of sophisticated equipment. Now it resembled several city blocks dumped haphazardly before them. The top of what they hoped was the door barely protruded over this metallic range.

"I suppose we couldn't spare the time to work our way around this!" Jefferies said as the group drew up before the mound.

"Sixteen minutes to go!" Thirkell said.

"I didn't think we could," Jefferies said to himself.

They began to pick their way over and through

the shattered mass. Luck favored them with a comparatively low and uncluttered valley between two colossal hills of wreckage. As they moved quickly through it, rugged pipes and other shards of metal caught at their legs and tore their clothing, but they had become inured to minor injuries and were soon standing at the peak of the rise.

"Hurry up so that you can put me down!" Anjanette said to Griffin, who was carrying her over the rough portions. "I don't want to tire you out in case we have to run some more!"

"My dear," he answered, carefully picking his way in the gloom, "please don't worry yourself! This close to that stoplight of a door, I could carry the entire assembly on my shoulders while tap dancing the rest of the way!" He looked up at the flashing doorway to realize that the entire panel was blinking in rhythmic, dazzlingly bright red bursts. It was at least thirty feet high.

"You have a gift of lyric expression!" Arbolada observed with a smile.

"A minor aptitude with which I have successfully bluffed my way through a large portion of my life!" Roger stated. He stepped carefully onto a piece of shattered machinery that was positioned on the edge of a slide-like chunk of metal which slanted sharply into the blackness of the floor below. Arbolada stepped beside him.

The clump of equipment gave way beneath them.

As Anjanette screamed, Arbolada desperately reached for purchase, but the three of them pitched forward into the darkness. The slide was extremely smooth, unlike the rugged plain about it, and they fell with no means of slowing themselves. Had the wedge of metal extended only to the floor of the room, they would have hit hard, perhaps hard enough to leave them unconscious, but the others could then have carried them the few remaining yards to the doorway. But the floor at this point had succumbed to the stresses placed on it by the events of the last few hours, and it had collapsed into the level below to create a black, gaping maw that waited to swallow the three.

Cries and the shrieking wind swirled about them as they fell, barely touching the angled metal. Griffin who had never thought of himself as athletic, saw the open death below them and threw himself wildly toward what he thought was the nearest edge of the hole.

He hit with the impact of a man being struck by a small car, and his shock was doubled when Arbolada came down hard on his back. The slender Spaniard slipped backward, away from Griffin and toward the gap in the floor. He stopped his fall by digging both hands into Roger's legs as he dropped into the opening. Roger felt himself being dragged from the narrow lip of the hole along with Arbolada and reached out with his left hand blindly, wrapping his fingers around a wrist-thick pipe.

Hold on! he screamed at himself. The entire lower portion of his body from the center of his chest was dangling in the nothingness that could have shot downward for two miles, for all he knew. His left arm felt as if it were being torn from his body.

But where was Anjanette?

Arbolada, screaming hysterically, clung to Roger's legs, but Roger suddenly realized that he had no

THE ASGARD RUN

idea what had happened to the young girl who was really responsible for his having come so far through this nightmare.

"*No!* Not her, not now!" he shouted madly.

Moments passed before he understood that he was holding the pipe with only his left hand because his right was closed firmly about one of Anjanette's wrists. She, too, was dangling below him in the darkness.

"Hold on, Anjanette!" he cried. "I can hear them coming to help us! Down here! Help!"

Normally the first to respond to emergencies throughout the run, Doyle, still carrying Patrice, was left behind by Jefferies, Thirkell, and Flanders. The three forgot about picking their way down the slope as they raced along the side of the treacherously smooth section of metal. They had seen Griffin and his companions fall onto it but had lost sight of the trio in the sharp shadows that cloaked the lower reaches of the room. The rescuers were within ten feet of the hole before they were able to see how precarious the situation was.

"Hurry! I can't hold on much longer!" Griffin yelled.

Jefferies reached the spot first and half-dived into the hole to drag Arbolada up over the head of the trembling Griffin.

"Where's the kid?" demanded Flanders.

"Down here!" Anjanette's voice called shrilly from the inky depths.

"I can't pull her up!" gasped Roger. "You'll have to pull us together!"

Slowly, carefully, and painfully Roger was pulled up over the edge of the hole and onto the floor.

When the girl's small hand emerged over the side, Jefferies again reached deeply into the hole to wrap both arms around her waist and hoist her to safety.

"Who's hurt and how bad?" Doyle asked upon arriving.

"My back," Arbolada gasped. "Wrenched it . . ."

"Anjanette?" asked Gloria.

The girl ignored the question and scrambled over to where Griffin lay. "Did you break any bones? That was awful! Can you go on? We'll carry you if we have to!" she said to him.

Roger struggled into a sitting position and chuckled slightly despite the new pain in his chest and back. "I'm fine, little one, just fine. You really don't believe that I'd allow my account of these peculiar happenings to end with the narrator being hauled out of the ship like a stranded whale do you?" He only hoped that he *could* still walk.

"If everyone's okay, we'd better be on with it!" Thirkell stated. "At most, we have twelve minutes!"

"It looks like a clear shot to the door!" Doyle said, "Let's go!"

Flanders and Jefferies helped Griffin and Arbolada to stand and made certain that the two could continue. Griffin knew that he could make it the rest of the way if he had to crawl on his elbows.

The remaining yards passed like inches. They had been subjected to dangers beyond all imagination in the twelve miles that they had crossed and now the goal that had drawn them through all of this was almost at their touch. The great door resembled all the others except for its peculiar, radiant color, but it represented to them a last shot at freedom.

A question that was vital to the moment hit Braam like a jolt of electricity. "Good God!" he shouted as they all stood at the foot of the door. "What's on the other side? We should have realized this at the beginning! We're *buried*! There's nothing on the other side but dirt!"

"No!" Kay Aymdahle shrieked.

"Wait! Don't panic!" Susan Leipnitz broke in. "It's all right. The UN scientific team maintains open shafts at both spurs! If we can open the door, we can climb out into the open! I thought you knew that!"

"Some of us did!" Gloria said with a touch of disgust. Arbolada nodded.

"Well, let's do what we came for!" Doyle said. He eased Patrice Rutherford into the waiting arms of Jefferies.

As they expected, there was a glowing panel at the right side of the door, though this one was much larger than the others, being a yard-wide bar that extended from the floor to a spot at least twelve feet above. It was beaming a steady, cherry red. Doyle used his right hand to press hard against the bar.

What did they expect at that moment? An explosion that would send the door smashing away from the ship? Or maybe the door would open to reveal a ladder that would lead them from the pit to salvation. Why not? Stranger things had proven real in this unearthly place.

Or did they expect *anything* to happen? Kenneth Braam had run with them all the way, but now, at the end of his tremendous effort, he thought that in another moment they'd be laughing and crying at the terrible joke they had played upon themselves.

The door moved.

With the timeless wailing of an alarm bell, the door began to rise from its eons of inactivity, slowly at first and then with a slick speed that carried it to the maximum height within half a minute. The group actually began cheering and clapping during this operation, and this outpouring of triumph continued as they crowded into the new opening.

But they weren't outside the vessel; they were in one more corridor. Although it was as tall and wide as those within the body of the craft, it was not another endless passage. This corridor was only about eighty yards long, and ended at another door, this one dull gray in color.

"Eight minutes!" Gloria shouted. "We have to get the second door open!"

"But I don't understand!" Susan said. "This doesn't look like an escape tunnel! What's it for?"

"I think it's a docking area!" Arbolada responded as he limped along next to her. "That room perhaps is for the transference of materials and this entire wall may open for easier access, but this tunnel was built in order to actually *insert* into other vessels in non-atmospheric conditions! It also serves as an escape dock! In space, lifeships could be launched through here in emergencies!"

They moved as fast as their injured bodies would carry them to the other end of the hall. There they found a control panel which looked identical to the one back in the tour room, the one which had failed to release them at the very beginning.

"The door could be designed to be operated on a special frequency broadcast from the lifeships, but we have to hope that this board also opens it!" Gloria said, studying the dozens of colorful squares on the panel.

"You can bet that it does," Aaron said, reaching by her, "just like you can bet that this is it!" He stabbed a red square at the very top of the board with his finger. Nothing happened. "Damn!" he spat. He began hitting all the squares viciously, in spite of Thirkell and Arbolada's cries of alarm.

In a near-repeat of the tour room experience, the lighting system went haywire, the temperature began to rise and fall wildly, and the noise level was multiplied by the new sounds that began to flow from the machinery around them. After an instant, Gloria and Antonio realized that this was their only hope and began to slam at the panel along with Doyle.

Jefferies, who had seen education and intelligence fail in situation after situation, had that feeling again. There was a lever next to the panel. It would have been considered small by the standards of the aliens, and there was nothing about it that was in the least significant; but that was it. Somehow, he knew. He flipped it unnoticed in the desperation that surrounded him.

"Something's happening!" Griffin shouted. "There's a buzzing—a hell of a noise, and it's coming from the other side, out there!"

Only a few dozen seconds had been wasted in the final corridor.

The buzzing noise must have had tremendous volume to be heard over the mad symphony in the hall and through the almost soundproof door, but

Roger could distinctly hear it in his right ear, the one pressed firmly against the door. And then he jerked his head away.

"It's stopped!" he shouted.

"What's happening now?" cried Braam.

"Nothing!" The writer's voice fell to inaudible levels. "Nothing."

With a tremble that they all felt, the final bar to freedom began to lift.

"It's opening, by heaven!" Griffin screamed in elation.

A wash of hot air was drawn from the burning room behind them and flushed through the opening, telling them that the way was not blocked on the other side. Most of them fell to their stomachs to peer beneath the edge as the door moved slowly and jerkily upward. When it had risen just over a foot, Jefferies wriggled under it to see what waited beyond. His joyous shout awakened a fountain of hope in their hearts.

"It's through! Christ, that noise must have been some kind of disintegration beam, because it's cut a round hole straight through to the side of the mountain, three or four hundred feet! I can see the sky and the stars!"

They could wait no longer. Copying Jefferies, all of them, even Arbolada, crawled beneath the sluggish door, with Doyle dragging the unconscious Patrice. The malfunctioning panel stopped no more than a yard above the floor, forcing the dozen survivors to leave the spacecraft in the same fashion in which they had entered it, twelve incredible miles back.

The hollowed cave was a technological marvel,

but none of them took notice as they made the last rush out of the side of the mountain and into a forest beneath a wonderfully wide and glittering sky.

Leaping into the fresh coolness of the night, the twelve injured and tired people continued down the incline of the wooded slope on which they found themselves. They were convinced that the ship that had been their prison was preparing to launch; five minutes remained before lift off, according to the calculations that had been made so long before in the tour room. They had come too far to die now in its tremendous exhaust.

As they ran, they saw that fires had broken out in the range above them and were being fought by aerial vehicles and hundreds of groundspeople. The portion of the mountain onto which they had escaped seemed to be free of fire, however, so they were surprised when they ran into the sweating and sooty crew of a jump tanker in a small glade several hundred yards from the spot where they had emerged. They came to a halt in an explosion of gasps and elated cries.

"Who the hell are you?" demanded the leader of the fire team. "Where did you people come from?"

"The ship . . . in the mountain," Doyle managed to spit out. He had carried Patrice Rutherford all the way down the mountain and never fallen a step behind the rest. Now he laid her gently on the ground. "We had to . . . go all . . . all the way through . . . Got out the rear emergency exit!"

Some of the crew laughed, but the leader remained serious. "What are you, crazy? That's a crock, mister. None of those people got out when that thing snapped shut, and they've even evacuated the digging crews because of the shocks and the fires! How did you get up here?"

Doyle stood away from the tanker and shook the man by the shoulders. "You damned idiot, I don't care what you believe, but that ship is going to lift in just about *three minutes*, so if there's anyone on top of it, you'd better get them off right now!"

"Everybody's been evacuated since the fire moved off to the north," the leader began. His dark-eyed men had surrounded the pair immediately.

"Chief," said one, "there are some projections on the end of that ship, and if they got back there somehow and opened one . . ."

Fear leaped visibly into the first man's eyes. "Holy Mother, if that's the truth, these people are contaminated all to hell! G team, into the jumper! You other people get back into the clearing and stay there until we send a decontamination crew!"

His men began flooding into the vessel, and Kay Aymdahle rushed toward them, crying, "Don't leave us here! We need help!"

Kenneth Braam added, "We're injured and hungry!"

The team leader drew a side arm from his belt and waved it at them in an extremely business-like manner. "Get back!" There was a touch of hysteria in his tone. He entered the vehicle last. "I hereby order you in the name of the United Nations to remain right in this spot until the proper officials arrive to take you into custody! Failure to comply with this order shall open you to immediate execution!" He ducked inside and yelled at the pilot, who sent the jumper soaring skyward in a rush of heated air.

Kay began to cry again, but Doyle merely grunted, "At least they'll know we're here," he said.

Jefferies found the energy in his mistreated body to extend his arms above his head as he laughed aloud. "I don't give a damn! We're out! We made it, man, we beat the Saucer!"

While the others joined him in this exuberant thanksgiving, Doyle remained silent. He stared toward the tunnel through which he had just escaped. He was thinking of too many things to sort them out neatly. There was a surface film of joy, of course, from the knowledge that he was free and he had done his job by delivering eleven others from certain death, but inside, where every man truly lives, he was also feeling a loss.

It wasn't Glynna who had caused the breakup, and, in all honesty, she had not torn him from a sea that he still loved. That had been in his past, emotionally if not physically, when they had met.

The truth, which he had been trying to deny in sheer desperation, was that he had outgrown everything—the sea, his business affairs, even poor Glynna. The future held nothing for Aaron Doyle, nothing that he had not already met, battled, and beaten.

He thought of the ship. Surely, it was crippled, the devastation they had encountered proved that, and it probably would not survive a launching even if one took place. The people trapped aboard it were as good as dead. How could they live through a trip across the depths of outer space? It was a lost dream.

"Time?" he asked softly.

Gloria Thirkell checked her watch out of reflex one more time. "You rushed it a little with that fireman," she replied. "It's just about three minutes and fifty seconds until zero hour. We should have a ringside seat from here."

"That's long enough," Doyle muttered, almost too low to be overheard.

Without explanation and apparently without reason, Doyle began to run again, back in the direction of the tunnel. Only Jefferies noticed this, and he stepped after Doyle to stop him.

"Aaron!" he shouted.

"No, son," Roger Griffin said, with a hand on his arm.

"But he's going toward the ship!"

As they spoke, Doyle's tall, broad-shouldered figure vanished in the dark shadows of the forest.

"We couldn't stop him if we tried," Griffin whispered. "Let him go." His writer's mind was working swiftly, and to the rest, who were just picking up on the unfolding actions, he said, "Mr. Doyle probably has his reasons for not wanting to be located by the officials, and after all he's done for us today, we really don't have the right to stop him."

"But that fireman was right, we *were* contaminated with alien bacteria," Gloria said. "We were in the *same room* with them, and Aaron could start an epidemic!"

"I doubt it. A miraculous automated intelligence

provided the atmospheric conditions for us throughout the vessel, and I'd be surprised if it hadn't taken care of the cross-contamination problem." Roger looked after Doyle almost wistfully. "There were many, many miraculous things on board that craft."

"Fifteen seconds," Thirkell said eagerly.

They were still in the glade, and no help had yet arrived, but in spite of their pain and thirst, they were excited.

"Ten," the woman said.

Kenneth Braam stared at the top of the mountain, wondering if he had lost or gained by the experience. Yes, he had witnessed supremely advanced technology in action and even met with a representative of another intelligent race, but all that he could force himself to feel was relief.

Antonio Arbolada felt joy that was deep, profound, perhaps even religious. He now truly believed in God for the first time in his adult life, and he knew that God would not have created the vastness of the Universe only to populate one—or even two—small specks of it, just as He would never have provided His creations with the marvelous affliction of unending curiosity if they weren't to be allowed to seek answers for it. The stars that Arbolada looked upon were so much more than they had seemed the night before. And they had been wondrous even then.

Kay Aymdahle had begun the retreat that allows individuals to live through the loss of loved ones, and she welcomed it. She had loved James faithfully and well, but now, hidden far below the insulation of shock, emotion, and conscience, there was a twinge of what might have developed into satisfaction had it been fed with anything less than love. James's only real love had been Jesus. It was fitting that he had finally met with Him hand to hand.

George Flanders might have come out of the ordeal with the most gain, at least so far as self-appreciation was concerned. He was definitely going to be famous now, and famous people commanded respect, which was what he had wanted more than anything all his life. Fame changes those who are touched by it, and not always for the worse. Yeah, George, wait until tomorrow comes.

Patrice Rutherford would recover, but from the first moment that she awakened and heard the tale from those who had lived through it with her, she understood that only a certain amount of oneself could be entrusted to another without danger of deep hurt. She would be careful in the future, much more careful.

Susan Leipnitz had undergone her Event, and she knew it. Everyone is entitled to one Big Moment during his or her life, and for the rest of that life it was fair to trade on that moment. She had always wanted kids, out of love, but now she *had* to have them, if only to tell them about this very day on some cold night during their childhoods. She wondered if Donnie Buckley had survived.

Bobby, whose last name was McCrory, was soundly asleep at last.

"Zero hour," said Gloria.

Nine pairs of eyes stared fixedly at the mountain range as the payoff arrived.

A light not unlike the one produced by the

rapturous death of James Aymdahle, but filled with all the colors of the spectrum, began to appear from beneath the earth. Beginning only a few dozen yards from where they stood and extending for more than twelve miles, it swelled upward as if struggling to return to its origin; it burned silently through the hundreds of millions of tons of soil and rock that lay above the craft which produced it. The ground, forest, and sky were suddenly filled with its power, and when it blinked off, in the fashion of a disconnected bulb, it had dissolved every ounce of matter that it had touched. The ship Roger Griffin had called Asgard lay revealed totally to human eyes for the first time in more than eighty thousand years.

No one spoke because they had no voices.

Light seemed to be the hallmark of the craft and the race that had created it. Within seconds after the obliterating glow had rid the vessel of the cage in which it had slept, the skin of the spacecraft began to give off a vibrant and brilliant whiteness comparable to the radiance of the sun. The watchers had to look away or shield their eyes with their hands, so strong was it, but they all managed to catch a glimpse as the ship rose in quiet majesty from the cradle of the Earth, floated to a point many miles overhead, turned slowly in place as if to set its bearings, and then slipped out of the atmosphere of the planet on its long voyage home. It was a blazing star for a time, then a plane's light, and finally a white pinpoint.

"I hope he made it back inside," Jefferies whispered.

"So do I," Griffin responded.

Gloria Thirkell was verging on jubilation. Science had been a large portion of her life, and she had just experienced more than she had ever had the right to expect. The coming years of evaluation of what she had discovered filled her with an inexhaustible sense of joy. This was not the ending of her adventure aboard the alien craft; it was only the beginning.

Anjanette Palmer felt a wild mixture of emotions at war within her. She knew that she had undergone perhaps the most unusual and important day in the history of Mankind, and she accepted this awesome responsibility gladly. But she also felt cheated in that there didn't appear to be anything in the future that could ever measure up. The adults would tell her that she'd forget it in time, but Anjanette was certain that her memory would never fail her on any point connected with the entire experience.

Coming back, fellows? thought Con Jefferies. You can't give us this taste of it and then leave us to ourselves forever. He was surprised that he was one of the lucky ones who came through it all the way. But one didn't question luck: one just accepted it. I'll be here, he broadcast to Them on the ether, whenever you get ready to check in with us and see how we've handled your legacy. Sure, we're a roughhewn bunch, a little conceited, a little cocky, and *always* ready to fight, with ourselves if no one else, but we are the future, too, you know. And you'd better not try to stop us from meeting with you out there. We're coming, even if you *don't* get back to us, laddies.

For no reason other than life, Con Jefferies laughed out loud.

Roger Griffin cherished many hopes for what had begun that night, including the hope that Daniel Levya had found Earl and they had escaped through the second spur. But one wish stood above all others: he hoped that the aliens had uncovered the secret of returning life to the dead, so that all those who perished—humans and aliens alike—most of all his beloved Maureen, could have life again. Bring her back to me he pled, and I'll tell the world of your greatness.

Goodbye, my love.

But right now, he had a monumental job ahead of him. How would he be able to present this to the reading public in its fullness and power? He respected himself as a writer, but he had to wonder if any author who had ever taken pen in hand could adequately relate the facts of those hours inside another world. That was his challenge, and he had never backed down before. I've got to begin as soon as possible, he thought. Tomorrow. No, tonight.

In the distance, the eleven people could hear the faint whirring of the military helicopter that was coming for them. The Asgard Run had finally come to a place of rest.

PREFERRED CUSTOMERS!

Leisure Books and Love Spell proudly present a brand-new catalogue and a TOLL-FREE NUMBER

STARTING JUNE 1, 1995
CALL 1-800-481-9191
between 2:00 and 10:00 p.m.
(Eastern Time)
Monday Through Friday

GET A FREE CATALOGUE
AND ORDER BOOKS USING
VISA AND MASTERCARD

LEISURE BOOKS   *Love Spell*